YOUNG BLOOD

Tricia Fields

SEVERN
HOUSE

First world edition published 2020
in Great Britain and the USA by
SEVERN HOUSE PUBLISHERS LTD of
Eardley House, 4 Uxbridge Street, London W8 7SY.
Trade paperback edition first published
in Great Britain and the USA 2021 by
Severn House, an imprint of Canongate Books Ltd,
14 High Street, Edinburgh EH1 1TE.

British Library Cataloguing in Publication Data
A CIP catalogue record for this title is available from the British Library.

ISBN-13: 978-0-7278-9246-1 (cased)
ISBN-13: 978-1-78029-693-7 (trade paper)
ISBN-13: 978-1-4483-0418-9 (e-book)

Typeset by Palimpsest Book Production Ltd.,
Falkirk, Stirlingshire, Scotland.

YOUNG BLOOD

ONE

Dr Oscar LeBlanc stepped into the room to find two little girls lying side by side on the examination table, eyes closed, black and blonde hair entwined. He closed the door and leaned against it, pulling air deep into his lungs, trying desperately to slow his pulse.

He shut his eyes against Ramone's frantic voiceover explaining his incompetence. The doctor finally lifted his head away from the door and forced himself to look at the little girls.

'What in God's name have you done?' he said.

'I had *no* choice!' Ramone's voice spiked.

LeBlanc snapped his fingers. 'Not so loud.'

'They can't hear. I swear to you, they're fine. Deeply sedated but their vitals are good. I assure you, they won't remember a thing when this is all over.'

'Do you understand what is at stake right now? You have put my life's work in jeopardy.'

'I made this decision to save *you*! The clinic just wasn't safe.'

'You should have known that before tonight. You had a simple job. You were compensated well to take care of the details, to keep me removed from' – he gestured toward the girls – 'from this kind of disaster.'

'They're fine.'

LeBlanc's eyes widened. 'You call this fine?'

Ramone brought his hands palms-down in the air, as if trying to push the doctor's anger to a more reasonable level. 'Medically, they're fine. Nothing much has even changed. We just do the procedure here, that's all. It's better here anyway. Less chance of someone being seen.'

LeBlanc's face reddened with anger. 'No, Ramone, there is a far greater chance of *me* being seen. Which is why you were paid to take care of this offsite.' Ramone started to protest and LeBlanc raised a hand to stifle him.

The doctor approached the table and looked at the girls, checking their coloring, examining their pupils and taking their pulse. Each girl wore an oversized hospital gown, intended for an adult. Dr LeBlanc had very little experience with children in his research practice, and just the sight of the girls caused him anxiety. He picked up the blonde girl's wrist to feel her pulse, noting the delicate skin and bone structure, and he wondered how he had gone from a Stanford med student superstar to a man barely hanging on to his sanity. He felt wronged in every aspect of his life – from the bureaucratic research horrors to his wife's increasing paranoia.

Now this. Months away from a medical breakthrough that would shake the scientific community like nothing else in the past two decades, and he was standing in the middle of his own worst nightmare.

He placed his stethoscope on top of the blonde girl's gown and slid it over her chest, listening to her faint, measured breathing. Despite the reassurances he'd received from Ramone, a pediatric anesthesiologist, he'd only performed the procedure on a child twice and wasn't at all comfortable with the situation. He moved around to the other side of the table to check the other girl, silently acknowledging the ever-present pull of risk against reward, imagining the countless researchers before him staring down disaster in the name of scientific advancement.

He slipped the stethoscope into his lab coat pocket and faced the technician. Ramone stood in the corner, a twenty-five-year-old manipulator whom the doctor had placed entirely too much trust in.

'You will not leave this room under any circumstance. You will not sleep tonight. If you need to use the facilities, you text me and I will take your place for the moment. Understood?'

Ramone nodded, looking relieved that the doctor had moved beyond fury to the next steps.

'How long before the girls will be ready?' LeBlanc asked.

'Thirty minutes.'

'Get them prepped.'

LeBlanc shut the exam room door behind him and walked across the hall to the restroom. He locked the door and felt the nausea pushing up into his throat. The room turned gray around the edges and he felt certain that he was going to pass out.

He dropped to his knees and grasped the commode, heaving up his dinner, hoping the patient in the waiting room couldn't hear through the walls. Once the heaving finally subsided and he felt his blood pressure stabilizing, he stood at the sink to splash cold water on his face, cupping water in his hand to rinse his mouth. Ashamed at his weakness, he stared at his sallow face and slapped his skin to revive some color.

At forty-two, his hair had prematurely turned a charcoal gray, but the long strands over his collar accentuated eyes so dark they appeared black. His wife, who claimed she fell in love first with his French accent, and then with his doctoral degree, said his hollow cheeks and pronounced nose gave him the look of an aristocrat.

He stood tall, forcing himself to look the part of the successful doctor, the aristocrat. 'This will not break me. I am doing this for the good of humanity.'

Dr LeBlanc stuck his head into the waiting room and waved at Thatch Roderick. 'Be right with you.'

Thatch was a seventy-six-year-old man who appeared to be in the prime of his life. White hair in a short crew cut, dress slacks and a white polo, tanned with the lightest scent of cologne. He presented himself at all times as one who took great pride in his appearance and his conduct. Thatch was a man with enough money to expect and get perfection – until his memory started to slip, causing the police to ferry him home on several occasions, with his wife frantic that he was in the beginning stages of Alzheimer's. Thatch had joined the study six months ago. He knew he was the first patient to receive the alternative treatment and was expecting a complete reversal of the symptoms.

The doctor logged into his receptionist's computer, then logged into his overseas account, double-checking that the deposit had been received that day. Dated 15 July, a payment of $100,000 was showing. He wouldn't have turned Thatch away from the treatment, but the money was certainly a relief. He sighed and grabbed a breath mint from a nearby candy jar. At least one thing had gone as planned.

The men shook hands and spoke briefly of Thatch's golf game, and his recent trip to Argentina.

LeBlanc led Thatch down the hallway, feeling his skin crawl as he walked past the exam room on the left that housed the little girls. Dr LeBlanc's practice was small, just two exam rooms and the procedure room, along with the customary receptionist and waiting areas, and the records and storage rooms. But it was large enough to conduct research that had the potential to skyrocket LeBlanc to the top of the medical field, giving his work the attention that it deserved. LeBlanc struggled with the irony of his situation: when funding for the research drove all else, decisions were made that were not always best for those involved, but were critical for the good of the masses. The work with children had taken much rationalizing, but he was confident that the potential for good far outweighed the negative. The children wouldn't be harmed in any way, and he felt he could sleep soundly at night knowing that.

Unlike the bright hallway, the procedure room was dimly lit, with large machines hulking along the periphery of the room, each with its own special function, highly technical and capable of miracles. The room felt serene, as if every item had been chosen with the utmost care, with cost of no concern. A patient had told him once that the room was like stepping into a church sanctuary, and LeBlanc often had that same sense, although not on this night.

LeBlanc pointed to the gown that his receptionist had left on the patient bed before she left. 'Everything off from the waist up. Gown open in the front and tied. After you've changed, go ahead and lie down and get comfortable. I'll be in for your exam in a few moments.'

'You're sure about this?' Thatch said.

LeBlanc paused at the door and offered a reassuring smile, allowing his accent to thicken. Oddly, he'd discovered that patients found his French accent even more credible than the summa cum laude degree from Stanford. 'Absolutely. Your first treatment went perfectly, yes?'

Thatch frowned but nodded.

'Then you have nothing to worry about. I'll give you time to get settled.'

Thatch pointed to the exam screen that was separating the room. 'Why the screen?'

LeBlanc hesitated. 'We're trying a different procedure tonight. We'll have as pure an interaction as is scientifically possible.'

TWO

At seven o'clock, Maggie Wise drove the Tamiami Trail to the east side of town for a drink with Danny Giardiello before he went onstage at eight. He played guitar and sang backup in a three-man band called The Blue Orchids. With his shirt unbuttoned to his hairy navel and his gray hair in a man bun, he appeared an unlikely best friend to Maggie, retired homicide cop turned talk show radio host.

The Blue Orchids played every Friday at Mel's Class Act, located in a strip mall in the low-rent area of Santa Cruz. The establishment was an Italian seafood restaurant, music venue and dive bar with an unmarked purple door that led to a strip club called The Foxxy Den. Maggie worked at the club on Saturday nights doing makeup and costume changes for the girls. Nothing about Mel's spoke of class. The restaurant entrance opened directly into a large room painted ocean blue with bright overhead lights and twenty tables of four that could be removed if the crowd was large enough to warrant the changeover from restaurant to dancehall.

Maggie parked on the side of the building next to Danny's Chevy Malibu and found him sitting in the bar nursing a beer.

'What's up, boss lady?' Danny said.

Maggie sat on the barstool next to him and nodded toward the bandstand. 'I see Agnus and her Pips have the front row sewn up.'

Danny gave an uninspired thumbs up.

From her vantage point at the bar, Maggie had a good view of the six women sitting at the table in front of the bandstand. Danny's groupies laughed full throttle at some outrageous story Agnus was telling. The women, ranging in age from mid-seventies to late-eighties, would drink their cocktails while they ogled the lounge singer, stuffing dollar bills inside the waist of his pants, catcalling at the lurid faces he made for their amusement. But the women had seen their share of heartache. Four of the six were widows, and the other two had husbands battling Alzheimer's in the same nursing home; it was how they had met and become friends. Collectively, they had lost children to disease and to murder, they had lived through a world war and survived the civil rights and wrongs of every stripe and color the United States had dished out over the last century. But they still got together every Friday night and found reason enough to celebrate life.

For Maggie, that was the beauty of Mel's. She guessed everyone in there was a stereotype of sorts, from her own down-and-out retired-homicide-cop guise, to her beach-bum, dope-smoking buddy Danny, and the old women groupies. But regardless of who you appeared to be, nobody cared who you really were. You didn't go to Mel's to judge or be judged. You went knowing you'd be accepted, faults and hang-ups be damned.

After her husband David died and she moved to Santa Cruz, Maggie spent the first month drinking herself into a stupor each night at Mel's, before walking across the road to the Moonlight Motel to sleep it off and start all over again the next night. After the first week, Agnus began leaving her girlfriends on Friday and Saturday nights to sit with Maggie at the bar during the intermission. She never bothered Maggie about her drinking too much, or tried to get her to share her story; Agnus simply became a friend, telling tales about her deceased husband who'd owned a string of auto-body shops across the south, or offering Maggie tips about getting around Santa Cruz, or telling her which grocery store gave the best deal on fresh fruit. Some nights, Agnus spent whole sets chatting away.

One night, four weeks into the drunken ritual, Agnus sat down next to Maggie and slid a key and a piece of paper with an address on it down the bar.

'You can't stay in that dump across the street anymore,' she said. 'You're moving in with me. I have a little house on the property that's empty. You can stay in it for free. Stay for a month and we'll see how it goes.'

That was three years ago, and Maggie was still living in the gardener's quarters behind the oceanfront mansion.

Danny tapped Maggie on the arm. 'You work early tomorrow?'

Maggie glanced over at him. 'Ten to noon. I have the interviews lined up. Should be a quick two hours.'

'Mark coming in tonight?'

Maggie nodded and raised a finger to Serena, the waitress who tended bar because Mel was too lazy to slide his ass off the stool behind the cash register. 'He's coming by at eight. But only if you get Whitney to sing "Don't Leave me this Way".'

'You got it.'

Serena put a tequila on the rocks in front of her. 'What's up, honey? You doing OK?'

'It's all good.'

Serena hustled off to grab sandwich orders from the restaurant side.

Danny leaned back and away from Maggie, staring for a moment before asking, 'What's got you down in the dumps tonight?'

'Who said anything about being down?' Maggie asked.

'I did. You look gray and pasty. Like you need vitamins.'

'Just a rough day.'

Danny nodded but continued staring. 'Agnus told me it's four years today since your husband . . .' His voice trailed off.

'Died?'

'Yeah. I just hated to say it like that.'

'How'd Agnus know?' Maggie asked.

'Agnus knows everything,' Danny said. 'How come you never talk about him?'

Maggie shrugged. 'It hurts. It makes me feel like shit.'

'So talk about the good times. Before the cancer hit.'

'That's not the way my brain works.'

'What was he like?'

'What I'm like. But exactly the opposite.'

Danny grinned and nodded.

'He was good,' Maggie said. 'He was just a really good

person. Up until the very end.' She glanced at Danny and felt the emotion she kept on ice heating up her insides. She swirled the last of the tequila around the bottom of the glass and figured she'd regret both the drink and the honesty, but she needed to talk. She'd thought that four years into David's passing she'd be over the physical pain, but her body still ached with the memory of him.

'Those last weeks,' Maggie finally said, 'when he was still smiling and acting cheerful, and I was so angry at the world for taking someone so good, I could barely function. All I wanted was to crawl inside a bottle. His smile though?' Maggie shook her head and downed the rest of the drink, signaling Serena who nodded and put a finger up. 'It never left. And the worst part of it? It pissed me off. That's what a horrible person I am.

'He'd be sitting by the sliding door in his wheelchair, wearing his ballcap to cover the clumps of hair that had fallen out, and he'd point at a bird he'd just identified in the *Birds of Santa Cruz* book. He'd smile at me from across the room and tell me to come look, and I'd think, how the hell can you be smiling at birds while this cancer is eating up your insides? I just couldn't wrap my head around it. I tried to smile, to look at the birds and encourage him, make small talk, but I couldn't make the words come out of my goddamned mouth.

'So he'd give me a pep talk. "I'm gonna beat this, baby." He must have told me that a thousand times. But I knew he wouldn't. I could see his body deteriorating by the day. So instead of enjoying those final weeks with him, I quit talking because I couldn't get the words out. I will hate myself for that until the day I die.'

Serena slid another tequila down the bar as she walked by.

Maggie picked it up and emptied it.

Danny said, 'Maybe you gave him the courage to smile. You ever think of that? All these good people in the world, they gotta have somebody to fix. So it's people like you and me that give them something to work on. He couldn't focus on his own pain because he had to drag your sorry ass out of the gutter each day. I don't know if that's such a bad thing.'

Maggie signaled for another and Serena raised her eyebrows

from behind the bar. Maggie nodded once and Serena reached for the bottle.

'You think that's what I am?' Maggie asked. 'A project?'

'Look. You're either the fixer or the fixable. It's the opposites attract thing. It works, as long as you don't get two fixables in the same relationship.'

'Who's fixing you?'

'Serena.'

Maggie grinned. 'You two seeing each other now?'

'Nah. We hook up when necessary. With us, we actually go both ways. Sometimes she needs fixing and I help her out.'

Maggie looked skeptical.

'I'm serious. She gets to freaking out about her life going by too quick. She doesn't have enough money in the bank, and she'll never have enough money to retire working at this shithole, and she's got a kid who's two steps from jail. I talk her off the ledge every six months or so. And then she's fine.'

Serena came by with a tray full of drinks and put the tequila in front of Maggie. 'How many is this?'

'You my mom tonight?'

'Somebody needs to watch out for you,' she said.

Danny put a hand out toward her. 'See?'

'I'm fine,' Maggie said. 'I'm gonna stay for the set. Mark's coming in after work.'

'Good. I get off at eight. I'll join you when Danny goes on.'

After Serena left, Danny asked, 'So how'd you end up in Santa Cruz after he died?'

'When David was first diagnosed he was chosen for a medical study. His doctor in Cincinnati said he was the perfect candidate. They were experimenting with a gene that could turn on some kind of receptor that would recycle damaged cells. He had to fly to Santa Cruz for treatment four times a year. He participated for a year before he died. I quit following the study afterward, but I never got the idea that the treatment did him any good.'

'You think participating could have hurt him?' Danny asked.

Maggie shrugged. 'I know the free plane ticket to Santa Cruz four times a year for treatment bought him a dose of sunshine and some hope. We spent a week in a condo each time. The study paid for it all. That was worth quite a bit. He was convinced, up until the day he died, that he was going to beat it. Or at least that's what he told me.'

'He had grit.'

Maggie nodded and watched Danny raise a hand in the air to someone walking in the front door.

'Whitney's here. I gotta go. She's like a drill sergeant.'

The Blue Orchids featured Danny on guitar, an octogenarian named Buffalo Bruce on the drum set, and a black woman who could sing Motown like no other on vocals. The band started each night playing Sinatra standards, but once the crowd cut loose, Whitney belted out Motown and got the old women shaking on the dancefloor. Even in the military and college, Maggie hadn't hung out in bars; a lifetime loner, it still surprised her some nights that she was a regular at Mel's Friday Night Orchestra. But outside of her twenty-year marriage, the people at Mel's were the closest friends she'd ever had. She credited the group of them with saving her life, although she'd never admit it publicly.

Maggie watched Danny disappear outside with Whitney to share a joint before going onstage. It bothered Maggie that Danny smoked, both cigarettes and weed, but she kept her opinions to herself. She had her own issues to avoid.

THREE

Mark Hamilton, Cypress City Chief of Police, walked into Mel's an hour late looking uncharacteristically disheveled. While Maggie typically bought her clothes online or in thrift shops, Mark dressed impeccably: his brass polished and shoes shined, his off-duty T-shirts smooth, his shorts and jeans crisp. They'd been dating for a year now, and he'd mostly given up trying to instill a sense of style in Maggie. He still bought her clothes every holiday, which was fine because it meant one less item she'd have to contend with getting for herself. She'd explained that it wasn't that she didn't want to look nice, she just didn't want the hassle. If he wanted the hassle, that was fine with her.

During her twenty-five years in law enforcement, she'd only dated one cop before learning her lesson. Between the erratic hours and stresses of the job, dating anyone was a challenge, but dating another person in law enforcement usually led to disaster. So she found it ironic that after she took early retirement and moved to Florida, the first man who had asked her on a date was another cop. After two divorces of his own, he liked the idea that she understood his work. Knowing she missed it, he often shared details and occasionally asked for input, and on most days even accepted her unsolicited opinions. In one of their worst fights he'd said the only reason she was dating him was because he was a lifeline to the job she missed. The accusation had stung. She loved Mark, but she also missed the job like a favorite bad habit.

Mark reached the table and forced a half-smile. His crisp white shirt and neatly trimmed hair didn't compensate for his red-eyed fatigue. He pulled a chair around the table to sit next to Maggie. She laid a hand on his thigh and he dropped his own hand onto hers with no warmth, just exhaustion.

'Bad day?' she asked.

'Missing ten-year-old girl. John Desmond's on it.'

'How long?'

'Since supper. She was at the park. Was supposed to be home at five.' Mark leaned his head back, then turned to peer sideways at Maggie. 'I'm getting nowhere with the family.'

'How so?'

'Mom says her daughter is never late. Never wanders off to see another friend or loses track of time. She would never run away from home. Which could all be true. I tried to explain that nine times out of ten it's something simple. The mother accused me of being a cold-hearted bastard because I don't have kids of my own.'

He shrugged, but Maggie could tell the comment had cut deep. Mark did care about the job, about his employees, about the people he served, about Florida water quality, his ailing parents, Maggie's poor eating habits, sea turtles, and God knows what

else; his care was exhausting to Maggie and not at all healthy
for him. In her opinion.

'Is John interviewing right now or canvasing?' Maggie asked.

'He's got three officers working it. He's following protocol.
If we don't hear anything by ten, I'll go back in.'

'What time did you go in this morning?'

He sighed but said nothing.

'Seven o'clock,' she said. 'It's now eight fifteen. You need a
break after twelve hours. A guilt-free break, Mark. You get that,
right?'

He smirked at her response. 'And you never worked a twelve
on a homicide over your twenty-five-year tenure?'

'This isn't a homicide.'

'God help us if it is.'

Maggie couldn't get Serena's attention, so she walked back to
the bar and got Mel to slide off his stool long enough to pull
a Perrier out of the cooler. Back at the table, she sat the bottle
in front of Mark and he smiled for the first time that evening.
She put a hand in the air to get Danny's attention and pointed
at Mark.

Danny finished with a tired version of 'Mac the Knife',
because one of the Pips requested it every Friday night, and
then announced it was time to heat up the joint.

Whitney sidled up to Danny and rubbed her hip up and down
his thigh with a suggestive look at the crowd who catcalled and
whistled for more. She wore a skin-tight black dress that
followed every curve and produced one hell of a convincing
vamp.

With Whitney's back pressed against Danny's side, she leaned
forward and put her lips against the microphone, her eyes as big
as Thelma Houston's. She started in with the slow hum that led
into the melody that sent the crowd crazy. Maggie looked over
at Mark, who grinned and squeezed her hand.

Whitney pointed a dark red fingernail at Mark and cooed,
singing the chorus directly to him.

Agnus was up, hands pumping the air, the Pips right behind
her, then the whole room was up and singing the chorus.

Mark leaned over to speak into Maggie's ear in order to be

heard. 'You're a good woman, Maggie Wise.' He pecked her on the cheek, then looked down at his cell phone buzzing on the table.

He read a text and stood. 'I have to go.'

Maggie followed him outside into the parking lot.

'What's going on?' she asked, rushing to catch up to him.

He clicked the unlock button to his cruiser and opened the door. 'That was John. Another girl reported missing.'

'I'll follow you.'

'I have enough to deal with right now. Don't do this.'

'I'll hear it on the scanner. The media will be all over this.'

'I need to understand what we're dealing with first.'

'Mark, I'll be there to help.'

He put the car into drive and stuck his head out the window. 'Stay here. Or go home. I'll call you when I can.'

FOUR

Once the girls were both prepped, Dr LeBlanc closed his office door and stared out the large window overlooking the lake lit up with fountains at night. He considered stopping it all: calling a halt to the whole fiasco. Too many grave errors in judgment had been made throughout the whole ordeal. The girls should never have been brought to his office. He would have Ramone deliver them home that night and find some other way.

He noticed Thatch's wife, Amy, walk outside the front of the office, swiping tears away from her cheeks. He stepped out the side door of his office and onto a dark path that led to the front of the building. She was sitting on a bench in an ivy garden, dimly lit by path lights.

'Amy?'

She looked up at him, obviously shocked to find herself not alone. She started to stand.

'No need to get up.' He sat down beside her. 'Why the tears?'

'I'm sorry. I'm fine. Just worried, that's all.'

'You know this is a very safe procedure for Thatch.'

She took a shaky breath and looked intently at the doctor. 'You have no idea how much we're counting on you right now. You are our lifeline. With Thatch's family history, it's all just so scary. We just appreciate everything you're doing.'

'This is so new, Amy, and one can never be sure with new treatments.'

She blinked away tears and nodded in silence.

'But I am as confident as I can be that this is the right treatment for Thatch.'

She nodded again, obviously too overcome with emotion to speak.

'All right then. You take care and we'll have Thatch ready to go home in no time.'

Dr LeBlanc entered his office again. He stood at the window and watched Amy pull her sweater tight around her thin back against the night air. He knew that he had no choice but to proceed. He could not turn away Thatch Roderick. And awful as it might be, the data was crucial.

He administered a light sedative to Thatch so that he wasn't aware the girls were in the room, and the procedure miraculously worked perfectly. By midnight, Thatch was alert, with his wife helping him into the car, her look of hope and heartache one and the same. She shook Dr LeBlanc's hand and promised to call if there were any issues.

The girls, however, were not responding as quickly as the doctor had hoped, or as quickly as Ramone had assured him they would. Ramone was a month away from starting his four-year anesthesiology residency. With eight years of med school behind him, and one hundred and sixty thousand dollars in school loans accumulating, he had been a loyal accomplice in the beginning. But the doctor realized too late that the young man's confidence outweighed his knowledge and experience.

After sending the Rodericks on their way, Dr LeBlanc entered the procedure room again to find Ramone standing at the head of the bed of the blonde girl, staring at the monitor.

'We're fine here. I just think we need another hour to be completely safe,' Ramone said.

The doctor had not asked about the girls' return trips home. He had wanted to stay as far removed from the details as possible, but these two beautiful little girls were lying in his patient beds under deep sedation and they had to be safely returned to their families. This should all have ended hours ago. He realized with each tick of the clock that the chances of getting these girls home without notice became exponentially more difficult.

'How can you assure me the girls are stabilized enough for transport?'

Ramone sighed. 'Look. I know this didn't work as planned, but I assure you these girls are in good hands. I would never put their lives in jeopardy by moving them before they're ready. You have to trust me on this.'

'It's one o'clock in the morning. You're running out of time.'

'I realize what time it is. I plan on—'

LeBlanc raised a hand to stop him. 'No details. Just explain to me how you know the drop off is still going to work this far into the girls' disappearance?'

'You just have to trust me.'

LeBlanc noticed the sheen of perspiration across Ramone's forehead and upper lip, and it gave him no confidence.

FIVE

Maggie had sent two text messages to Mark, one at midnight, the other at 1:00 a.m. At 3:00 a.m. he finally responded. She'd been dozing on the couch when her phone vibrated against her chest.

You awake?

How's it going? Maggie wrote.

Going to my place to grab sleep. 2 still missing. Looking for connection.

Want company?

Just a quick nap. Press conference at 9:00 A.M. Hope it's not needed.

When Maggie awoke at seven, she resisted the urge to call for an update. She checked the Cypress City Police Station and Sheriff's Department websites but found no news bulletins. At ten o'clock she would be interviewing the mayor to discuss urban sprawl in Collier County, and the city's plans to thwart it, but she suspected her topic had just changed. Mark would have called if he had good news.

Maggie called Mayor Phil Brattain's cell phone and left a message. 'I may need to do a last-minute cancellation on your interview this morning, Mayor. Call me when you get this.'

With coffee in hand, she walked outside to breathe in the salty air before the heat of the day wilted her good humor. Her home, as Agnus now called it, was a one-bedroom, one-bathroom bungalow with a sign hung above the front door that read 'Gardener's Reprieve'.

For the first two years Maggie had attempted to leave rent checks of various amounts in the main house, but Agnus had always returned them. She finally stormed up to Maggie one evening, the latest rent check flapping in her hand. She told her that she had more money than she could ever spend, and Maggie's money was a nuisance.

'I have no kids. Like it or not, you're as close to family as I've got, so you'll be getting all these silly checks back in the end anyway. So knock it off.'

Agnus had offered to deed the gardener's house over to Maggie that afternoon, but she'd protested, promising to never mention rent again if Agnus would drop the matter. Consequently, Maggie had taken to her role of protector, checking on Agnus at least once a day, offering the occasional unsolicited safety tip, and cat-sitting when Agnus flew to Omaha once a month to visit her sister.

Maggie's one splurge on her new home had been the addition of a wall of windows in the living room and the bedroom, both of which faced the ocean. Agnus had a multimillion-dollar view behind her home, and Maggie intended to make good use of the kindness. She imagined David smiling down at her from heaven, pleased with her circumstance.

Maggie carried her coffee across the small dune, everchanging with the winds off the Gulf of Mexico. A day didn't go by without her thinking about David on her walk. She loved Mark, but she couldn't shake the feeling that their relationship was limited. David had been her first real love and she'd shared twenty years of joy and heartache with him. Mark didn't have that kind of history with another person. He'd undergone two grueling divorces, and Maggie doubted that he'd ever had the all-encompassing love that she and David had experienced. Although, in her more introspective moments, she wondered if time and grief had made her remember her own past with such an exaggerated sense of perfection that she would never be capable of starting over.

When she reached the water, she lifted a hand at the neighbor a hundred yards down the beach out walking his Shih Tzu. Knowing she would have to talk to the scrawny dog if the neighbor caught up to her, she opened her buzzing phone and took off walking in the opposite direction.

'It's bad,' Mark said, skipping a greeting. 'Two girls disappeared out of thin air. One from Cypress. The other from Santa Cruz.'

'Any leads?'

'Nothing. Just that they're the same sex and similar ages. The girl from Santa Cruz is white. The girl from Cypress City is biracial. And they were both taken from parks.'

'That's odd. You think they're related?'

'It's hard to imagine they aren't. We don't often see missing kids that aren't custody related. And that's not the case with either of these girls.'

'Do they know each other?'

'I don't think so. The girl from Cypress, her family barely puts food on the table. The other girl goes to a private school in Santa Cruz. Lives in a million-dollar home. There doesn't appear to be any connection.'

'Did either girl have a cell phone to track?' she asked.

'The Cypress girl didn't own one. The girl from Santa Cruz left hers in the car when her mom dropped her off at school. She convinced her teacher to call her mom from school to request she bring it. The mom is beating herself up now, thinking the phone might have allowed the girl to get help.'

'What can I do?' Maggie asked.

'You're on the air this morning?'

'Ten to noon,' she said. 'I've already sent the mayor a message and told him I might be canceling his interview.'

'Can you devote some time to the story?'

'Absolutely. Can you come on for an interview?'

'I'll try. I'm on my way to Santa Cruz this morning. The Chief there has the media coming at nine. We're approaching it as a multi-city investigation within Collier County. I'll send you an email with everything we know so far. If I can, I'll stop by the station with an update. Maybe around eleven.'

'Anyone else I should talk to?'

'I'll have John give you a call if he has time. He's lead investigator.'

'What's your gut telling you?'

She heard him exhale slowly, could imagine the worry lines across his forehead. 'That's what's eating at me. They seem so random, so unconnected, other than the girls' ages. The Cypress girl is ten and the Santa Cruz girl is eleven. But I don't want to spend all our resources looking for a connection when maybe it's a freak coincidence.'

'You think the Santa Cruz girl could be a ransom?'

'It makes sense, but there's been no contact with the family. Obviously, that's not an issue with the Cypress City girl.' He paused and said, 'I've got another call. I'll email you a fact sheet when I get to the PD.'

WKQE radio station was located in a strip mall in downtown Cypress City, sandwiched between a jewelry store and a discount liquor mart. The station produced local programming for the Collier County area at key times during the week, with National Public Radio filling in with national news. Several large benefactors from Santa Cruz kept the station afloat.

Cypress City was located twenty miles inland from the coast, between Naples and Santa Cruz to the north, and Marco Island to the south. People associated Cypress City with its wealthy neighbors, assuming it benefited from the affluence, but the town had much more in common with Everglades City to the south. Cypress City was quite a bit larger, but both towns were still struggling to rebuild after flooding from Hurricane

Irma took out hundreds of homes. Maggie's zip code placed her in Santa Cruz territory, but she related more closely with the hardscrabble folks from the swampland.

Maggie had talked to the mayor on her way into the station and rescheduled the interview for the following weekend, then called her producer, Tiger Dennison, with a heads up on the content change. Tiger said he would line up law enforcement call-ins with commentary or updates on the investigation. Maggie was also fairly certain that Tiger would contact a few call-in regulars and provide them with the topic. New callers were good, but the regulars kept the show moving. Tiger was a publicity whore, and had no problem convincing natural-born talkers to call the station to participate in a discussion. 'We need your input,' he'd say. 'Listeners know you by name. They tell me they love it when you call in to the station and give Maggie a run for her money.'

Fifteen minutes into her show that morning, Arnie Havershine, a retired tomato farmer, called to argue. Regardless of the stance Maggie was taking, Arnie would take the opposite. After Maggie provided the information the police had released on the kidnappings, she opened the lines for callers, asking for any information someone might have about seeing either of the girls, or any suspicious activity in any of the area parks.

Arnie cut Maggie off midsentence. 'We are the biggest county in the state of Florida, and we don't do jack squat to take care of nothing but rich folks.'

'Hold on,' Maggie said. 'We're the largest county land-wise, but half our county is the Big Cypress Reserve, plus the state park and state forests. The largest city in our county is barely over 25,000 people. So we don't have the resources that—'

'The only reason you're talking about these missing girls is one of them's from Santa Cruz. You and I both know that's the truth. If both those girls had been from Cypress you wouldn't even have brought up their names.'

Arnie's politics couldn't have been further from Maggie's own, and his voice was like nails on a chalkboard, but it was a good call; it kept listeners tuned in, and better yet, calling in. Tiger had hand-lettered a small plaque that he hung above the radio booth: 'The crazies make the ratings. Keep 'em on the line.' He was currently spinning his finger in the air behind the glass for Maggie to drag it out, but this was two little girls' lives, not some senator's latest bumble.

'Why would you think a missing child's zip code would make a difference to anyone? The police want both these girls found as much as you and I do.'

'OK, then. You think you know it all, how about this?' Arnie said.

Maggie glanced through the window to catch Tiger shaking his head, grinning.

'Take a look at that story on the Mexican brothers that got kidnapped from Immokalee last year,' Arnie said. 'Count up how many lines of copy that got in the local paper. Then count up how many lines that boy from Santa Cruz got a couple of years ago. The one whose dad owned the power plant. They talked about that for weeks, even after the kid was found. Tell me the cops spent as much time on those two investigations. Tell me you talked about those Mexican brothers on your radio station.'

'The brothers were taken from school by their father over a custody dispute. Custody disputes aren't news. They happen all the time. The boy from Santa Cruz was abducted from his bedroom, inside a heavily guarded home.'

'So what? A kid's a kid! Who cares why they took those boys? You still need it on the radio. You need to let people know what's happening so they can get involved.'

Maggie pressed the end call button and flipped Tiger off for mouthing, 'What's wrong with you?'

'Which is exactly what we're doing here today. We have to keep the focus,' Maggie said. She modulated her voice, low and reasonable. 'We've got two missing girls from Collier County. I don't care what city these girls are from, they both deserve our best.'

Maggie went through the details again, describing the girls, their clothing, where they were last seen. She received an endless string of calls that morning, mostly from listeners who had stories to relate about kids who had wandered off at the shopping mall, kids who took the wrong bus home from school, kids who decided to walk to a friend's house and got lost on the way. The general message from callers was, don't worry, it will all turn out OK.

Maggie had been tempted to share her background with callers like Arnie, to let him know she understood poverty firsthand, but her privacy remained a priority. She'd never been ashamed of her background, and had used it to direct many of the decisions she'd made as an adult. She'd worked hard to make a life for herself with resources that her mom had never had, but she didn't regret the experiences she'd had growing up.

Her mother had been a stripper in Dayton, Ohio in the seventies, when Maggie was in grade school. Her father had never been part of their lives, so her mom had chosen a career path with a fairly consistent paycheck. She'd never been ashamed of her body or her ability to make money from it. It had been a wild time and Maggie had seen her fill of strange men and abusive situations growing up, but her mom had never been one to complain or harbor regrets.

In 1980, when her mom had saved up enough money to choose a different lifestyle, she opened her own strip club called Madame D's. Maggie was fourteen. She spent weekends at the club and became close to several of the dancers who treated her like their kid sister. It was through watching their chaotic lives that Maggie developed her own desire to become a cop. And while she'd never been ashamed of her childhood or the life her mother had chosen for the two of them, she also determined to not make the same choices herself.

Late one Friday night at Mel's, while Serena counted the till and Danny loaded up the instruments, Mel had sat next to Maggie at the bar and reminisced about his expansion from Italian restaurant to bar to strip club. Maggie told Mel about her mom's experience, from stripping to club owner, and how at seventy-three she still went into work each evening to check on the girls. Mel said he needed a female to watch over the girls working The Foxxy Den. He said their lives were a mess and they needed a female to give some much-needed advice. Several tequilas later and Mel had convinced Maggie to work the dressing room on Saturdays, their busiest night, helping the girls with makeup and costume changes, and offering an occasional piece of advice. A House Mom for the strippers. Having no kids of her own, Maggie had fallen in love with the girls and looked forward to her Saturday night ritual. Several of the girls had tried to talk her into having them on the radio show to spice things up – a late night program. She smiled at the thought of Arnie Havershine sputtering his way through a phone call with one of Maggie's favorites, a rough-talking girl who called herself Sassy.

SIX

The office was in chaos. Olivia Sable, the doctor's receptionist, a pretty twenty-nine-year-old who could pass for eighteen in the right clothes, had gone from shock to rage to throwing records and medical instruments when she'd shown up at work that morning and the doctor had taken her into the examination room to find two little girls comatose on the tables. It took her only a moment to recognize the girls from the photographs that were all over the news that morning.

After ten minutes of LeBlanc and Olivia yelling at each other, Ramone entered the office, apparently to defend his actions.

He walked in pointing a finger at Olivia. 'I can hear everything you're saying. You don't know what you're talking about.' And then to LeBlanc, 'I told you not to bring her in here. She's nothing but added trouble.'

LeBlanc felt his blood pressure spike. 'I told you to not leave those girls, for any reason. Get back in the room!'

Olivia stood behind her office chair at the front desk where she had already called to cancel all appointments for the day, telling patients that the doctor had fallen ill.

She lowered her voice. 'How could you trust him? He's an idiot! He's here for the money, that's it.'

'You knew the risks but agreed the ends justified the means,' he said.

'But I told you he was too big of a risk and now look what's happened.'

LeBlanc pulled her into his chest, folding her arms into him, and placed his hand behind her head, cooing to her like she was a child. Given his small office, he'd had no choice but to confide in Olivia about the alternative research. As office manager, she knew his business down to the last dime, so including her in the details was crucial, but getting her to buy in to the research involving children had been lengthy. He trusted her, but he was wise enough to put certain safety nets in place. He knew very well that one wrong word from Olivia would cause everything he cared about to come crashing down around him.

When the fight finally left her, he placed his hands on her arms and gently pushed her away from him to grab a tissue off her desk.

'Olivia. Why do you think I had you come to work early today? You have supported me through this whole ordeal. And I need you now more than ever.'

He watched as she turned her back and rubbed the tissue under her eyes, trying to fix her makeup. Olivia used her beauty like a tool, disguising her cunning intelligence under a head full of bleach blonde hair when it suited her, but just as quickly using it like a master manipulator. He had hired her for her looks, but it hadn't taken him long to understand her far greater value.

'Oscar, you have done some things in the past that I haven't agreed with, but I've kept quiet. I respect what you're doing. I understand how important the research is to you.'

'How important it is to humanity. This isn't just about me, Olivia.'

Olivia's expression had turned from anger to weariness. 'Can we please not talk about that right now,' she said. 'Your life is falling apart and you are dragging me into your mess. The least you can do is tell me you have a way to get those girls out of here without all of us getting arrested. Because it is all over the news. And I refuse to go to jail for you.'

'You can't be serious.' He looked at her with compassion, trying to soothe her worries. He needed her calm and thinking rationally. He leaned casually against the wall and considered her for a moment. 'You know the French have a saying.'

She banged her hand against the desk, her eyes wide and full of fury. 'I don't give a damn what the French say! You can't charm your way out of this. You are screwed. Unless you do something to help the moron in the other room figure a way to get those girls home without being seen, you will go to jail.'

'What do you suggest?'

She choked out a laugh. 'How the hell am I supposed to know? This is not my problem. I did nothing to create it, and I'll do nothing to fix it.' She stood and grabbed her purse.

'You can't leave me. Sit down.'

'Screw you.'

'Sit down!'

Olivia stared at him for a moment before speaking. 'Where's Jillian? Why isn't she here?'

'She has nothing to do with this.'

'She has as much to do with it as I do! She's your wife! Let her save your . . .' She let the words trail off when she saw the anger on LeBlanc's face.

He said nothing, trying to control his anger while everything else in his life was spinning dangerously out of control. He'd had no sleep and was terrified of the physical stress the long-term sedation was placing on the girls. Years of research were in danger of disintegrating over one man's ineptitude.

SEVEN

Mark arrived at the radio station at a little before two o'clock, just as Maggie was walking out the door to her car.

'Good news?' Maggie asked.

'A few decent leads.'

'The radio segment didn't turn up much either.'

'Actually, our best tips came from a woman from Fort Lauderdale. She caught your show on her way out of Cypress. She was here visiting her mom. She saw a black-haired girl at the park last evening and noticed a white transit van pull up to the curb where she was walking. It was odd enough that she pulled her car off to the side of the road to watch what was happening. I texted her a photo of Amaya O'Neal, the little girl missing from Cypress, and she confirmed it was who she saw.'

'Why didn't she call it in to police when she saw it?'

'She said she felt terrible about not calling it in. She said it looked sketchy, but the girl smiled at the man and climbed in without any issue. This was at four forty-five yesterday afternoon.'

Maggie pointed to her car. 'You have time to sit a minute?'

He nodded and she unlocked the doors and cranked the AC.

Mark climbed in and cursed. 'God almighty, please stop this heat.'

Maggie handed him a napkin from inside her glove box and watched him wipe the sweat off his forehead.

'It's a start, but we're twenty-one hours into this,' he said. 'It doesn't appear to be a domestic issue. Neither of the families can imagine why their daughter would get into a transit van with someone, or who their daughter would know who would even be driving one.'

'Tiger can interrupt programming. You want to get this information on the air, about the van?' she asked.

'I do. I'm headed in to talk to him. We have a photo of a similar van and pics of the girls running in tonight's paper. But I have another favor to ask you.'

'You name it.'

'I've talked with Amaya's mom twice now, and John Desmond did the first interview with her last night.'

'Amaya is the little girl from Cypress City?'

'That's right. Her mom's name is Kelly O'Neal. She's tough. Has a chip on her shoulder. She clearly doesn't trust the police.'

'Is there a dad in the picture?'

Mark nodded. 'I didn't get a good read on him. I had a conversation with the mom and dad both. He was upset but didn't seem fully engaged. Like he couldn't express himself.'

'Suspect?'

'Too early to tell. They live over on Howard Street next to the river. It's pretty obvious they're struggling. The wife seems completely overwhelmed with life. She didn't relate to me at all. She seems to think the cops couldn't care less about her kid. Even though I'm standing in front of her trying to help.'

'You want me to talk to her?'

'I do. Since you aren't an officer, but you know what we're after, I think you could do us some good. I just couldn't get her to open up about anything personal going on with her daughter. I got the feeling she thought I was judging her. She thought I was asking questions about problems she might be having because I was going to blame the kidnapping on bad parenting or poor decision making. I couldn't get her to understand I was asking questions to try and figure out who would have taken her little girl.'

Maggie heard the frustration in his voice. 'I get it,' she said. 'What's my MO?'

'Just be honest. Tell her you work for the radio station and you'd like to have her on. That you're also working with the police to help sift through connections that might lead to something.'

After Mark went inside the radio station, Maggie called Kelly O'Neal from her car.

'Mrs O'Neal?'

'Yes.'

'My name is Maggie Wise, I'm a radio host for Collier County Weekend. I'm hoping you might let me drop by to talk to you about your daughter. I did a show this morning about the missing girls. I'd like to run another segment with information you might be able to provide.'

She didn't speak for long enough that Maggie pulled the phone away from her ear to make sure the line was still connected.

'I heard your show this morning,' Kelly said. Her voice was edgy, hesitant. 'Someone called and told me you were on.'

'I'm pleased to say the show did some good. I just spoke with Chief Hamilton. He said they received a tip from a caller this morning about a transit van.'

'Officer Desmond called a little while ago and told me. I can't imagine Amaya getting into a van with someone. I just don't get it. She knows better than that.'

'I realize it seems like the police are spending their time

asking you questions when they should be out looking for your little girl.'

'It's so frustrating.' Her words were stilted, as if trying to talk around tears. 'It seems like we ought to be out *doing* something, but all we do is sit around *talking*. And nothing is happening.'

'It's the tips from people, like the listener today, and the small things that you might know as her mom, that can lead the police in the right direction. Walking the streets of Cypress City isn't going to find Amaya. Figuring out who would want to take her and why they would want to is going to find her. That's why Chief Hamilton is asking so many questions.'

'Did he put you up to this call?'

'He asked me to talk to you. He got the impression that you didn't trust him.' The woman said nothing so Maggie continued. 'Let's talk for a few minutes. If you don't like what I have to say, you can send me down the road.'

'That's fine. If you can do something to bring my girl back then I'm all for it. We live on Howard Street.'

'What's your house number?'

'You don't need one. It's the house with the lawnmowers.'

EIGHT

E conomic inequality in Collier County was a frequent topic on Maggie's show because it lit up the phone lines. She dropped the statistics at least once a year, and they never failed to work. The top one percent in Collier County earned over four million per year, while the remaining ninety-nine percent earned less than $58,000 per year. There were over 1,000 homeless children in Collier County; hard to fathom with the number of billionaires living in Santa Cruz and Naples. Yet every time Maggie cited the statistic, someone from Santa Cruz would call and dispute it, claiming that she was lying to garner ratings. But the residents living on Howard Street had no problem believing it.

Howard Street ran parallel to Snake River, so-named because

of the cottonmouth water moccasins found along its banks. The houses were a mixture of run down and abandoned. As Maggie drove down the street, it didn't take long to understand the landmark description that Mrs O'Neal had provided. The one-story box with chipped white paint was surrounded by dozens of push mowers parked haphazardly in the front and side yards. A garage with its doors wide open was located in the back of the lot. Maggie parked in front of the house and noted that the man standing behind the workbench in the garage didn't bother to look her way.

Kelly O'Neal stood several feet back from the screen door in the shadows of her house and watched Maggie get out of her car. She was aware that Kelly was watching her, probably looking for judgment in her behavior.

When Maggie reached the porch, Kelly walked outside and shook Maggie's hand as she introduced herself.

'I'd take you inside, but we don't have air conditioning. At least there's a breeze out here.'

With a heat index that day of 112, Maggie couldn't imagine being without air conditioning.

'I'm fine. It's nice to sit outside.'

Kelly motioned to one of the two lawn chairs and Maggie took a seat.

'I'm so sorry for what's happened, Mrs O'Neal. I can't imagine how terrifying this must be for you and your husband.'

'Thank you. And call me Kelly.'

Maggie nodded. 'Any new information, other than the transit van?'

Kelly shook her head then looked down, watching the tears splatter on her thighs.

'I appreciate you talking with me,' Maggie said.

Kelly swiped the tears away and adjusted the ponytail that caught up her long blonde hair. She cleared her throat, obviously struggling to keep from falling apart. 'I didn't mean to sound ungrateful before. I appreciated you doing the radio show.'

Maggie nodded, giving her time to finish.

'I just can't help thinking if the Santa Cruz girl wasn't missing too, that this wouldn't even be a story. That's what pisses me off.'

'I'm not sure why you think the police and the community wouldn't do everything they could.'

Kelly made a dismissive noise. 'I heard the guy on your radio show this morning. Obviously I'm not the only one who thinks that way around here.'

'The police don't care where your child lives. They just want those kids back home.'

Kelly gave her an incredulous look. 'I drove up to Santa Cruz this morning. I wanted to see where the other family lived. The Baxters.' She sat up straight as she pronounced their name, offering a knowing look, as though the name alone spoke volumes about their privileged life. 'I just thought maybe something would click about how Amaya and the other girl might know each other. Have you seen their house?' She waited until Maggie shook her head. 'They got their manicured lawn. Their edge-trimmed sidewalks with each blade of grass the same three inches tall. Not a freaking dandelion in sight for miles.' She gestured to their front yard. 'You know how many mowers we're up to?'

Maggie shook her head.

'Forty-seven. We don't have a pot to piss in and Andre bought another mower to fix last week. He can't fix the forty-six that he has, but somehow this new one he brought home is gonna be different. And you think people are gonna drop everything they're doing to find *my* kid?' She rolled her eyes. '*Please.*'

'Ma'am.'

Kelly pointed to the shack next door. 'I went and told Marleen what was going on last night. Asked her to keep an eye out for Amaya. She says, "Honey, I'm so sorry to hear that. You bet I'll keep an eye out for her. And listen. If you're going into town later, do me a favor and pick me up a carton of Marlboros. I'll pay you back on Friday."'

'Kelly.'

She turned to stare Maggie in the eye. 'Nobody gives a shit about my girl. Not even my neighbor.'

'I do.' Maggie stared her down. 'I'm here, right now, ready to help.'

Kelly looked back over at Andre, still bent over his workbench, muttering to himself around the cigarette dangling from his mouth. 'It looks like he doesn't care about Amaya, but Andre's ate up over this. He just can't show it.'

'Can you or your husband think of anyone who would want to hurt Amaya? An ex-boyfriend or girlfriend, someone Andre did business with who's out to get him now?'

Kelly shook her head.

'No one who's acted odd around you lately? Or someone different hanging around the neighborhood you might have noticed?'

'I can't think of anyone.'

'Amaya hasn't mentioned someone at school who was giving her a hard time?'

'No.'

'Look. You're being straight up with me. So I'm going to be straight with you. Is that OK?'

'Well, hell yes. You better be,' Kelly said.

'I get that you're angry at everyone right now. The most important person in the world to you has been taken, and no one has any answers for why it happened.' She paused and wiped the sweat dripping down the sides of her face with her shirt sleeve. 'I get that. But I suspect you're holding back. You don't think people care so you refuse to put yourself out there.' She paused and considered whether she should continue. 'I think you've been disappointed one too many times in the people around you, so you don't give anybody credit for anything. Do I have it about right?'

Kelly said nothing. She felt the tears slide down her cheeks and grit her jaws against the comment.

'I think you believe the officers aren't doing their jobs. You already know they're going to let you down. But I promise you, that's not the case here.' She waited a moment but Kelly remained silent. 'Let people help you. Come to the radio station to talk about Amaya and your family. Tell people how desperate you are to find her.'

Kelly gestured to Andre. 'So we can get some news anchor out here filming this shit show? Who would take us seriously?'

'Come up to the station today.' Maggie glanced at her watch. 'Plan on three o'clock unless you hear otherwise. I'll get someone from the local cable station there too. You bring a framed photo of Amaya and I'll get it on our radio station website, along with the one the police posted. People want to hear from you. It's one thing to see a missing girl's picture on TV. It's another to hear the girl's mom making a plea for help. That's what you have to do. OK?'

She nodded.

'Meanwhile, when Chief Hamilton contacts you again, answer the questions. He's not trying to embarrass you. He's just trying to find Amaya. He put in a twenty-hour workday yesterday. You can't tell me he doesn't care.'

Kelly raised a hand in the air to stop her. 'I get it.'

NINE

Over the next hour, the interview at the radio station morphed into a community search at the park where Amaya was abducted, with several media outlets sending crews to film the event. They wanted a statement from Kelly. Maggie called her several times, talking her through the updates, attempting to convince her each time that she was capable of talking in front of a microphone, and that everyone coming was doing it to help her daughter.

When Maggie arrived, she saw one of the Cypress City officers working with a cameraman to set up a makeshift staging area shaded from the late-afternoon glare of the sun. Mark and several other officers were organizing the search party, gathering the volunteers in an open grassy area by the park's entrance and just below the media stage. Word had spread through the crowd that the girl's mother would be speaking, and the atmosphere was charged with a mix of excitement and overwhelming sadness. It was similar to a crime scene investigation, minus the world-weary knowledge that the odds weren't good for a positive resolution. Maggie could sense that the crowd in front of her still believed in happy endings.

Kelly wore a skirt and tank top and clutched an eight-by-ten-inch framed school photo of Amaya to her chest. She'd fixed her long blonde hair and pulled it into a bun behind her head. Her husband stood next to her, but she'd already told Maggie that Andre wouldn't come up to the podium. 'He can't talk in front of people.' Maggie saw Kelly's nausea playing out in her expression.

'Can I see the photo you brought?' Maggie said, hoping to calm Kelly's nerves.

She hesitated and then handed it to her.

Maggie smiled and found herself tearing up at the sight of the little girl. She looked more like her father, with his dark skin and tightly curled black hair, but she had Kelly's lopsided smile and freckles.

'She's beautiful,' Maggie said. 'She looks like both of you.'

Kelly attempted a smile at the compliment but Andre turned away, his expression full of anguish.

Maggie handed the photo back and asked, 'Are you going to be OK? Talking to the crowd?'

She shook her head. 'People keep talking about me making a statement. I should have written something out. I don't have anything to read. I just figured you'd be asking me questions and I'd answer them. I don't have any idea what to say when I get up there. I get this one chance to do this for Amaya, and I'm going to screw it all up.'

'You can do this. Take deep breaths before you walk up to the podium. It will help slow your heart rate. First thing, thank everyone for being here. Tell them a little about Amaya, what she looks like. Describe what she was wearing. Tell them if they know anything about the white transit van that they should find a police officer immediately.'

Kelly nodded her head as Maggie spoke, staring intently at her, trying to absorb her words.

Mark walked up behind Kelly and laid a hand on her back. 'We're ready for you. I'll introduce you first, and then I'll come back up and explain how the canvas will work. OK?'

Kelly stared at Mark, her eyes wide.

'I'll stand right behind you,' Maggie said. 'You're going to do just fine.'

As they walked to the staging area, Maggie was surprised at

the number of people who had gathered on a Saturday afternoon in a matter of hours, just based on a social media callout. She hoped Kelly could see beyond her nerves to the caring people standing in front of her.

One of the news crews had produced a podium which now had several microphones attached to the front of it. Mark thanked the volunteers for offering up their time and asked them to join him in a moment of prayer. The group of about 200 people grew silent, and Maggie scanned the crowd of bowed heads, looking for anyone or anything that appeared amiss.

Mark turned and motioned for Kelly.

She set the photo down gently, then clenched either side of the podium, drawing her shoulders in tight. She cleared her throat and leaned in to the microphone. 'Hi. I'm Kelly O'Neal. Amaya's mom.'

Maggie watched the expressions of the men and women standing in front of her. The concern, the heartbreak, was evident. A cop needed occasional moments like this to realize the world wasn't full of monsters.

Kelly turned back from the podium and stared at Maggie, and she saw the tears streaming down Kelly's face.

She moved behind Kelly, placed her hands on her shoulders and whispered in her ear. 'You're doing great. These people just want to help. You take your time. Start by thanking them for being here.'

Maggie watched Kelly's shoulders raise and lower as she took a long breath. 'I'm sorry,' she said. 'I've never done something like this.' Another long breath. 'I just want to thank you all for coming here. I never imagined this many people would show up.'

She paused and Maggie leaned into her ear again. 'Say you want to tell them a little about Amaya.'

'So, Amaya is ten years old. She's in the fifth grade. She's pretty quiet, but she's not shy when you talk to her. She loves school. I brought a picture of her.' She held it up with both hands. 'I'll leave it up here if you want to look at it. The day she—' She stopped and turned back to Maggie, shaking her head as if she couldn't continue.

Maggie placed a hand on her back again and leaned in to

her ear. 'Come on, you can do this. Tell them what she was wearing.' She motioned toward the microphones.

Kelly turned and took a tissue from Mark. After a long moment she wiped her eyes and bent toward the microphone again. 'Yesterday, at the park, she was wearing khaki shorts and a navy-blue T-shirt with a yellow smiley face on the front of it. She was wearing white sneakers.' She turned and gestured to Andre who suddenly looked like a deer in headlights. 'She has black curly hair like her dad. She's thin and has lots of energy. She likes to play basketball with her friends. She's a tomboy, but she's polite with a real sweet side.'

Maggie scanned the faces in the crowd, watching men and women swipe away tears, and she wondered again at the chance that one of the faces might be the abductor. Coming out to gather information on what the police know, or to gain the perverse pleasure associated with having such a horrific secret, maybe coming to watch the pain of others because they can't experience it themselves?

'So if you could just tell everyone you know about the white van in the park. Ask them if they might have been at the park. Or maybe you've seen a white van in your neighborhood that you think looked suspicious? Just please tell the police. And thank you again for coming here today.'

As the volunteers formed the ranks that Mark described in his briefing, Kelly and her husband began walking toward the front line. Before they could join the group, John Desmond stopped them and asked them to remain at the news table in case they were needed to answer questions. Maggie knew the police were trying to protect the family from a possible devastating revelation in the woods.

As Maggie left to walk alongside Danny on the canvas, she noted that the Baxters had arrived and were talking to Kelly and Andre, although Andre stood about three feet back from the conversation, looking off into the distance. Maggie wondered if Kelly had softened enough to benefit from the support that she hoped the other family could provide.

The canvas through the park was somber. Groups split up to cover grassy patches, woods and swamp, a creek, the campground and a picnic area. Volunteers were staggered in ten-foot increments and made the walk in relative silence, only occasionally remarking on an object found on the ground. Maggie and Danny's group made their way down a walking path to a thick band of cypress and walked just a few feet into the dense thicket to scan for any signs of color outside of the dark gray swamp and bright green leaves. Deeper into the swamp, the mangrove was mostly impenetrable, and too dangerous to walk through even in the occasional clearings. Caution signs were posted around the area, warning of alligators. By the time they circled the two-mile perimeter of the swamp, Maggie's boots were wet with sweat and her shirt and shorts soaked through.

As she and Danny made their way back up the walking path to the park entrance she received a text from Mark.

They found Brooke Baxter. In Santa Cruz. Dropped off at a park.

Maggie felt cold bumps raise on her arms. She passed the cell phone to Danny.

'That's great news.'

Maggie texted back, *Unhurt?*

Appears to be

Amaya?

Nothing yet. Telling Baxters now

Danny had been looking over Maggie's shoulder. 'You gonna tell these people?' He gestured to the group of twenty sweat-soaked volunteers, now slogging back through the stifling parking lot to the staging area to check in.

'The police may not be ready to let that out yet so don't say anything.'

As they approached the area where the TV vans had been parked, Maggie noticed the reporters rushing to grab cameras and straighten ties and smooth blouses, attempting to wipe the perspiration off their faces as they made their way toward the area where the police huddled with the Baxters. The wife called out, crying first and then laughing. Maggie watched the husband pull her into a hug, cradling her head against his chest.

Maggie turned from the scene, searching for Kelly and Andre in the crowd, and found them watching the commotion, Kelly standing from her seat near the podium. Maggie ran toward her and she turned, her eyes wide and expectant.

'Did they find something? Did they find the girls?' She started to take off toward the group of cops surrounding the Baxters, but Maggie caught her by the arm.

'Hang on.'

She jerked her arm free and looked as if she was ready to throw a punch.

'Kelly! Just listen to me.'

'Oh my God. Tell me Amaya's OK.'

'It's not Amaya. They found Brooke. Someone dropped her off at a park in Santa Cruz. But Amaya wasn't with her.'

Andre, who had been standing behind Kelly, grabbed her arms and held her as she slid to the ground, falling on to her hands and knees, sobbing.

TEN

'At five-twenty this afternoon, an eleven-year-old girl, Brooke Baxter, was found by a jogger in a remote section of the Santa Cruz Golf Club in south Florida. Police stated that the area, located just out of sight of the range of play, can also be accessed by a gravel road that runs about three hundred feet from the site. When the joggers found the girl she was sitting against a tree looking dazed and confused. She stated her name, but wasn't able to communicate much else. The girl, who had been missing for twenty-four hours, has been reunited with her family. Another girl, Amaya O'Neal, age ten, was taken from a neighboring town around the same time and remains missing.'

Maggie watched the TV screen as the number for the Cypress City Police Station was displayed. She flipped the TV off and wondered how Mark was coping. Once the double kidnapping had reached CNN and FOX that evening, he'd received a phone call from the governor of Florida asking for an update.

Mark had explained that the girl's clothes were intact and, after a thorough medical examination, the Baxter girl had been deemed physically unharmed. The girl had told her parents that her last memory over the twenty-four-hour period was climbing into a white van. The next thing she remembered was waking up on the ground in the park. Mark hadn't spoken with the girl, but the Santa Cruz Police Chief had said she had never heard of Amaya, and hadn't recognized her photograph. The case was half solved but with no more information now than they'd had before the girl was found.

After the search, Maggie went home to shower and dress for her shift. Wishing Mark would call with an update, she was surprised when her cell phone rang and it was Kelly O'Neal.

'I'm sorry to bother you. Do you mind?'

'No, course not. I told you to call any time.'

'I keep thinking about the van, and trying to think of someone that Amaya might have gotten in with. I feel bad even saying this, because I'm sure it's nothing, but it's the only thing I can think of.'

'Anything, Kelly. The police will decide if it's worth pursuing.'

'The police keep asking me about anything at all that was different over the past month or two. I can't get the van out of my head. It just seems so weird to me that Amaya would have gotten into a van with someone she didn't know. And the only thing I can even think of that might count as that sort of different in the past month was at the blood clinic.'

Maggie muted the remote. 'What kind of blood clinic?'

'I give blood for money a couple times a week. Actually plasma. Amaya comes with me sometimes. She says she likes to watch those blood machines. So she came with me a few weeks ago, and one of the techs asked her if she wanted to find out what her blood type was. I thought it was odd because they're all business in there. They wear their plastic masks. I go through the same questions each time I go in. It's not like they try and get to know you. It's the exact same procedure each time. We're like cattle moving through. And then out of the blue some guy is all friendly with Amaya. Asking her about school. Asking her what she wants to be when she grows up. Then he says he'll type her blood for her and Amaya got all excited. I wasn't so sure afterwards, you know?'

'Why weren't you sure?'

'Cause there's some real perverts out there. I was afraid he was a molester, but he didn't have that vibe, you know? But maybe he was a pervert. Maybe he looked Amaya up. He had our address from my medical forms.'

'With your address it would have been easy to figure out what school Amaya attends.'

'That's what I thought. He could have watched her for a week or two, and figured out most afternoons after school Amaya goes to the park.' She exhaled shakily. 'You know, maybe that would explain Amaya getting into a van.'

'The guy could have said he was picking Amaya up to take her to the clinic. Maybe he told Amaya that you asked him to pick her up.'

Kelly moaned. 'I should have told the police this. It just didn't come to mind. The next time I went to give blood I didn't see that guy, and Amaya hasn't been back with me since. It was just that one time. I don't know if I'm making a big deal out of nothing.'

'Do you know the man's name?'

'No.'

'Did you watch him take Amaya's blood or hear the conversation?' Maggie asked.

'No. I was on the machine when they figured her blood type. It takes me longer than a fresh vein. It's actually the Three Region Plasma Center. Takes about two hours to drain the blood, remove the plasma, and then put the blood back in. When we were driving home, Amaya said the guy she was talking to before I left showed her the lab in the back. And then he offered to tell her what blood type she was. He told Amaya she was O positive, the universal donor, like that was some prize. I'm thinking, no. My girl is not going to be selling her plasma someday. I got bigger and better plans for her than that.'

'Amaya didn't seem to think anything odd had taken place?'

'Not at all. She was excited. And, honestly, I thought it was pretty nice that this guy was showing her around. It's a long two hours for her to sit there.'

'You didn't think it was odd that they would take a sample of Amaya's blood without asking you for permission? Without you signing some kind of consent form?'

'I don't know.' Her voice took on an edge. 'I didn't think

about it. When Amaya told me what had happened, we'd already left. And Amaya thought it was great. It just didn't seem a big deal.'

'I understand,' Maggie said, afraid Kelly would shut down for fear of being judged. 'Can you give me the exact date you were at the plasma center with Amaya?'

'Not off the top of my head.'

'I need you to work on that. Figure out the exact date Amaya was with you. Use old receipts, credit card statements from some shopping you may have done that day, a school function around that time. I have to work tonight, so I may not answer my cell phone. As soon as you get it, text me when this happened.'

On Saturday nights, Maggie took the side door to The Foxxy Den to avoid the men and occasional women in the club. She rarely ventured out into the bar area, which smelled like stale alcohol, weed and body odor, with a lavender deodorizer that mixed with – rather than masked – the smells. The dressing room, located down a short hallway to the right of the side door, was so saturated with hairspray and gels and body sprays that the rank bar smells couldn't penetrate the air.

Maggie worked the dressing room from eight to midnight each Saturday, applying makeup and checking costumes for dress code violations, or helping the girls into the dresses and strings and patches of fabric that Florida code deemed sufficient to count as clothing. Mel had four dancers on Saturday nights, with several of them working the club circuit all the way to Miami on other days of the week. Mel didn't charge a stage fee, and instead offered an hourly wage with all tips split evenly between the bartenders and the entertainers at the end of the night. Some girls wouldn't work for the even split, but Mel had a loyal following who liked the sense of family it cultivated.

Maggie stored her purse in a locker just inside the door and found three of the girls crowded around Cassondra, a sophomore at Florida Gulf Coast University majoring in business administration. She made more stripping on Friday and Saturday nights than her roommates made working thirty hours a week as waitresses. It was fast cash but hard work.

Sassy, the fiery red-haired senior dancer of the group, waved Maggie over to the girl who was sitting in the makeup chair, staring at her puffy eyes and red, swollen face in the mirror. 'Her mom found out. Called her a slut and disowned her. The help she'd been getting with rent? Gone, as of today.'

'So she can trick on the side now too? What a stupid thing for a mother to do.' Ana Sofia had emigrated from Honduras to the US three years ago, and had been dancing at Mel's for almost a year. She had an angry temper and an unrealistic sense of justice that the other girls found humorous.

Maggie put her arms out and Cassondra dissolved into tears and came up out of the chair for a hug. Maggie squeezed the girl tight and promised it would work out in the end. She finally put her hands on Cassondra's shoulders and pushed her back to look at her more closely. 'Do you need to take tonight off?'

She choked out a laugh. 'I don't even know if I can pay my rent. I can't afford a night off.'

'Look. There are kids all over the country who pay for their own college. You don't need your parents' money. You'll take out loans and get another job. Maybe you change schools or take a semester off.' Maggie glanced at Ana Sofia and back at Cassondra. 'You don't trick, though. You know that. It's not safe. You make two hundred dollars and end up with some disease you'll be paying on for the rest of your life.'

Ana Sofia, who worked for an illegal escort service in Miami, rolled her eyes and walked over to the dressing area where she pulled her dress off in one fluid motion and dropped it to the floor. 'Fifteen minutes, Cassondra. Better get makeup on those eyes.'

Maggie was still holding her by the shoulders. 'Are you OK to go on?'

She nodded.

'Have a seat and I'll get you ready.'

Maggie took a concealer stick and swiped it under the girl's eyes, then used a makeup sponge to apply a layer of foundation to cover up the red splotches while she offered advice on applying for financial aid and contacting the bursar's office for help. After ten minutes of pep talk and makeup, Cassondra appeared ready to face the men waiting in the bar.

'You got this. You shake it off tonight and figure out a plan in the morning.'

She stood, and Sassy brought her little yellow dress over. 'Let's go. You're on first. You got two minutes to get dressed.'

Maggie and Sassy helped her step into the strappy dress and then into her heels. Ana Sofia grabbed her by the arm and kissed her on the cheek. 'Come on, girlfriend. We're up.'

After the other two had left, Sassy, who was still wearing her bathrobe, plopped into the makeup chair. 'Do me up, Maggie May.'

Maggie handed her a makeup wipe to clean her face. 'You need to watch out for her. Don't let Ana Sofia take her down that road. She's vulnerable and hurting. I don't want to see her turn to sex for money. You be the big sis and watch after her. You hear?'

Sassy grinned and pitched the wipe onto the counter. 'Yes, ma'am.' She pointed to her eyes. 'Do me up good tonight. Antonio's bringing friends. The guy tips like no other. He's an arrogant jerk, but he's rolling in it. Lap dances all night long.'

Maggie told her to close her eyes and swiped white powder across the crease under the brow. 'Did you watch the local news today?' Sassy was a news junkie. Maggie was certain she'd be following the story of the kidnappings, and if gossip was available, Sassy would know it.

She grabbed Maggie's hand and pulled it away from her eyes in order to open them, her expression shocked. 'Can you believe that about those little girls? I swear, if it's some pervert man that took them, we will hunt him down and castrate him on the spot.'

'Have you ever heard of the parents of the Cypress City girl?'

She moaned. 'I feel so bad for them. The dad, Andre O'Neal?' She fanned her face with her hand. 'So hot. He played ball in school. My older sister had the biggest crush on him. But he was too quiet. I don't even know if he dated anyone until he hooked up with that young girl.'

'Was the young girl Kelly?'

'Yeah, she's still older than me, but she was a lot younger than him. She's the only girl I can ever remember him with.'

'You know much about him?'

Sassy closed her eyes again and lifted her face back up to Maggie. 'He went into the military and came back different. He was one of those quiet boys all the girls had crushes on. I am not kidding. My sister thought he was the hottest man walking. But when he came home, he wasn't the same. Still quiet, but more angry than shy.'

Maggie stepped behind the chair to look at Sassy in the mirror. 'How's that look?'

Sassy opened her eyes and grinned. 'You are a miracle worker.'

Maggie leaned in to peer at her own reflection in the brightly lit room. 'This is why I don't use lights like this in my own bathroom. I swear I sprouted another three wrinkles since last weekend.'

Sassy feigned shock. 'Are you kidding? When I hit sixty—'

'I'm not sixty!'

'I'm kidding. You look wonderful. Pretty black hair. A body that still rocks.' She gave Maggie a long look. 'You remind me of a working-class Sandra Bullock.'

Maggie laughed. 'You girls know how to make someone feel good.'

'That's a compliment!'

Maggie glanced at her watch. 'You better get dressed. Fifteen minutes and you're up.'

The girls had thirty-minute sets before they switched out. Felecia, Sassy's partner, was just walking through the door, hair and makeup half done, cussing her babysitter for being late again.

Maggie sat her down in the chair and made her take three long breaths without talking before she would start on the makeup. Felecia, whose real name was Ann, was highly strung, always late, and usually angry. Before she could start in on the babysitter again, Maggie asked if either of them had ever donated plasma.

'No way. You get junkie arms and the men don't want any part of you,' Sassy said.

'I did a few times before I started dancing. But the pay sucks and you just lay there for two hours. It's boring as hell.'

Sassy grinned. 'Sounds like your last boyfriend.'

ELEVEN

The next morning, Maggie woke early and checked her phone for messages as she shuffled out to the kitchen to make coffee. No word from Kelly O'Neal. She tried Mark's phone but it went straight to voicemail. Same with John Desmond's. She decided Kelly's plasma information didn't warrant a phone call that would drag either officer out of bed. She called Mark's phone again and left a detailed message for him, suggesting he should contact the Baxters to see if they had ever donated blood at the Three Region Plasma Center, or if their daughter had ever received blood.

After a quick shower, she drove twenty minutes to the plasma center, located in a strip mall on the outskirts of Santa Cruz. She had been surprised to find they were open on a Sunday, and at ten after eight in the morning, shocked to find the parking spaces in front of the business filled almost to capacity.

After getting off work from the club the night before, Maggie had driven home and searched the internet to find out the process for donating her plasma. She discovered plasma centers weren't actually about donations. People were being paid up to $400 a month to sell off a portion of their body. She discovered a twenty-billion-dollar global industry, with ninety-five percent of the sales coming from the US. And the industry, fueled by expensive medical treatments and research, was built on the bodies of the poorest people. Donors in the US were allowed to sell up to one hundred and four times per year, while donors in Europe maxed out at forty-five times per year. Maggie wondered if Kelly used the money she earned from selling her plasma to put food on the table for her family.

Inside the plasma center, Maggie took a paper number and sat in a row of plastic molded chairs, waiting twenty minutes for her number to be called by a woman sitting at a desk with one chair in front of her. They clearly were not welcoming of multiple family members participating in the process. Or, she wondered, maybe privacy laws dictated a private place to discuss medical history.

'First time donor?' the woman asked.

'Yes, ma'am. A friend of mine is having surgery. I thought I should do my part.'

She glanced over her glasses at Maggie, her expression kind but harried. 'Please just answer the questions with a yes or a no so we can get through this process and get you over to medical.'

'I have to have a medical exam in order to donate?'

'Yes, ma'am.'

'Every time I come here?'

'No, ma'am. Just once.'

'Do you tell me what my blood type is?'

'Ma'am, let's just get through your basic information. Then I'll need you to sit in those chairs by the exam room and Ramone will be with you shortly. He does the exams. He'll answer your questions.' She turned back to her computer. 'Address?'

Thirty minutes later, Maggie sat on an examination table behind a screen answering multiple questions about her sex life, the tattoo on her back that she'd received while in the service, and her lack of travel to a foreign country. Next was a thorough oral examination. Ramone was friendly, asking her questions and marking off answers on a form stuck to a clipboard while he went through a cursory physical exam.

When Maggie could see the examination was coming to an end, she said, 'You know, it was a neighbor's kid that got me to come in here today.'

'Oh yeah?'

'Yeah. A little girl by the name of Amaya. She comes with her mom. She said you told her what blood type she was a few weeks ago. She said she was the universal donor.' Maggie was fishing. She had no idea if Ramone was the person who'd told Amaya her blood type, but she noticed his efficient hands hesitate when she mentioned it. The information clearly caught him off-guard, and caused him to process the news before moving on.

'You remember her?' Maggie asked. 'That same little girl has been kidnapped. It's just awful.'

'Yeah, I heard about that. She comes most weeks with her mom when school is out. I couldn't believe it.'

'I thought it was odd that you took her blood, since she's a minor.'

Ramone avoided eye contact and his smile was gone. 'I felt bad for her sitting around. Thought I'd give her a tour. She seemed happy about it. The poor kid has to sit for a couple hours each week. I just hope they find her soon.'

Maggie felt her phone buzz and saw it was from Mark. The blood tech continued talking, adeptly changing the conversation to law enforcement dropping the ball on important cases. Maggie nodded, feigning interest as she glanced at the text.

Found Her. Can't call. Check WXBQ in 10 min for update.

Maggie stood from the exam table. 'Listen, I'm sorry. I just got an urgent text. Save my paperwork. I'll be back.'

Ramone looked surprised at the sudden change, and said nothing as Maggie left the room, straightening her shirt as she exited.

Inside her car, Maggie pulled up the TV station's live feed on her phone and listened to the update.

TWELVE

K elly and Andre sat in the waiting room at Lee Pediatric Health with their hands clasped between them, caught somewhere between immense relief and paralyzing dread. Kelly pointed to the TV monitor hanging from the wall across from them.

'Andre, look. It's the park where they found Amaya.'

He grabbed the remote on the table beside them and pressed the volume button. A news anchor was providing a summary of the events over the past thirty-six hours while law enforcement jostled around the podium in the background, arranging microphones and cameras from different news outlets. After several minutes, the camera cut to the officer who'd come to their house early that morning with the news that Amaya had been found.

'Good morning. I am Mark Hamilton, Chief of Police with Cypress City, in Collier County, Florida. I will be making an official joint statement for the Cypress City and Santa Cruz Police Departments this morning.

'On Friday fifteenth July at four forty-five p.m., Amaya O'Neal, a female, age ten, was taken from the Cypress City Park, located two blocks from the elementary school where she had attended earlier that day.

'Also on Friday fifteenth July, at six forty p.m., a second female, Brooke Baxter, age eleven, was taken from the Bike and Board Park located in Santa Cruz.

'Brooke Baxter was recovered Saturday sixteenth July, at five twenty in the evening at a golf course in Santa Cruz, located on the outskirts of the city. The girl was discovered in a remote area not often used by the public. She was discovered by a walker who found the girl in a confused state.

'Amaya O'Neal was recovered at six twenty this morning, on a walking path just outside of Cypress City, on an unmarked logging trail by a city maintenance worker. She also was confused and lethargic when discovered.

'At this time, the police believe the kidnappings are related but a motive has not been established. The girls are being treated by doctors and have been returned to their families. Both families have asked that I thank the public for their support in helping to find the girls, and both families have asked for privacy as the girls recover. We ask that the media and well-wishers do not contact the families or visit their places of residence during this stressful time.

'I will now answer a few questions, but I have no additional details that I can provide on the investigation.' He looked up from his notes and stared hard at the camera. 'What I can promise you is that both departments are allotting every available resource to finding the person or persons responsible for these horrendous crimes. They *will* be brought to justice.'

Kelly drew in a ragged breath. An older couple across the waiting room was staring at her, but had apparently not made the connection that she and Andre were Amaya's parents.

Andre wrapped his arm around her shoulder as the officer took questions from reporters in the newsroom.

'Can you tell us if the girls were hurt during their time away from home?' a female reporter asked.

'I'm not prepared to answer additional questions about the investigation at this time.'

A male reporter shouted, 'There have been rumors that the O'Neal father is a suspect in the kidnappings. Can you confirm or deny?'

'Unbelievable,' Kelly said, turning in shock to look at Andre. 'After all we've been through, and now they turn on *us*?'

Andre pulled his arm away and turned to her, his face deep red with anger. 'Has anyone talked to you about me being a suspect?'

'No! Of course not. They're just trying to make more of a story.'

Kelly pointed back at the screen.

'I've already explained,' the officer told the reporter. 'I'm not prepared to answer additional questions about the investigation at this time.'

'Why couldn't he just say no? That I'm not a suspect,' Andre said.

The officer turned and talked with another officer behind him, then faced the podium again. 'This concludes the briefing. We'll be in contact as soon as new information becomes available. Thank you.'

The camera whirled back to the young woman with the microphone who instantly started talking.

'How can she have anything more to talk about?' Kelly said, her tone incredulous. 'She doesn't know anything more than what the cop just said. They use our little girl like she's some form of entertainment.'

A female doctor in a long white lab coat walked into the waiting room and approached them. 'Amaya is stabilized and is resting comfortably. We're ready for you to go back in with her, but I'd like to talk with you both first.'

Kelly nodded and they both stood. She walked beside Andre and grabbed his hand. Before they followed the doctor into the conference room, Kelly touched his arm to get his attention and whispered, 'Are you OK? Can you do this right now?'

He fixed his brown eyes on her, full of worry and heartache. 'Just sit beside me. And hold my hand. OK?'

She nodded.

They sat at a round conference table and Kelly was struck by how young the doctor appeared. She didn't look much older than Kelly at twenty-eight.

The doctor said how sorry she was for the scare they had been through, and that their initial assessment showed good news, that Amaya appeared to be in overall good health.

'Then why did the person who found her say she looked drugged?' Kelly asked.

'We believe she was drugged, for an extended period of time, probably the entire time she was away from home.'

Andre turned his head and placed a fist against his eyes, looking as if he was trying to keep the anger and tears from escaping.

The doctor reached an arm across the table toward him. 'I do have good news. We don't believe that Amaya was physically assaulted. We see no signs that she was sexually or physically abused while she was away. The only sign of anything amiss is that she has needle marks behind both knees.'

Kelly shuddered.

'We believe she received long-term sedatives intravenously behind her knees.'

Andre moaned and stood abruptly. He left the room, looking as if he were about to be sick.

THIRTEEN

Maggie had been a homicide cop in Cincinnati for twenty years of her marriage, and while she'd understood David worrying while she was on the clock, it had been easy to overlook given the stresses of the job. Her own stress, and the importance of the job, had trumped his fears – at least in her own mind. She remembered him asking her to take sixty seconds out of her night to call and let him know that she'd be late getting home, but she rarely did. She ignored the hypocrisy of her current situation and broke the cardinal rule of a cop's significant other, calling to check up on Mark.

'Actually, I'm headed to your house,' he said.

'That's great. I'll be home in about half an hour.'

'A sheriff's deputy called and said there's a news van camped outside my house. I can't deal with it tonight.'

'Bastards,' Maggie said. 'Then sleep with me. Make the buzzards roost outside in their van tonight.'

When Maggie pulled down her driveway, she found Mark sitting on the patio behind Agnus's house, drinking a beer with her.

'How's life, neighbor?' Agnus said.

Maggie grinned. 'I'm now in the presence of my two most favorite people on the planet, so life is good.'

Mark tilted his head to receive a kiss on the cheek and patted the arm of the chair next to him. 'Take a load off. Ten more minutes to finish this beer and then you can carry me to your place and put my comatose body to bed.'

'Gladly.'

When Agnus went back inside to pour Maggie a drink, Mark didn't waste any time. 'Tell me about your meeting with the lab tech at Three Region Plasma Center.'

Maggie described the place, and the med tech who'd hesitated when she mentioned him taking Amaya's blood type.

'It has to be against protocol to take a kid's blood without some kind of parental consent. He probably figured you were there to cause trouble.'

'Could be. I was in the middle of my intake physical when I got your text that Amaya had been found. I left mid-exam.'

'I need you to keep this quiet.'

'Mark. Come on. You really need to tell me that?'

'We just can't let this out. Both girls were checked out this afternoon at Lee Pediatric Health.'

'In Santa Cruz?'

He nodded. 'Both families agreed to share the medical findings with law enforcement. As much as they want to shelter the girls at this point, they're desperate to find out what happened while they were away from home.'

'I don't think I want to hear this.'

'It's not what you're expecting. They didn't find any evidence of sexual assault. But they found needle marks on both girls behind their knees. The doctor at Lee said he suspects the girls were given some kind of drug that put them under for an extended amount of time. He could tell as much from examining the vein that was used.' Mark tipped his beer back to drain it. 'My theory is they drugged those girls and took photos. Put them in compromising positions. I don't know.'

'But they weren't molested?'

'It doesn't look that way. People get their kicks in a number of different ways.'

'What about the Baxters? Any connection to the plasma center?' she asked.

'No. But the parents both donated blood at a community blood drive five weeks ago. I've got someone tracking down the workers on that day. If we can connect the worker from the O'Neals' plasma center to the Baxter's blood drive, we might be on to something.'

'So what would the blood tech have to do with child porn?' Maggie asked.

'He'd be able to safely knock the girls out and keep them unconscious for however long the session took. Whatever is going on, I feel confident there are multiple people involved.'

Maggie thought about the information for a moment. 'One girl coming home lethargic and confused is awful. Two is enough to send the community into a panic. You'll have schools asking if they should shut down classes.'

'We've had news media calling and asking about serial kidnappings.'

'The scary part is, if there's any truth behind that, by the time the police connect the dots there's usually other victims in the past and new victims in the making. Have you been able to question the girls at all?'

'No. The hospital brought in a psychiatrist who's monitoring their case. He won't allow any law enforcement near them for twenty-four to forty-eight hours, until he's sure they're stabilized and can handle talking about it.'

Maggie nodded. 'Those poor kids.'

'What bothers me most,' Mark said, 'is the long-term doping. It could be as simple as a method to keep young kids quiet in order to drop them off with no memory of where they came from. But with no ransom note or demands of the parents, it's apparent that the kidnappers received what they wanted from the girls. And what does a girl of ten or eleven have to offer an adult?'

After Mark fell asleep, Maggie filled a cocktail glass with ice and poured it to the rim with tequila. Two long draws later, she poured it to the rim again, then pulled her laptop out of her backpack and slung a folding chair over her shoulder.

On the beach, Maggie sunk into her chair and let the unopened laptop rest on her thighs as she took in the sound of the waves crashing on the shore and breathed in the briny moist air of the ocean. She would never take for granted what Agnus had gifted her. The surf at night under a half moon was one of the most exquisite feelings on earth.

Maggie acknowledged her good fortune, but couldn't shake the feeling that something was missing. She missed her mom. She missed being a cop. She missed David. She missed the routines and traditions of her former life: the Cincinnati Reds baseball games she and David attended each summer, Saturday afternoon visits to Findlay Market. David's eggs Benedict on Sunday mornings. Fifty years of her life had turned into a memory, with nothing to grab hold of anymore. She loved the ocean and Mark and Agnus and her friends, but they were all new. It felt as if she'd abandoned her old life, and part of herself had been left behind with it.

She breathed in the saltwater air and exhaled slowly, forcing her thoughts to settle on the rhythm of the water. She sipped at the tequila, feeling the burn down to her gut and the final release, as if a lever were pulled on her spine and the tension of the day finally loosened its grip.

After a twenty-minute reverie, Maggie was glad to have a task to focus on. She opened her laptop and started an internet search, focusing on the needle punctures behind the girls' knees. Aside from the obvious necessity to hide the marks away from parents' and doctors' prying eyes, she tried to find a reason why someone might use that specific location. The only information she could find was that the area behind the knee was simply an alternative option for drawing blood or providing intravenous medicine.

After determining that the knee was an accepted location for introducing chemicals into a child's vein, Maggie searched for reasons why a person would want to inject drugs into a juvenile. She searched predatory websites, looking for trends or illicit groups. She'd found through her years in law enforcement that the degenerates of the world liked to connect to one another, to feel better about their behavior, she assumed, or perhaps it was simply a more-the-merrier mentality. She was amazed at some of the depraved information people posted in chat rooms. The sick underworld of perversion left little to the imagination, and it made Maggie glad she wasn't doing that kind of work for pay anymore. She discovered drugging juveniles was certainly a means to an end and there were plenty of people happy to offer guidance.

After creating an account on a site that 'virtually' explored the human body while 'at rest', Maggie connected with a self-described 'retired surgeon' who posted nightly. He was clearly enamored with the human body, 'fully functioning and alive, but at rest'. And the only way to view a body in such a way was through drugs. Repulsed at even communicating with such a person, Maggie was amazed at how simple it was to connect and get a discussion going with this doctor who referred to himself as a 'sleeper expert'.

Amazingly, the doctor seemed concerned about her ability to safely puncture a vein in a child, but apparently had no problem with the emotional trauma of what he was most likely putting a child through.

'And if you're taking blood be just as careful,' he said.

'Why would you take blood?'

'Young blood? Maybe you're too young to get it, lol.'

Hoping to draw out the 'expert', Maggie lied. 'I'm seventy. Anything young has my attention.'

'Certain plasma centers mark blood from teenagers. Research

has shown young blood, given in regular doses to people in their seventies, can reduce aging. Mental and physical. But it's controversial so you don't see much information on it.'

Maggie leaned back in her chair. Young blood.

When Mark walked out of the bedroom the next morning, Maggie was at the kitchen table typing up notes.

'You're up early,' he said.

'Not really.'

'I never even heard you come to bed last night.'

'You must have slept well then.'

He sat across from her at the table and gave her an appraising stare. 'You never came to bed, did you?'

Maggie spent the next hour giving him a rundown on the various possibilities for why two adolescent girls, from differing backgrounds, could have been kidnapped, drugged and returned with no other physical alteration than a prick where something was either put into or taken out of a vein.

'We were looking for commonalities between the girls and their families in terms of the kidnappings. Maybe the commonality was their age and blood type.'

Mark pulled his phone out and called Mrs Baxter, putting the call on speaker.

'Good morning. I hope I'm not calling too early,' he said.

'Not at all. I'm making breakfast. Steven took the day off. We're just trying to have a normal day at home. It's more difficult than you might think.'

'I won't bother you then. I just have a quick question, although it's a bit odd. Can you tell me what blood type Brooke is?'

'We've been asked so many questions the past few days, nothing surprises me anymore. She's Type O because Steven and I are both Type O. We learned that at the blood drive. Does this have something to do with the case?'

'I'm not sure yet. Please don't mention the question to anyone at this point. But I promise to let you know if something comes of this.' Mark hung the phone up and turned to Maggie. 'You think the plasma center is involved somehow?'

'If not the plasma center, then at least the tech that typed Amaya's blood.'

'There are medical research companies all over this area. Anti-aging is huge,' Mark said. 'Do you have any contacts? Anyone you know who's into that kind of stuff?'

'Agnus has a friend who takes weekly shots. Agnus gives her grief over it. Says it's not natural.'

They found Agnus in the side yard, talking to her cat as she filled up her water bowl.

Her smile turned to a wince. 'You two look like hell. I hope you at least had a good time to look that bad.'

Maggie grinned. 'I always appreciate your honesty.'

'No you don't. Nobody does. But I can't shut my pie hole, so you just have to deal with it.'

'What can you tell me about your friend who takes the anti-aging shots?'

She rolled her eyes. 'Nadine? She's obsessed. Spends a fortune on her vitamin cocktails. She claims all the stars get them. She calls it her B12 Bomber cocktail. She goes in and they hook an IV bag up to her arm and drip in these high-powered vitamins. She claims it gives her energy. I told her taking a walk would give her energy too, but she won't listen.'

'Can you do me a favor and call her? See if she'd meet with me today?' Mark asked.

An hour later, Maggie and Mark were traveling to Old Santa Cruz to take Nadine out to lunch at her favorite café.

On the drive into town, Maggie searched the internet on her phone for information about donating blood in Florida. 'You can't donate blood if you're younger than eighteen.'

'That's blood. See if the same applies to plasma.'

'Looks like same rules apply. This says blood banks don't pay people to donate because they don't want them lying about their health status, about tattoos they have, traveling out of the country, and so on. The plasma banks have to pay people in order to maintain a large enough supply.'

'What happens if somebody lies about their health and gives their plasma anyway?' he asked.

'It looks like taking the plasma is pretty sophisticated. But this says blood from donors is pretty much used as is. And there aren't enough controls to ensure the blood is clean.'

Mark winced. 'As a potential recipient of that blood, that seems entirely too unscientific.'

'Wow. Listen to this. Back in the sixties and seventies, plasma companies used prisoners, paying five or ten dollars a pop for plasma donations. But when AIDS hit in the eighties, much of the blood plasma they received from the prisoners was tainted. This says fifty percent of the hemophiliacs in the US contracted AIDS from the bad supply. They had to file a class action lawsuit in order to have the shielded plasma companies finally deal with the bad supply.'

'This is no longer an issue, I take it?' he asked.

'It looks like there's more testing than there used to be.'

'But what about new diseases that pop up?'

Maggie nodded. 'Think about Zika or West Nile Virus. Couldn't viruses get into the blood supply for a time before we have them identified and know how to test for them? Maybe we think the new disease is getting spread by mosquitos, but it's actually being spread through our blood supply?'

'A twenty-billion-dollar industry is an awful lot of incentive to keep it coming.'

Mark pulled into the parking lot of Julie's, advertised as the best chicken salad and iced tea in Florida.

Maggie and Mark knew Nadine from Mel's Class Act, so they were well into lunch before Nadine was sufficiently caught up with Santa Cruz and Cypress City gossip to wonder why they wanted to meet with her.

'Agnus gives me hell for it, but I don't see it's any of her business. You know how bossy that old woman can be. I told her, "would you rather I spend my money on booze and gigolos, or vitamins and masseuses?"'

Mark agreed that Nadine's option sounded much healthier, and certainly more legal. 'How often do you get your vitamin drips?'

'Each week. It's a social thing too, if you want the truth. There's three of us that have standing appointments each Monday.' She dropped her voice. 'Listen here. Agnus thinks my cocktails are a big deal, but one of my lady friends at the clinic is trying to get me to participate in a medical study. You have to pay to be a part of the study. It has to do with blood.

It's anti-aging. But I was so caught up in the cost I didn't pay much attention to the rest of it. She's paying ten thousand dollars to be a research participant. Can you imagine?'

'I thought the researchers paid the participants, not the other way around?' Mark said.

'If you can't get money for your research, you can convince private donors that you have a great idea and they'll fund you. She said some billionaire from China outfitted the initial study, and now they're signing people up to participate. But at least if you pay, you know you're actually getting the goods.'

'Meaning, there's no variable group?' Maggie said.

Nadine looked at Maggie like she was crazy. 'If I pay ten thousand dollars, then I'd better get the goods and not some sugar pill.'

'But it's experimental, so you still don't know if it will work? Or its dangers?' Mark asked.

Nadine shrugged it off. 'Look at the crap people eat and drink all day long. And they know that crap is killing them. I take a few chances, but at least mine make medical sense.'

'Makes sense to me,' Maggie said. She glanced at Mark. He looked as if he wanted to argue the point, but thankfully didn't.

'Do you know what kind of blood research she's participating in?' Maggie asked.

'My friend used the term "young blood". That's when I tuned out. Too strange for my taste, but to each her own.'

'I'd like to talk to your friend. Can you connect me?' Mark asked.

Nadine dug through her purse, pulling out bags inside of bags, until she found a stack of business cards that she flipped through. 'Here! She wrote down who to contact if I'm interested in participating in the study. His name is Doctor Oscar LeBlanc. She said to call this number to set up a consultation.'

Back outside, Mark said, 'Young blood? How bizarre is that?'

'That's too big a coincidence for this not to be related.'

Maggie watched as he started the car, but put her hand on his arm to stop him from pulling into traffic. 'How about I visit the doctor?'

He immediately began shaking his head. 'You quit police work when you left Cincinnati. You retired for a reason.'

She felt her face flush. 'I retired because my life was miserable and I needed something new.'

'I understand you miss the job, but I can't help you. The prosecutor would have my hide if I started letting my girlfriend interfere in cases.'

'I'll go in as myself. The narcissistic radio host who wants to stay young forever.'

'As yourself? The narcissist?' He grinned, and she knew she had him. 'You said it, not me.'

'I'm serious,' she said. 'If anyone asks, I'm doing this for the radio show. It's research. It has nothing to do with police work.'

'You're killing me.'

'No I'm not. You know I was a great cop. You just wish you could hire me.'

He laughed. 'Not a chance. We wouldn't last a month.'

'I'll make an appointment. See what it takes to participate in one of his studies,' she said.

'When he talks about young blood, find out how young he'll go.'

'If a patient pays ten thousand dollars to participate in a study with lawfully donated teenage blood, imagine what they'd pay for blood from a ten-year-old.'

FOURTEEN

D r Oscar LeBlanc's office was located in Doctor's Park, an area of Santa Cruz known for medical offices and hospitals. His was at the end of a tree-lined drive, where several black and white brick office buildings nestled around a lake shaded by weeping willows. LeBlanc had commissioned an etched glass sign for outside his office that read 'The Institute for Life and Longevity', with his name listed underneath. It had been one of the proudest days of his life the day the sign was erected; a dream realized.

Leaving the family law business in Paris for an American

medical school had been considered a traitorous move. His specialization in geriatric medicine was considered a waste of a brilliant mind. What his parents and three older siblings hadn't counted on was his determination to change the world. Coming from a family of wealth and privilege, his three older brothers were certainly successful in their own right, but Oscar had found their effort complacent. He expected more of himself. With his acceptance into medical school, he left France and never looked back. When his father began suffering the vestiges of dementia, Oscar had him transferred to Stanford, where Oscar was completing his residency. His commitment to finding a cure for the disease that destroyed his father's mind was sealed.

When LeBlanc arrived at work on the Monday after the final little girl had been delivered to the location in which she was found, he forbid Olivia to mention it. He would find a way to further research without placing himself or his practice in that kind of jeopardy ever again. He'd learned one critical lesson living among some of the nation's wealthiest citizens: there is nothing that enough money and time cannot fix, including life and death. He would find a better way.

The phone on his desk lit up and Olivia announced that Maggie Wise was ready. He wasn't happy about the quick appointment, but she had explained to Olivia that she needed to meet with the doctor that day because she was going out of the country for an extended trip. It wasn't that he didn't have the time in his day, but it prohibited him from conducting any research on her before the first meeting. A sound bank account was obviously a key factor for a new patient, but just as important were their background, their presence on the web, their position in the community and network of friends. He'd found plenty of information about Maggie Wise's work on the public radio station, but she had no web presence before her retirement to Florida. With her oceanfront address, money was likely a nonissue, but it was much easier to court a prospective participant when their background was understood.

For the initial consultation he preferred to meet in his office, allowing the patient to get to know him in a more relaxed setting. Olivia opened the door and introduced Ms Wise, then showed her to a seat in front of his desk. He allowed her a moment to take in the tastefully decorated room and expansive windows overlooking the lake. She was an attractive middle-aged woman dressed in cream pants and a light pink silk blouse with stylish jewelry, nothing flashy. She smiled politely but had the look of a woman who wasted little time. He gave her his typical introductory speech about his move from France to the United States, his medical background, and a bit about the research. She nodded politely but offered nothing to the conversation so he cut it short.

'So, what brings you to the Institute?' he asked.

'I'd like to learn how to participate in your blood study.'

He raised his eyebrows. He found an abrupt manner one of the most unappealing traits a woman could possess. He made an effort to temper his response. 'It's a bit more complicated than that. Why don't you tell me what you know about the study, and what you hope to gain by participating?'

'I hear you've found a way to use young blood to halt, and maybe even reverse, the aging process. Is that true?' she asked.

The doctor's eyebrows rose. 'I think that's a fairly accurate statement. Yes.'

'Then I want to participate. It's as simple as that.'

'Because you want to halt the aging process, as you put it?'

She hesitated. 'Dementia runs in my family. On top of that, I've started feeling run down lately. I don't have the stamina I used to. I just feel like I need a boost.'

'I have a family history of dementia as well. I understand the pain that this disease causes families. It's the driving force behind my passion to find a cure.'

Maggie nodded. 'Then I think I'm the perfect candidate for your research.'

'You realize the research is privately funded?'

'Pay to play.'

Dr LeBlanc frowned. 'Pay to participate.'

She tilted her head and apologized. 'Semantics. Payment is involved. I understand.'

He nodded once, propped his elbows on his desk, and steepled his fingers in front of his lips before launching into a lecture about the goals of the research and what the funds would be used for.

After several minutes she leaned forward in her chair and said, 'Dr LeBlanc. I get the basics, and I've done my own research. Just explain what it will take to become a member.'

He pressed his lips together in a thin line, wishing he could stand and show her the door.

'All right then. You'll need a thorough medical examination and blood work. My receptionist will get you scheduled, and she'll collect payment up front for participation. After that, we'll schedule your first session. It's as simple as that.'

She nodded slowly and seemed to be considering something. She finally said, 'I understand there are actually two studies concerning young blood.' When he didn't respond, she continued, 'I've read that there have been interesting results using the blood from prepubescents.'

The doctor leaned back in his chair to consider Maggie. 'Let's take this one step at a time. We'll get you set up in the study and see how you perform with the first round. Then we can talk about other alternatives. How does that sound?'

Once she agreed and he had ushered her back to the front desk to talk with Olivia, LeBlanc came back to his office to dig into Ms Wise. He pulled up the patient record that Olivia would have started during her intake before the appointment, but most of it was left blank. No social security number, which would have made things much easier. It wasn't just her rude manner that bothered him, but he couldn't put a finger on what it was. He hoped it was simply paranoia clouding his judgment.

FIFTEEN

Before Maggie had time to report what she discovered while talking to Dr LeBlanc, Mark called her cell.

'You were dead on with the med tech,' he said. 'John Desmond confirmed that the same man you talked to, Ramone

Anderson, was working the Three Region Plasma Center the day Kelly O'Neal said she was there with Amaya. And Ramone was also working the blood draw the day the Baxters gave blood. The company faxed the forms from the blood drive this morning, and Ramone's initials are on the Baxters' paperwork. He performed their intake. He would have known that Brooke Baxter, who was with her parents that day, was an O positive based off her parents' blood type. The same blood type as Amaya O'Neal. Our universal donor.'

'That's a great connection. But does it prove anything?'

'It gets better. John and I picked up Ramone from the center to question him about taking blood from a minor.'

'Is that legitimate?'

'We were just asking questions, although he took it as a little more serious than that. During the interview he broke down sobbing. He turned on the doctor without a second glance. Blamed the whole thing on your Dr LeBlanc.'

'No kidding?'

'Ramone eventually wized up and requested an attorney. The attorney says Ramone will cooperate fully in exchange for leniency.'

'What's the prosecutor say?'

'We're scheduled to meet with him and Ramone's attorney in about thirty minutes. So far, everyone's on board. And the doctor is screwed.'

'How so?'

'What we suspected about the prepubescent young blood appears to be accurate. Ramone explained something about the proteins in the younger blood being capable of reversing some process or another. But they need young kids, under the age of thirteen, with a known blood type. It's not like you can approach a parent and ask for a volunteer.

'Once Ramone found two girls whose blood type matched what he needed, he picked them up in a white transit van, immediately drugged each girl, and delivered them to the doctor's office. Supposedly, the girls were to have been delivered back before dawn the next morning. But the media attention forced the doctor to keep them longer than expected.'

'Jesus. This is sick. So who gets the blood?' she asked.

'I don't know. That's all the attorney allowed before he shut the questioning down.'

'Any idea what happened to the girls over the two-day period?'

'We know a piece of it. Ramone said the doc wanted the girls for a specific amount of time. Ramone's job was to put them to sleep and monitor their vitals. Do the blood exchange. Then drop them off at a safe place. But once they had the girls, there wasn't anywhere to return them to. The city went crazy. Things spun out of control. That's when Ramone's attorney put a stop to questioning. We don't actually know where they were kept. I'm assuming on patient beds in the doctor's office.'

Maggie winced, imagining two young girls lying comatose in the examination rooms next to where she'd met the doctor that morning. As a cop, she'd witnessed bizarre and sometimes harrowing scenarios played out in the homes, apartments and businesses that next-door neighbors could not even dream of; the old saying, truth is stranger than fiction, was never truer than a cop's nine to five.

Maggie drove home and sat on the couch with her laptop to see what she could dig up on young blood. Research had been one of her favorite tasks in a homicide investigation. Pulling the details apart and putting them back together again, the problem-solving, tracking and talking to witnesses, digging into the dark side of the human psyche; Maggie had excelled in those areas. Her struggle had been with the human side of the investigations. Walking away from victims whose lives had been destroyed without dragging their pain with her had been impossible after David died.

Without him, she'd been unable to keep her promise to stay away from alcohol. He had been the one who had separated her from the job, who had forced her to leave it at the doorstep. After he died, between her grief and the loss of his reasonable voice, the drinking had spun out of control. It had been her shift boss who had finally convinced her to leave both her job and her city behind for a new life. After three years in Florida, most days left her feeling that it had been the right decision.

Once she moved to Santa Cruz and found a place to stay,

Agnus helped Maggie get a grip on the drinking and clean herself up to the point that she could look for work. Financially, she was fine. She had her own pension, as well as David's pension and the insurance settlements, but shutting down her brain long enough to begin to heal had felt impossible. She'd thought the sunshine and physical activity would be enough, but nothing could stop the downward spiral of her thoughts. When the radio job had opened, she'd thought she'd found the perfect alternative to police work; a job she could lose herself in. The research and prepping for interviews had helped, as did her Saturday night job at the strip club, but nothing gave her the satisfaction she'd felt as a cop. And Mark didn't get it. He'd told her repeatedly that he would trade places in a heartbeat, but given his alimony and child support payments, early retirement was not in his future. He thought Maggie had life made. She wished she agreed.

Maggie forced Mark out of her mind and typed the term 'young blood' into the search engine. After scrolling past results for several pop songs with the same name, as well as a few posts utilizing the seventies-era slang term, she was surprised to find quite a bit of research detailing the use of young blood in various aging studies. She came across the term 'heterochronic parabiosis' and shuddered at the definition: surgically connecting two animals of differing ages to create a shared circulation system.

An article published in the scientific journal *Cell Cycle* stated, 'Ludwig and colleagues published a study in which old rats that were joined in heterochronic parabiosis with young rats lived four to five months longer, which is a 20% increase in longevity. In many of these early experiments, the old animals shared circulation with young animals for years; thus, they both continued to age, and at times, several young rats were connected to one old rat in an attempt to have the prevalence of young blood . . .'

Maggie knew the mental image of the two rats sewn together and sharing a circulation system would stay with her for quite some time. More disturbing was how this research might be connected to the two young girls who appeared to have been kidnapped for their blood.

*   *   *

At four o'clock that afternoon, Maggie received a phone call from Kelly O'Neal asking if she had some time to talk. 'Sure thing. What's up?'

'Chief Hamilton just called me. The man you date?'

'Yes?' Maggie wondered how Kelly knew that information.

'He wants me to go with an undercover officer to the doctor's office tomorrow to confront him. I'm freaking out about talking to him. I just need someone to talk to.'

Maggie wanted to ask where Kelly's husband was, but decided against it. 'Why don't you start by telling me exactly what the police want you to do.'

'They had a big meeting today with police from Cypress City and Santa Cruz. They're trying to figure out how to get the doctor to admit he was involved in the kidnappings before he knows the police are after him.'

'So they haven't made any arrests yet?'

'They were questioning Ramone, the blood tech, but I don't know if he's been actually arrested. The doctor doesn't know that Ramone was picked up. That was part of the deal Ramone made with the cops, that he wouldn't talk for forty-eight hours. Chief Hamilton said if the doctor gets a big money lawyer, they'll turn it all around and make it look like Ramone was to blame and that the doctor didn't have anything to do with it.'

'I'm sure that's right. He could walk free,' Maggie said.

'So they want me to visit his office tomorrow morning. Along with an undercover cop who will do all the talking. He'll go in with me and say he's a friend of mine, looking out for me.'

'For what purpose?'

'They think if I go in there and say that I'm Amaya's mom, that it will shock him. He'll know that I could go to the police and ruin everything for him. With me sitting there, they're hoping the doctor will admit to having contact with the girls. They're hoping that he'll assure me that he took good care of my daughter. Once they have that information, then his lawyer can't say that he knew nothing about the kidnappings.'

Maggie nodded. 'Makes sense. How do you feel about it?'

'Terrified.'

'Of seeing him?'

'Of what I'll do. Of saying the wrong thing. Of crying or

screaming. I just can't imagine how I'll handle it, or if it's even a good idea.'

Maggie was quiet a moment, not sure how to respond. She didn't have any children of her own, but it wasn't hard to imagine what this mother had endured while her child was missing. 'What does your husband have to say about it?'

'He's furious that the police even asked me. He says it's their job to solve the case, not mine. He doesn't want me to do it.'

'Have you given them an answer yet?'

'No. Chief Hamilton was nice about it. He told me not to feel pressured to say yes. But he needs to know today. He said the word will get back to the doctor about Ramone and then we're screwed. We've got one shot.'

'Listen. No one will be angry with you for not going through with this. You've been through enough.'

Kelly cut in. 'But I feel like this is my chance to do what's right for Amaya.'

'I'm not sure what you want from me right now.'

She sighed audibly. 'I guess I want a pep talk. Andre told me not to do it. He left the police station furious at me. I want to help though, I just don't know if I have the guts.'

'I can tell you the answer to that. Without a doubt, you have the guts to do this. I hate to go against what Andre is telling you, but I think talking to the doctor is a great idea. It puts you in charge. It isn't very often that victims actually get to confront their attackers. And if you're able to say something that puts him behind bars—'

'That's what I told Andre! He's just afraid for me. The chief told Andre that the doctor isn't violent, that I wouldn't be put into a dangerous situation, and that the undercover cop would be with me the whole time. I don't even have to speak.'

'Just keep in mind, you may go through with this, and he may not admit a thing. He's obviously a smart man. If he senses in any way that the person you're with is undercover, then he won't say a word.'

'I get that. But when he sees the mother of one of the girls he violated walk into his office, he'll sure as hell pay attention.'

SIXTEEN

K elly did not grow up in a house where the police were trusted or respected. The police represented the power elite: they crashed parties, handcuffed and arrested innocent people, searched cars, busted down doors for entrance into the homes of law-abiding people. Kelly's dad hated the cops and told anyone who would listen that the world would be better off without them. 'Let people take care of their own damn business. I don't need a cop protecting my family. Somebody walks up to my house with bad intentions, then hell is coming to breakfast.' As a kid, Kelly had loved to hear her dad rage on about the bad world, and how he would keep his family safe at all cost. But her dad was shot and killed in a bar-room fight when she was thirteen years old. And her family's response? Where were the damn cops when you needed them?

When she met Andre two years later, he had been a quiet voice in a world of chaos. Kelly's family reveled in righteous indignation and she had begun to find the anger exhausting. Even as a teenager, when she walked into Andre's house she would feel the tension melt away. The first year she spent hanging out at his house they never touched. His place was a haven away from the madness. There were Saturday nights when she was in high school when they would stretch out on the couch and read books for hours, and there wasn't any place else she'd have rather been.

When Amaya was born, they'd both promised her a childhood free from drama, and now here they were. A stranger walking through their house would see nothing wrong, just a typical young family with a little girl who loved basketball and books and pink unicorns. But outside, news crews were parked and their life was becoming a circus.

Andre had taken Amaya fishing at dawn, not wanting her around when Kelly left for the police station. He was still upset with her for going, but he had finally relented and agreed that it was Kelly's decision to make.

Kelly arrived at the police station at seven o'clock and was taken to the conference room where Chief Hamilton and several other officers were waiting for her. The chief introduced Kelly to Sam Delaney, the undercover officer who would be going with her.

'I'd tell you my real name, but I did that once with an informer in a drug buy and he called me by the wrong name in the middle of the handover. Fortunately, we don't typically arrange drug buys with rocket scientists, so the whole thing went unnoticed.' He winked at Kelly. 'But I find it easier for everyone if we just stick to Sam.'

Kelly grinned and nodded. Sam was a rough-looking man in his forties who seemed as if he spent most nights hanging out at biker bars. He definitely didn't look like a cop. But he was friendly and easygoing, and he was obviously trying to get Kelly to relax.

He explained that they had been looking into the doctor's research, and then described the line of questioning he planned to take with the doctor, along with the information he hoped to glean.

Sam showed Kelly the digital recorder that he would be wearing and explained how it would work.

Chief Hamilton said, 'Sam is your protector and negotiator. He will ensure you're safe at all times. We will hear every word that is said, and Sam will be armed. You have nothing to fear while you're in the doctor's office.'

Sam gave Kelly a long look. 'If you get in there and get scared, then you don't have to say a word. It's completely understandable, given what happened. But I caution you against anger. You can't lose control. That's when things get said that can't be taken back. The last thing we want is to tip him off that you're working with the police.'

Kelly walked behind Sam into the Institute for Life and Longevity. Sam had told her that her job wasn't to get information, it was to serve as the catalyst that would scare the doctor into offering it up. They had agreed upon several questions she was allowed to ask, and he had made it clear that he wanted her to stick to the script.

A young receptionist explained that the doctor wasn't available without an appointment. Sam told her it was an emergency and that it was 'in his best interest' to see them. Ten minutes later, the receptionist returned with her smile still in check. 'Doctor LeBlanc will see you now.'

Kelly followed behind Sam and took the seat next to him in front of the doctor's desk.

'This is highly unusual, Mr Delaney. I don't appreciate the intrusion.'

'I think you'll agree it was warranted. I'd like to introduce you to Kelly O'Neal. Amaya O'Neal's mother.'

The doctor looked at Kelly for the first time, and the reaction was brief but obvious. His eyes widened, clearly shocked, followed by a look of panic as he tried to form an appropriate response. 'I don't understand.'

'Yes, you do. Mrs O'Neal is visiting because she has questions about what you did to her daughter.' Sam kept his voice calm and sensible, as if talking to someone who needed simple explanations.

'I have no idea what you are talking about.'

'We don't want the police involved,' Sam said. 'We want answers. If you cooperate then we don't go to the police. We work this out between the three of us. If you don't cooperate? Then we call Santa Cruz PD.' He held his phone in the air. 'And endless social media outlets. Your research, your reputation? Obliterated in a matter of hours.'

'This is absurd.' Dr LeBlanc's expression was stuck somewhere between nausea and panic.

'Did you feed her? While she was here?' She kept her eyes trained on the doctor, her voice quiet and determined.

The false indignancy drained from his expression, leaving a man sitting in the midst of his own lies. 'This has all gone wrong,' he said. 'We're doing work here that can change the lives of thousands of people. I never intended to hurt anyone.'

'You never intended to hurt anyone? You kidnapped two girls from their families,' Kelly said.

'Your daughter was taken care of. She never even realized

she was away from home. Her safety was never once comprom-ised. I swear that to you. It should have been a matter of hours and the whole process would have been over.'

'Tell me what you did with my daughter. From the time you picked her up, to the time you let her go.'

'I did not pick your daughter up. The blood from juveniles was critical for the research. As awful as it sounds, this was all necessary.'

'Bullshit,' Sam said. 'You kidnapped two little girls so you could make a profit. You have one more chance before we go to the media.'

'You asked for the truth. It's what I'm telling you. I had no idea how the plasma was being obtained. It wasn't my concern. I was simply trying to take care of my own patients.'

'How can you say that two children in your care were not your concern?' she said.

LeBlanc sighed, but his expression revealed that he knew he'd misspoken.

'Did you ever see Amaya or the other girl?' Kelly said.

He opened his mouth as if to speak, then closed it again.

'All I want is the truth.'

'The person I hired was supposed to have taken care of all of this.'

'Ramone Anderson?' Sam asked.

The doctor nodded once, his eyes widening at the use of the tech's name. If he'd not believed they had come with details, he did now.

'They couldn't use the plasma center. Ramone worked there, but one of the doctors was in the office unexpectedly that night. It was too risky, and the girls were already . . .' He paused, and avoided the obvious. 'Originally, I was promised they could take care of those details on their own. Then the details changed. They had to perform the procedure in my office. I'm telling you the truth when I say I had no idea where the girls were coming from.'

Kelly shook her head. 'You say it like it's an excuse. You're a doctor and you don't care about the details of two young girls' lives?'

He sighed again, as if she had misunderstood his point.

Kelly went on. 'Those girls were kidnapped, drugged, and left alone on a park bench in a remote area for God only knows how long. Amaya wakes up at night calling out my name, terrified that she's not in her own room.'

'I understand. And I am sincerely sorry for what happened. But the research that is being conducted could add years to people's lives. Your daughter will save lives.'

'What you mean is, you can add years to rich people's lives while you destroy poor people in the process,' she said.

'It's not that simple. There's no source for plasma from donors under the age of eighteen. Eventually, that can be handled with synthetics, but not before I have evidence that the process works.'

'What process?' Sam asked.

'There's research as far back as seventy years ago where doctors surgically entwined a young rat to an old rat so that they shared the same blood supply. Basically, allowing the old rat to benefit from the fresh blood supply. The cartilage in the old rat began to repair itself. Researchers expected the rat's mental functions to improve, but the physical improvements were shocking. The aging process literally reversed itself in the older rat. And the research has been replicated since. But we've never had plasma from patients younger than eighteen.'

'If it's against the law for kids to donate their blood, then what good will any of this do you? It's not as if you can publish it in a scientific journal,' Sam said, 'so what's the point?'

'Once I have proof, then I can get the backing for research using synthetics. But I can't get the pharma companies to buy into this until I have the biologicals in place.'

'Who backs the next round of research?' Sam asked.

'It's a complicated process.' LeBlanc looked frustrated with Sam's simplistic questions. 'This is being funded by several private donors. It's pay to participate. This allows me to step outside the normal confines of the scientific community.'

'How is that scientific research?' Sam asked.

'Don't be naïve. Every research study has bias. Whether conducted in a university by a professor pushing for tenure, or a pharmaceutical out to make a million, or a researcher like me who is on the cusp of a scientific breakthrough. It's all the same. Just different avenues for funding.'

'So how does your private donor benefit?'

'I have two patients, both men in their seventies, who are receiving plasma infusions from donors younger than thirteen. Medically, the proteins in the blood of juveniles are special. I don't think you want a medical lecture, but there it is. That's why the girls were a necessity.'

Kelly listened to the conversation and appeared to grow impatient with the details. She finally broke in. 'You never answered my question. I want to know what happened to my daughter while she was gone. She spent two days with you. I deserve to know what happened to her.'

He turned and faced Kelly, crossing his arms on the desk, making a show of devoting his full attention to her. 'The procedure I performed was called plasmapheresis.'

'I know about plasma removal. I do it to buy groceries for my family.'

'Then you know she wasn't hurt. Your daughter basically slept for two days.'

Sam laughed. 'You are one sick bastard.'

LeBlanc looked frustrated at the turn of the conversation. 'If you've ever given your plasma you know how simple it is. The blood is removed, and a machine separates the cells out. The blood is scrubbed several times and given back to the donor. With especially young donors the process is more involved, takes more time. Extreme care is taken with the veins.'

'You talked about your own patients. How do they fit into this?' Sam asked.

'My patients receive the plasma the same day. As a patient, there is no other procedure that can guarantee results like those I'm providing. My patients know that what they are getting is genuine young blood.'

'Oh my God,' Kelly said. She looked as if she might vomit.

The doctor looked annoyed at her response. 'If you donate, then you know the process. Your child was not hurt in the least. And I guarantee my office is much more sanitary and sterile than that center you visit.'

'You personally saw that her daughter was safe during the procedure?' Sam asked. 'That she was not harmed in any way?'

'I promise you. I was by her side, monitoring the transaction the entire time. Every care was taken.' The doctor lowered his voice and seemed to be pleading for her to accept his vision. 'Your daughter is part of groundbreaking research that could affect not only the longevity of the human race, but more importantly the quality of life. The implications for Alzheimer's research alone are infinite.' He leaned toward Kelly, his eyes boring into hers. 'I can make this right for you and your family. I have two donors paying $100,000 per session to participate. You should be compensated for your daughter's participation. I get that. I'm not out for the money. I need the money to proceed, but I have to have donors. I can compensate your family with a $25,000 payment each time your daughter participates. We would do the procedure in my office. It would take just a few hours every other month.'

Kelly said nothing so the doctor continued. 'Think of what this could mean for your daughter. This could be college tuition. Think of the future you could give her for a few hours of her time.'

Kelly appeared unable to speak.

'How would she get the money?' Sam asked.

The doctor leaned back into his seat, ignoring Kelly. 'However she likes. I can wire it into a bank account. I'll make the first wire payment tomorrow, to reimburse for the first donation.'

Kelly's gaze remained on the view out of the doctor's window, the rippling lake water and shady willow trees. She nodded once and stood.

As she walked out of the office, the undercover officer said, 'We'll get back to you on the details.'

SEVENTEEN

Maggie received a text from Kelly O'Neal asking if she would be able to give her a ride home. Fifteen minutes later, Maggie pulled up in front of the Cypress City Police Station. Kelly got into the passenger seat and stared out the front window.

'What's going on?' Maggie asked.

'I went. Everything went the way the cops wanted. Andre was supposed to be here, waiting for me to take me home.'

'He left you here with no ride?'

'Yep.'

Maggie pulled onto the Tamiami Trail. 'How about we go get an early lunch and you can tell me what happened?'

Once they were seated at a diner across from the police station, Maggie could see the tension and anger gathered in Kelly's shoulders and around her eyes.

Kelly started in immediately. 'I wanted to rip him apart. He represents everything that I hate about this world.'

'Take a deep breath. It's over with. Why don't you take a minute before you talk about it. Tell me how Andre's doing. I take it he wasn't happy you went today, since he left you at the police station.'

'He actually came around. He finally admitted last night that he thought it was wrong that I was going and that he wasn't. He said it looked bad. But he couldn't have gone. He'd have blown up, attacked the doctor. I convinced him the police thought a mother would stand a better chance of getting the doctor to talk. Andre finally agreed. Or I thought he did.' She shrugged. 'He's not doing well with any of this. It's eating him up inside. He's usually such a calm person. That's what I loved most about him when we first met.'

'How did you and your husband meet?'

She laughed. 'At least you have a little tact. My mom usually asks me how I *ended up* with him.'

'No judgment here,' she said.

'Everybody judges.'

Maggie grinned and lifted her hands up. 'I surrender. It was just a simple question. I didn't intend to offend you.'

'Andre's ten years older than I am. I was sixteen when we actually started dating. With the age difference, and him being black and me white, we were a scandal. I had the school guidance counselor calling me into her office every other week. I didn't care. I just wanted out of the house. I hated my mom back then. His place,' she put her sandwich down and glanced up at Maggie, 'where we live now, was my refuge. I stayed there more than my own home my last two years of high school. Then I got pregnant.' She shrugged again.

'Your mom didn't make you come home?' Maggie's own mother had been anything but conventional, but she couldn't imagine her mom allowing her to move in with a man ten years older than she was.

'Everyone judged my mom. And I can't imagine making the same decision with Amaya. But at the same time, if my mom had dragged me home and locked me up, I'd have run away. I think she recognized Andre was a good man. He didn't do drugs, didn't drink, didn't allow it in his home. My mom new it was a safe place for me to stay. Better than on the streets.'

Maggie had never had kids, so she changed topic to avoid saying something she would probably regret. 'Has he always found it hard to talk to people?'

'It's gotten a lot worse. He got exposed to some bad chemicals while he was in the military. The burn pits. The VA won't acknowledge the neurological problems, but I know it's what happened to him. It did something to his thinking. He can only focus on one thing at a time. When he gets around people, he gets overwhelmed. He loses his temper when he never did before the war.'

'Does he lose his temper with you?' Maggie asked.

'When it's just me and him together, he's OK. But it's hard, you know? I'm twenty-eight years old. I want to go out with friends and socialize. I'd like to have some fun.' She shrugged again.

'Is Andre seeing anyone about his issues?'

'Does he seem like the kind of guy who'd see a shrink?'

Maggie grinned. 'Maybe if you didn't refer to the therapist as a shrink, Andre might be more inclined to listen if you asked him.'

She tilted her head and smiled. 'Maybe. My mom tells me I have a chip on my shoulder.'

'Do you agree?'

'Probably.' She was quiet a minute before picking up on the idea. 'You know what cracks my ass up? All these rich people walk around looking at us with their noses in the air. Walking on the other side of the street so they don't catch a whiff.'

'Oh, come on. It can't be that bad.'

'You think I'm exaggerating? You come to Santa Cruz and walk through Old Town with Andre, Amaya and me, and tell me some of those old women don't walk the other way.' She shook her head at some not too distant memory before continuing. 'But the funny thing is, those same people are walking around with my plasma inside of them. My blood keeps their raggedy ass hearts pumping.'

Maggie laughed. 'That does have a nice ironic twist.'

'How many of those people in their million-dollar ocean homes do you figure donate their blood or plasma on a regular basis? They maybe donated blood once, forty years ago, thinking they were doing their good deed for the world. I give my plasma two times a week. Those old ladies don't have any idea it's my blood pumping through their veins during their open-heart surgery.'

'Karma,' Maggie said.

'You bet your ass.'

Maggie glanced over at Kelly's thin arms, trying to imagine how she could produce enough plasma to sell that often. 'You can't weigh much over a hundred pounds. Twice a week you donate?'

'One hundred ten pounds is the limit. I try and stay around one twenty. There's an old woman who comes in wearing ankle weights to reach one ten.' Kelly held her arms out. 'See these holes? They never heal over all the way. I have dreams sometimes about these open holes into my body.' She shuddered and put her arms down. 'And now there's some doctor who wants even younger blood. Because some old narcissist thought his life was more important than my daughter's.'

'For some people, personal wealth equals personal value.'

'Then I hope I never get that wealthy. I know there wasn't anything sexual in what they did to Amaya and the other girl, but it feels so awful. They kept Amaya drugged for two days. That's why I went today, to get answers from that bastard.'

Maggie nodded, leaning back in her seat. 'And did you get any answers?'

It took her a moment to respond. 'Nothing that helps. It's just a rich bastard thinking his patients are more important than my little girl.'

After lunch, Maggie drove Kelly back to her home on Howard Street. The drive was quiet. Kelly had still not been able to reach Andre on his cell phone.

Maggie pulled up in front of her house and saw the garage door was shut. 'Is this bad news for you, that Andre isn't here?' she asked.

Kelly shrugged. 'It's not good news. I got a text that Amaya is with her grandma, so he's dropped her off and left.'

Maggie followed her up to the house. Kelly glanced back at her as she unlocked the living room door. 'I'll just follow you in,' Maggie said. 'Let's make sure everything looks OK.'

The living room was spare and clean, decorated with antique lace cloths and framed photographs, antique books and small potted plants. The furniture was worn but well cared for, the wood floors swept clean. It was the house of a woman who cared for her family.

Maggie followed her through the two bedrooms and out into the backyard where they opened the door on the empty garage. They stepped inside, smelling the engine oil and grease in the enclosed space.

'Is this Andre's only job?' she asked, glancing around the room strewn with tools and mower parts.

'He has a small military disability, but this is his job. Small engine repair. He's not been out here today,' Kelly said, shutting the door behind her.

Maggie followed her back into the house.

'He'll be gone a day or two. He just needs to get it out of his system,' Kelly said.

'Get what out of his system?'

'The demons. The anger.'

Back inside, Kelly stood in front of the kitchen sink and picked up the dishcloth folded next to it. She ran the cloth down the neck of the faucet, polishing the silver between the handles. Maggie stepped behind her and watched her tears hit the chipped porcelain basin. Maggie placed her hands on Kelly's shoulders.

'If he comes home tonight, is he going to hurt you or Amaya?'
She shook her head. 'He's not like that.'

'When things get bad for Andre, when the demons hit, what happens?'

Kelly lifted a shoulder. 'I don't know. He leaves. He doesn't want me to see him angry.'

Maggie ran her hands down Kelly's arms and Kelly let her hands fall to her sides, leaning back against Maggie's body.

'I want to be happy. I want Amaya to be happy. I just don't know how to do it without destroying Andre.'

'He needs help. He needs something that you and Amaya can't give him. Living in a house with no happiness isn't doing any of you any favors.'

Kelly turned and laid her head on Maggie's shoulder. 'I want to feel safe again,' she said, her voice just above a whisper. 'What happened to Amaya? Listening to that doctor today wanting to prostitute my own daughter? And me agreeing to it, even if it was only said for the police. I still feel dirty and disgusting.'

Maggie put her arms around Kelly and stroked her hair, holding her for a long while. 'What you did was brave. You haven't done anything wrong in any of this, OK? What happened to Amaya was terrible, but you can't let it destroy you and your family. You need help. All of you.'

EIGHTEEN

Maggie's drive into Santa Cruz was all the more disconcerting given the time she had just spent on Howard Street. Growing up, she'd not experienced the hardship she'd just left, but her mom had survived paycheck to paycheck, and they'd never had it easy. When she married David, a high school biology teacher, they had lived conservatively and saved with the intention to retire and travel. Driving past multimillion-dollar homes on the way to her own oceanfront home still gave her the feeling of a tourist ogling the wealthy, wondering what people did to earn that kind of lifestyle.

She pulled onto Chantilly Drive, the neighborhood before
her own, and slowed her car to a stop. The scale and visual
perfection of the homes that curved around the brick drive was
what amazed her the most. While she didn't know many of the
homeowners as friends, she knew enough of their backgrounds
to understand that most of them were retired couples, or parents
with no more than two children. Why would two people ever
need a six-thousand-square-foot home? And beyond the extrava-
gance of space were the perfect proportions, from the palm
trees and gardens to the multi-tiered Key-West-style homes with
plantation shutters and soaring interiors; mansions whose colors
were deeper, creamier, whiter than anywhere else Maggie had
ever been.

She watched a trim woman in yoga pants and a sports bra
pass her by on a power walk, her tiny dog on a leash prancing
along beside her. Maggie had a vision of the lawnmowers in
Kelly O'Neal's side yard. The woman turned her head to glance
at Maggie so she eased the car into gear. She still couldn't
shake the notion that the neighbors viewed her as riffraff.

A half-mile around the curvy drive she passed the sign for
Oceanview Estates and pulled in front of the gate house, one
of the few remaining with an actual person instead of a swipe
card. She waved at Mr Aaron, a seventy-something-year-old
retired librarian who knew every person by name, as well as
their address and personal history. He tipped his baseball cap
and buzzed Maggie through.

Agnus's home was located six houses into the estate, one of
a dozen oceanside mansions. The gated community boasted a
helipad, golf course, boat slips, pools, tennis and walking trails
for the residents, although Maggie rarely saw people venture
outside. It was the kind of wealth that made her feel uncomfortable, as if the money ought to have a greater purpose than
stimulating the senses of a few dozen people, but here she was
living among them, her brain soaking up the emerald colors
and ocean smells like a junkie on crack.

She eased her car down the driveway and couldn't help
smiling at the beautiful two-story white stucco home with shutters the color of key lime pie. Agnus and her husband had, in
her own words, worked their asses off to grow a company worth

this kind of fortune, and she didn't feel an ounce of guilt for enjoying the fruits of their labor. Maggie drove down the lushly landscaped driveway lined with towering Royal palm trees, and parked her car beside the gardener's shack, marveling at the dunes leading out toward the ocean. She imagined David sitting beside her, holding her hand, telling her that Kelly and her daughter and Andre with his demons would all make it through to the other side; that justice would be handed out and Amaya wouldn't battle her own special set of demons for the rest of her life.

Maggie looked down at the pint of tequila sitting on the seat next to her. She'd stopped at the liquor store and rationalized that a small bottle was no big deal, and would limit the amount available to consume, thus limiting the guilt she felt in the purchase.

She flinched as she saw a hand raise against her driver's side window.

'What the hell are you doing in there?' Agnus hollered, banging on the glass.

Maggie pressed the down button on the window and Agnus tilted her sun visor up to better see her. Agnus leaned closer to peer in at Maggie. 'Where have you been? We expected you hours ago!'

'Who expected me?'

'We all did! Danny G signed a gig in Vegas. It's supposed to get down to seventy degrees tonight, so we're throwing a party on the beach. Go grab your flip-flops and get your ass down there.'

Maggie stood at her living room window, looking down at the bonfire blazing on the beach where Danny, Serena, Agnus and Mark were swaying their hips to a song Whitney appeared to be belting up to the skies. It was a happy sight. She wondered if she could hold up her end of the party.

When she reached the beach, flip-flops in hand, a chorus of, *Hey Maggie*, rang out as she made her way across the sandy dune. The smile came to her in spite of the melancholy she couldn't shake.

Agnus organized a round of celebratory tequila shots for Danny and the band. Danny explained that they had gotten a one-night gig in Vegas in September that he hoped would be their chance to break into a bigger market. They fantasized aloud about what the gig might mean for the band, the possibility of going on the road as an opening act, and who they might tour with. Maggie hoped the best for them, although the idea of taking the band on the road sounded exhausting to her.

After a dinner of hotdogs roasted over the fire they walked out into the surf, enjoying the cool breeze and the last orange rays of sunlight.

Mark laid his arm over Maggie's shoulders. 'This is a party. Why so quiet tonight?'

She kept her gaze on the boat that appeared to be straddling the horizon. 'Just enjoying the evening.'

Mark moved from her side to stand in front of her, then held her face in his hands to force her to look at him. 'I'm a cop. Remember? I can smell bullshit from a mile away.'

Maggie sighed and leaned her head into his chest. 'I've been out of it too long. I lost my defenses.'

'Defenses against what?'

'I spent the day with Kelly O'Neal. I picked her up after she got back to the police station and drove her home.'

'We tried to give her a ride home but she wouldn't take it,' he said.

'I think she just needed someone to talk to. And her husband took off to blow off steam somewhere. She seems lonely.'

'What about those lectures you give me about worrying too much?'

'I give you those lectures because I can relate,' she said.

'You sure you want to get sucked into their mess?'

'The dysfunction in that family . . .' Maggie struggled for words. 'A lot of people have a way out. They just don't have the guts to take it. Break the ties. Whatever. But this lady wants out and she's stuck. It depresses the hell out of me. She loves her daughter and her husband, so she stays, but they're in chaos. Her husband knows he's on the verge of losing everything he loves, but his head is so screwed up from who knows what kind of chemicals he breathed in from those burn pits in the Middle East. I get the feeling the little girl spends her days trying to do whatever she can to make things better. She's the fix-it girl, the peacemaker. But she's not fixing this one.'

Mark moved back to Maggie's side and pulled her toward the water to walk along the shore away from the others.

'Kids like Amaya are resilient. Kids like her turn into the cops and nurses of the world. Amaya will grow up and know how to walk into chaos and not turn and run. She'll solve problems for people.' He glanced down at her. 'It's probably how you ended up a cop. I'm sure you managed your own share of drama with a mother who ran a strip club.'

'I get that. It's probably why I'm so drawn to the family. I see myself in Amaya at that age. But her dad needs help. He seems like he's not engaged, and then you look again and see rage in his eyes, like it's barely contained. I saw it at the park, after we did the walk through and we told them that the Baxter kid had been found.'

'I didn't notice. I guess my focus was on her, on Kelly.'

'I'd like to convince him to go to the VA for help. At least fight for some compensation.'

'Do it. Go talk to him.'

Maggie shrugged, finding it hard to imagine a conversation with Andre.

'This should make you happy. They officially charged Ramone Anderson with kidnapping today, among a host of other things.'

'At least someone pays for what happened to those girls.'

He squeezed her hand. 'Now, let's leave it alone for a while. Be with me tonight.'

Maggie stopped and wrapped her arms around Mark. 'What's the term the yuppies use? Be in the moment? I need to work on that.'

He grinned. 'First of all, the term yuppies hasn't been used in several decades. But I would agree that enjoying the moment would be a good strategy for you.'

'Maybe I should sign us up for Saturday morning yoga classes,' she said. 'You could buy me some cute yoga pants and we could de-stress together.'

'Or we could eat bacon and eggs on the beach on Saturday mornings. Equally as relaxing, but way more enjoyable.'

NINETEEN

At eleven the next morning, Maggie grabbed her buzzing cell phone off the floor beneath the couch where she had been reading a historical novel on the Everglades. 'It's Kelly. I need your help.' Her voice was frantic.

'What's going on?'

'The police are here. They're talking to Andre right now. They won't let me in the same room.'

'Talking to him about what?'

'The doctor. He's dead. They said he slashed his wrists, so I don't know why they're talking to Andre. No one is telling me anything.'

'Doctor LeBlanc is dead? He killed himself?' Maggie sat upright.

'Yes. That's all the cops said. They asked where Andre was last night, and then said they needed to talk to him and took him into the kitchen. They told me to stay in the bedroom. I don't know what to do.'

'Andre shouldn't be talking to anyone without a lawyer. Get up. Walk into the room where they have Andre and tell him to stop talking. Tell the cops he's not saying another word without an attorney present. Do it right now.'

'We can't afford an attorney!'

'It doesn't matter. You get a court-appointed attorney, assuming they have anything on Andre. The cops are probably following up on rumors. If they had anything serious they'd have taken him in for questioning. Go put a stop to this before Andre says something he'll regret later.'

She listened as Kelly took a breath. Maggie imagined her standing taller, bracing herself for the encounter. It was unsettling, sitting on the other side of the phone, encouraging someone to shut down an interview.

Kelly hung up and Maggie called Mark, whose phone went to voicemail. Finding nothing but old sitcoms on the local news channels, Maggie searched the doctor's name on her phone and found the breaking story.

Dr Oscar LeBlanc, a hematologist specializing in age-related diseases, was found dead in his Santa Cruz office this morning of an apparent suicide.

Maggie looked up at banging on her door. Assuming it was Agnus or Mark with news of the doctor's suicide, she was shocked to find two uniformed Santa Cruz police officers standing on her front porch.

'Maggie Wise?'

'That's me.'

'I'm Officer Todd Weston. This is my partner, Officer Darrin Kilbourne. We'd like to ask you a few questions.'

'Absolutely. Come in.' Maggie opened the door for them to enter her living room. 'What can I do for you?'

She watched as the younger officer took the long way around the couch to look at the photos hanging above Maggie's desk. The other officer walked to the wall of windows in the back of the living room to take in the ocean view. She'd made the same moves in countless homes through the years, taking inventory and scanning for anything amiss, but only now did she fully understand the fury that people had felt over the intrusion.

'Nice place on a cop's pension,' Weston said.

'Why don't you have a seat and explain why you're here?' Maggie sat in the club chair opposite her couch and waited for the officers to sit.

'Have you heard the news this morning?' Weston said.

'I read all kinds of news.'

'Then you read about Doctor LeBlanc's suicide.'

'I did.'

Weston nodded and leaned forward to place his forearms on his knees, clasping his hands in front of him. He looked to be in his late twenties and Maggie wondered if the kid had been reading books on interview techniques. Kilbourne sat on the other end of the couch saying nothing.

'What do you make of it?'

Maggie stared for a moment. 'What do I make of what?'

'Of the doctor committing suicide. We know you spent time

with Kelly O'Neal last evening. I'm sure you talked about her visit to the doctor's office. Surely you have an opinion.'

'His life was unraveling. His medical practice was in jeopardy. I'm sure he worried the police were steps away from finding out what he'd done. He was a man who a month ago was on top of the world, making millions, and in the course of a week had turned into an identified kidnapper. So I think his mental state was a mess. What do you think?'

Kilbourne said, 'The doctor's receptionist found his body this morning. She called 911 at seven thirty-five. She said she gets to work at seven thirty to start the coffee and open up the office. The doctor usually arrives just before eight. She turned the light on in the exam room and found him sitting in a chair, both wrists slit. Bled out. A fifth of Old Crow whiskey on the counter, half empty.' Kilbourne stared at Maggie for a moment. 'What do you make of that?'

She considered the officer for a moment. 'Why do you care about my opinion?'

'Because we talked to his receptionist. She said you were the last patient he saw.'

'Not yesterday.'

'That's right. She said you were the last patient he had scheduled. And then Kelly O'Neal goes to confront him with the Cypress City police the next morning. You end up driving Kelly O'Neal home from the police station, and then spend time at her house. Then the doctor commits suicide that night. We're just trying to understand how you're involved with this,' Kilbourne said.

'Other than you're an ex-cop dating the Chief of Police in Cypress City,' Weston said, grinning widely.

Maggie looked at him with confusion. 'And why is that humorous?'

Kilbourne stepped back in. 'It's just that his receptionist brought your name up straightaway. She said, Maggie Wise, the arrogant talk radio lady – those were her words, by the way – showed up at the office asking to participate in the blood study, completely out of the blue. Were you serious about participating?'

'I was curious. I went to gather information for a possible radio show.'

'You weren't there representing a law enforcement agency?'

'No.'

'Does the suicide seem surprising to you?' Kilbourne said.

'From the one meeting I had with him, it doesn't seem the doctor's style. The whiskey and the mess.'

'Just what we thought,' Kilbourne said. 'We're not here to harass you.' He glanced at his partner and back to Maggie. 'You spoke with him the day before his supposed suicide. We'd just like your opinion. His wife claims he came home last night after she'd already gone to bed, and she didn't hear him leave.'

'She didn't see him at all?' Maggie asked.

'No. But he used the code to enter the house through the front door. And he entered the code when he left as well because it was engaged. We've subpoenaed the records from the alarm company to get exact times.'

'Not much of a marriage?'

'Hard to say. She seemed legitimately upset. She said he was career obsessed. She said they did their own thing, but that they loved each other. That they might go a day or two without seeing each other, but it was no big deal.'

'Were there signs of forced entry?' Maggie asked.

Weston cut back in before his partner could respond. 'We're not able to release those details.'

'We're just interested in your appointment with the doctor. If he gave any indication that he might be suicidal,' Kilbourne said.

Maggie shrugged. 'I don't know what to tell you. He just explained the blood research program he was conducting and how I could participate.'

'What happened with Kelly O'Neal's meeting with him?' Kilbourne asked.

'You'll need to bring that up with the Cypress City PD,' Maggie said.

'We'd like your take on it, with you being a former cop and all,' Weston said.

Maggie said nothing, letting the silence drag out. Kilbourne finally stood and thanked Maggie for her time.

As soon as the door shut behind them, Maggie texted Kelly. *Are the cops still there?*

Yes, Kelly responded.

Did you tell them you want a lawyer?

Yes. One of them is on the phone about a lawyer. The other one is talking to Andre.

Tell them to stop. Tell them the interview is over. Immediately. Won't we look guilty?

No. You'll look smart. Do it now.

Maggie called Mark again and he picked up.

'What the hell is going on?' she asked.

'Drop it down a level,' he said. 'I've got mess enough without you yelling at me.'

'I just had two Santa Cruz PD at my door. Kelly had the same. You don't think a courtesy call would have been in order?'

'I'm sure you can imagine things have been a little crazy this morning.'

'So how did Kelly and I end up on the shortlist? This is being reported as a suicide. Why the interest in us?'

'The doctor is dead, and you were two of the last people to talk to him, outside of his receptionist. Obviously, the police want to talk to you.'

'Kelly said they've got Andre in a separate room, grilling him on his whereabouts.'

'So what, you and Kelly are a team now?'

'What the hell is that supposed to mean?' she said.

'I just can't believe you have an issue with this. I could present this case to any other cop I know and they'd have Andre O'Neal on the shortlist in a heartbeat.'

She bit back a smartass comment and said nothing. Maybe Mark had a point. Maybe she'd been off the road too long to be impartial.

'Maggie. His only alibi is his wife. And from what the chief says, she didn't sound any too confident about his whereabouts last night.'

The hair prickled on the back of her neck. 'What do you mean?'

'I just got off the phone with Chief Osbourne from Santa Cruz. He said one of his deputies started out with both husband and wife in the room together. Big mistake. He asked where Andre was, from the time he dropped Amaya off after fishing, to when he arrived home. The first thing he did was look at his wife. She stared back at him, wide eyed. Then he finally turned back to the deputy and said he was out driving until about ten when he came home and went to bed.'

'Did she corroborate?'

'Of course she did. I can't believe they didn't separate them. Osbourne said the deputy didn't want to freak them out and get attorneys involved before he got the basics.'

'What makes you think Andre's lying?' Maggie asked.

'I'm not saying he is, just that he's got motive out the ass. If somebody kidnapped my daughter and stuck needles in her for two days, I'd want to kill him too. And I don't buy the suicide for a minute. The set up was all wrong. That doctor, who was so careful with his appearance, is not going to drink a bottle of cheap whiskey and then bleed all over his meticulously maintained white office.'

'Just because a guy has a doctorate doesn't mean he can't like whiskey.'

'Rotgut Old Crow? Maybe someone brought the whiskey to him,' Mark said.

'Even if someone brought whiskey to his office, you can't force someone to get drunk.'

'Sure you can,' he said. 'Put a gun to my head and I'll drink monkey piss.'

She grinned, feeling her anger begin to abate. 'So you think Andre lured the doctor to the office, put a gun to his head to get him drunk, and then slashed his wrists and watched him bleed out?'

After a moment's pause, he said, 'I know it's a stretch.'

'Let's go back to me for a minute. This cop that showed up at my door decided that since the receptionist thought I was a jerk with the doctor, that I was apparently involved with his death. How long are you going to let this guy hound me?'

'Because you never hounded anyone as a cop.'

'I'm not smiling.'

'Was it Todd Weston?' he asked.

'Yep.'

'He's an ass. He treats everyone like they're pond scum. And you know I have no control over what he does. He's from Santa

Cruz. Did you tell the officers you met with the doctor because I wanted you to?'

'Of course not. I said I was gathering information for my radio show.'

'Good.'

'So what's next for Andre and Kelly? She helped you out yesterday. Now you're going to let her husband hang?'

'Maggie. The murder took place in Santa Cruz.' He spoke slowly, as if to a child. 'This isn't my jurisdiction, so stop giving me hell. You have an issue with this, call the Chief in Santa Cruz. I have to go.'

'You stopping by after work?'

'No.'

TWENTY

Kelly O'Neal was a woman in crisis looking for comfort. Her husband was a suspect in a possible homicide and was disappearing for hours at a time, leaving no word with his wife on his whereabouts. Maggie and Kelly may not have been suspects, but they were certainly persons of interest with the Santa Cruz Police Department. Mark had hinted at concerns about Maggie's involvement with Kelly, which she had found both absurd and insulting earlier in the day, but which now seemed at least somewhat justified.

Kelly had called after supper and asked Maggie if she would stop by her house. She'd said she was scared and needed someone to talk to.

When Maggie arrived at the O'Neals' house, Kelly walked out to the car carrying a large bag. She said she didn't want to stick around in case Andre came home 'in a mood', that there was a quiet place down by the river where they could talk. When she slid into the passenger seat, Maggie was taken aback by the pale-yellow sundress that skimmed Kelly's thighs and the sweet smell of perfume.

'I appreciate this,' Kelly said. 'I couldn't stay in that house another minute without going crazy. Amaya went to stay with her grandma tonight, so all I had to think about was Andre and this mess.'

Maggie pulled away from the curb. 'It's no problem. You want to go get a cup of coffee somewhere?'

She lifted the handle on the bag that she'd hoisted onto the floor of the car. 'Nope. We're all set. I pack Amaya and me a bag all the time. We go down to the river to fish or swim, usually just to hang out. Just follow this road along the river to where it curves right, but take the dirt path straight instead.'

Maggie did as instructed, passing a half-dozen small homes before the road gave way to an empty, overgrown weed patch that eventually grew into thick woods to the right of the road. Scrub brush and scattered trees lined the left side of the road and gave no indication of the river beyond.

'Just pull off here. Nobody ever comes back this far.'

They walked several hundred feet down a dirt path that finally gave way to a grassy opening that led down to the river.

'People put in here to kayak on the weekends sometimes, but mostly it's deserted.'

'No gators?'

'Occasionally.' She gestured to the sandy flat leading into the river. 'It's our own private beach. Amaya and I hang out here in the evenings when Andre's in a mood.'

She opened her bag, shook out a blanket and laid it on the sand. 'Have a seat. I won't bite.' She smiled at Maggie's hesitation and pitched her a can of bug spray. 'If you don't put a blanket down, the sand fleas eat you alive.'

Maggie sat next to her in the middle of the blanket and watched as she pulled two juice glasses and a thermos out of her bag.

'This is the only cocktail I can stomach. Cranberry juice and vodka. Would you like one?'

'Sure.' Maggie scanned the slow-moving water, smelling the murky decay from the banks, and realized she'd not been to a river since she'd moved onto Agnus's property. The ocean was beautiful and soothing, but the river had a mystery to it that she'd always loved.

'A friend of my mom's used to take me night fishing for

catfish when I was a kid,' Maggie said. 'That's when I fell in love with the night. It's why I liked third shift homicide. Even when things were quiet on the street there was still a charge in the air. You could feel it when something big was about to break open.'

'I've never lived in a big city, but I think I'd like the night too. The mystery of it.'

Maggie pointed toward the remnants of half-burned logs in a fire pit twenty feet away. 'You have bonfires down here?'

'Amaya does. That's her favorite thing, building the fire. She watches the survival shows on TV and then wants to come down here and try out what she learns. She's such a good kid. She deserves way better than what her dad and I have given her.'

'How's she coping with the kidnapping?'

'She saw the school counselor but she didn't like being pulled out of class. She doesn't want to talk about it with me.' She handed Maggie a drink and sipped at her own. 'Amaya is partly why I asked you to meet tonight. I wondered if you might talk to her.'

'About what?'

'She says she wants to be a police officer. You said you used to be one. I thought maybe you could meet with her for that reason. But then, if it comes up, ask her how she's doing with the kidnapping. With the kids at school. That kind of thing. I just think she needs to spend some time with someone other than me, and her dad is off the charts.'

'I'd be glad to. But what's Andre going to say when he finds out I'm hanging out with his kid?'

'I don't really care at this point.'

'I care. I don't want an irate Andre confronting Amaya and me and making things worse.'

Kelly stretched her legs out on the blanket and rested her drink on a bare thigh. 'I'm sorry. That was rude of me. I'm just worn out with Andre right now. He wouldn't even notice.'

'Then why are we hiding out at the river?'

She sighed, obviously frustrated with the direction of the conversation. 'Just trust me on this. Andre won't be a problem. I was thinking you could pick Amaya up after school. She used to go to the park each night after school and shoot baskets with some other kids, but she won't go now. I thought maybe I could let her know you were a cop, and that you offered to talk to her. I'd be there to introduce you.'

'Andre won't do this for her?'

'Andre's so lost in his own head that he can't deal with Amaya. I hate Andre for it some days, because I see how much it hurts Amaya. And other days I see the misery in Andre's face and it breaks my heart. My world is crumbling around me and I can't stop it from happening.'

Maggie watched the water, motionless on the surface, and wondered what might be lurking underneath. She had no idea what to say. Kelly's problems were far too big for a pat on the back or some meaningless platitude.

She opened the thermos and refilled their glasses.

'Do you feel like telling me what happened with Andre this morning?' Maggie asked.

She was quiet for some time. 'I want to tell you. I need to tell someone how terrified I am before I go crazy. But you were a cop. I think you're friends with cops. I don't know if every-thing I say will be held against me later.'

Maggie felt as if the sand underneath her was shifting. She'd been nervous about meeting with Kelly, but not for this reason. 'Do you know something about the doctor's murder?'

'No! Nothing like that. I don't think Andre did it or anything, I just don't know what's going on with him.'

Maggie nodded slowly, feeling as if she was straddling a line and being asked to cross it. 'Let's approach it like this. If LeBlanc was murdered, and I know something that would lead to his murderer's capture, then I'm going to share that information with the police. But I'm not the interrogator or the investigator. And I think you could use a friend right now, and probably some decent legal advice. So how about we navigate this conversation carefully. Does that make sense?'

'It does. And I'm fine with that.'

'Then I'm just going to cut to it. Do you know where Andre was last night?'

'No. He wouldn't tell me.'

'Was he gone all night long?'

Kelly hesitated. 'I don't know.'

'Were you at home all night long?'

'No.'

'OK. This is where we navigate carefully,' Maggie said.

'I was at the doctor's office last night.'

'Shit. That is not being careful.'

'I know. But I need to tell someone. I had nothing to do with his death! When I left he was fine. And he definitely didn't look like he was going to commit suicide.'

'What were you doing there?' Maggie held her glass out and Kelly drained the rest of the contents into it.

'The more I thought about the way the doctor just assumed he was going to get away with all of this, by getting me to sell my own kid, it just infuriated me. I thought about killing him. I swear I did. I wanted to walk into his office and blow a hole right through the center of his arrogant forehead.'

'Jesus, Kelly, stop it. This is not good.'

'But I didn't! Obviously that wouldn't have helped Amaya. So I kept thinking what could I do to make this right for her. And then I figured, the cops were going after the doctor. The prosecutor said she had to get things in order before she filed charges. So I figured I had one night to take care of things.'

Maggie leaned back on her hands to watch Kelly, intrigued now. Her voice had lost the fear and sorrow she'd come to associate with her situation. Kelly turned on the blanket, crossing her legs underneath her to face Maggie.

'I found his phone number online. I paid twenty-five dollars to one of those online white pages sites and actually got his cell phone number. I called him last night at about seven o'clock. Amaya was in her bedroom and Andre was gone. I told the doctor who I was and asked him to meet with me. He quickly hung up then five minutes later he sent me a text message.'

Kelly pulled her cell phone out of her bag and opened up her messages. She handed Maggie the phone.

When and where? I don't want to meet at the office during the day.

Tonight at the office? Kelly had responded.

Yes. Meet me at 8:00

OK

Maggie handed her the phone back. 'This isn't good, Kelly. If the cops subpoena his phone records you're screwed.'

'This isn't my phone. I ran to WalMart and bought one.'

Maggie took a deep breath. This was not the person she thought she'd been dealing with.

'Look. I know it sounds bad. It sounds like I was trying to be sneaky. But I didn't want him calling my cell phone. I didn't want Andre to see me texting with the doctor. And I especially didn't want Amaya to see anything. She uses my phone to get on the internet. I didn't want her to accidentally see some strange communication with this psychotic doctor. So I bought a cheap throwaway phone.'

'So you met the doctor at eight last night, in his office?' Maggie asked.

'Yes.'

'Why?'

'I thought you'd have figured it out by now. He offered me $25,000 in payment for what he did to Amaya. And Amaya deserves that money.'

Maggie choked back a response, and then laughed at the smile, barely visible, on Kelly's face in the fading light.

'You went to collect before the cops could arrest him.'

'Exactly. They wouldn't let me keep that money.'

'Where's the money?'

'He helped me set up an overseas account.'

'Son of a bitch. Are you serious?'

Her grin widened.

'Who are you?' Maggie said, laughing.

'I'm a pissed off mother wanting justice for my kid.'

'How did you accomplish this?'

'I just went in and told him I wanted paid for what he did to Amaya. He asked why Mr Delaney didn't come with me, and I said I didn't need his help, that I was taking care of myself. Then he started giving me his line of bullshit about his all-important research and I cut it off. I said I didn't care what he was doing, what he did to my daughter was terrible, and I wanted Amaya to have that money. So then the bastard wants to negotiate having Amaya come back in for another blood draw next month! Obviously he couldn't continue getting blood the way he did it this past time, and he said his patient had doubled his payment when he heard what had taken place. So he said he'd pay me in advance to get Amaya in his office again. He gave me twenty-five thousand for last time. And fifty thousand, half of what his patient offered to pay, for next time.'

'He paid you seventy-five thousand dollars last night?'

She nodded.

'How do you set up an overseas account at eight o'clock at night?'

'In French Polynesia it was only two o'clock in the afternoon. It's where the doctor has his own accounts. It took about two hours to set it up. He pulled up my bank accounts online and walked me through it. It was the most bizarre night of my life. And I couldn't tell anyone! I was selling my plasma for grocery money last month, and now I have seventy-five thousand dollars sitting in a bank account that I can't tell anyone about.'

'So why are you telling me this?'

'Because I don't think it was illegal. He offered me money and I accepted. I guess I want you to tell me that what I did was OK.'

Maggie laughed again at the audacity of what she'd done. 'You are asking a retired homicide cop from Cincinnati. I don't know what kind of Florida laws exist for selling your child's plasma. A child can't donate at a plasma center, but that's not what happened here. But the money *was* gained as part of a criminal investigation, so I just don't know.' She could feel Kelly's eyes on her. 'This is where we navigate carefully. I'm not going to say a word about this to anyone, and you aren't either. OK?'

'Yes.'

'Don't tell Andre. Don't tell Amaya or your mom or some friend. I'm not calling you a criminal, but that's what gets most crooks a trip to jail. They can't keep their mouths shut.'

'Which is why I'm talking to you and not someone else.'

'Then you get my point. Just leave that money where it is. I'll do some looking into this for you later, but not just yet. Let's see where this all shakes out.'

'OK.'

'One more question. Does Andre know you met with the doctor?'

'No. At least I don't think so. Andre came home about four in the morning, showered, and stumbled into bed reeking of alcohol. I went to work for two hours this morning. I clean houses on the side. I got home at the same time the police were pulling up to the house. The police asked Andre where he was last night and he told them he was with me all night. I didn't know what else to say, so I just agreed. I really don't know where he was.'

TWENTY-ONE

Maggie wanted a drink from Mel's, but she knew the conversation she'd had with Kelly would ruin the night. She needed a plan, or at least a way to rationalize the information she'd heard and not yet reported.

On the beach behind her cottage, tequila in hand, she let the waves splash up against her shins, eventually moving out into the water, letting it slap against her thighs, threatening to push her down into the surf. The noise of the waves, the icy water and taste of the salt, the sand rubbing against the soles of her feet, all helped to drown out the distractions in her head. She realized that it wasn't the content of what Kelly had said that was bothering Maggie the most; it was that she'd lost her read on the woman. Maggie had summed her up as a struggling wife and mom, overwhelmed by life, stuck in a situation that had left her helpless. But she wasn't helpless. She was cunning. And gutsy. Two traits Maggie would not have associated with her two days ago.

Within a few hours of confronting the man who had kidnapped her child, Kelly had been savvy enough to figure out a plan to turn the screws on him. She'd taken a huge risk. If the doctor had not died, he could have told the police about Kelly's visit. He could have claimed he was being blackmailed. When Maggie had asked Kelly about that possibility, she had said she'd considered that, but she figured in the end, him admitting to paying Kelly off would only make him look guiltier. Maggie wasn't sure about that, but her decision had certainly worked. It had worked to the point where Maggie had begun to question the motives of everyone involved. How does a woman on the verge of a meltdown hours earlier manage to fleece a doctor for $75,000 and have him deposit it in an offshore bank account just before he was murdered, thus leaving all traces of her actions obliterated?

But if she was guilty of something more sinister, why tell Maggie anything? And, in the end, the $75,000 may help Amaya someday, but it certainly wasn't going to solve her current family problems. Her life was still a shit show, as she had called it.

Most troubling was finding out that Andre had arrived home at four in the morning, drunk, the night of the murder, after telling police he'd been with his wife all night. If he had just been out drinking, why not tell the cops that? Maggie had not heard there was any video footage at the doctor's office, so she assumed Kelly's visit was safe, at least on that account. She figured the doctor wouldn't have wanted video cameras anywhere near his offices, given the nature of what he was doing after hours. So, again, he'd screwed himself. If Andre had visited the doctor, there was probably no video to prove it.

Maggie weighed her duty to inform Mark about what she'd learned with her desire to keep Kelly as far removed from the investigation as possible. Maggie wanted Amaya to get that money. She agreed with Kelly: the little girl was owed the money. Maggie had no idea if the police would seize it, so why open that door? The way Maggie had it figured, the cops already thought Andre was lying about being at home the night of the murder, so Maggie confirming the fact wouldn't change the trajectory of the investigation. She decided to take her own counsel and navigate the conversation carefully.

When she finally turned the lights out for bed, she stared at the ceiling for an hour, trying to imagine how a doctor could make the leap from using plasma to research diseases plaguing the elderly, to kidnapping juveniles to steal their blood. Her thoughts turned to other research that initially started with one person's bizarre hypothesis. She thought about how the tissue from aborted fetuses had been used for stem cell research for years, both with and without patient consent. And look at the medical breakthroughs that one perverse decision had led to. So using blood from young children maybe wasn't that big a leap.

And, as was always the case with two in the morning ceiling sessions, Maggie's thoughts turned to David. It had been over a year since she had heard any news on the research study that he had participated in. The doctor had provided updates in the beginning, but Maggie had quit responding, and she figured the doctor had decided the news was too difficult for her to hear. While she wanted the research to succeed, she'd also been struck by blinding jealousy when she heard of other patients experiencing significant improvements and even remission.

Maggie got out of bed and went to the living room where she opened the filing cabinet under her desk and pulled out the expandable folder filled with David's medical records. She'd requested the documents shortly after his death, packing them away when she received them. She'd not had the courage to review them as she had imagined.

She wondered briefly what David would have thought of her current dilemma, but she knew. There would have been no internal debate: he would have helped Kelly and her daughter and dared someone to stop him. David had called himself a rule follower, but his rules were never governed by policy and procedure, rather by a sense of morality that informed every decision he made. He had been one of the most stable, kind people she'd ever known. Back in Ohio his sickness, and then his death, had made her job in homicide unbearable; how could someone so good be taken from the world, while so many horrible people continued to travel through life, spreading hate and disaster everywhere they landed, free to ruin countless lives in their wake?

After downing one final shot of tequila, with an internal promise to drink nothing the next day, she pulled the stack of papers out of the file and sat down on the couch to read. Much of it was lab orders and test results, combined with research updates and publications. About halfway through the stack of papers, a page of handwritten notes caught her eye. Each of

David's visits had been accompanied by lab work, a physical exam, and the more interesting anecdotal records detailing his progress. It was the quotation marks that caught her attention.

The doctor detailed David's failing organs, his plummeting white blood count, and a host of other problems that read like Greek to Maggie. And then she read:

> *The patient was informed he was not bound by the research project. If he was in pain, then he should terminate. He stated, 'I'm doing it for my wife.' He knows he's dying, 'can feel it in my soul', but he's at peace. He doesn't want the needles and drugs, but he does it for her.*

Maggie let the papers fall to her lap. Tears burned her eyes with the shame of what she'd read. She remembered the last argument they'd had a few months before his death. They were back in Cincinnati after his checkup in Santa Cruz. They'd been sitting at the kitchen table where she'd made him a cup of hot tea to soothe his stomach.

He'd told her, 'We've had a good run. We've had joy and sorrow, but we did it together. We loved each other. Do you know what a gift that is?'

She couldn't answer. She'd just stared at him.

'I am ready. God wants to take me.' He'd reached over and laid his hand on hers. It had been dark outside, a blustery night in February that made them regret leaving Florida. Maggie had stoked up the woodstove, but it had still felt cold sitting at that table. 'My time here is coming to an end. I want to bow out gracefully. To say thanks to my friends for their support, but mostly to enjoy a few more quiet evenings with you here at home.'

His defeat had fired up an anger inside her belly that she would only later understand was pain. 'We are a team,' she'd said. 'We do this together. You can't quit when things get bad. You can't give up on me like this. I need you to be strong and mean and fight like hell. How do you know if you can beat this thing if you don't believe? The doctor told you that attitude is a huge part of recovery.'

Maggie's face burned with the shame of that night. He'd been asking for her help. He'd wanted Maggie to let him go, and she'd been too selfish to grant his last request.

She drained the remaining tequila out of the bottle into her glass and leaned back into the couch. Her body felt numb. She needed one more drink to get her to sleep. She thought about the dive bar, The Last Straw, located a block off the ocean in Fort Myers. She'd been thinking about it quite a bit lately, and she'd been less inclined to suppress the thoughts.

Maggie had found the bar a year ago when she'd promised Mark she'd given up alcohol. She had assured him that her drinking was no problem, that she could stop when she wanted to. It had solved a problem at the time, gotten him to acknowledge that she wasn't an alcoholic, that she could take it or leave it. Two weeks into her abstinence she'd told him she was going to visit an old friend in Miami who'd flown in for a conference. Instead, she'd driven to Fort Myers Beach on Estero Boulevard and found The Last Straw, a dark little hole in the wall where she could sit at the bar for hours and not a soul would judge her. She'd been several times since, making friends with the bartender, an old guy named Kenny who'd put her in a cab and had her delivered to a motel the last time she visited.

She knew Mark would do more than disapprove, which she figured was part of the reason she went. Screw the world was her frame of mind when she thought about The Last Straw, which was exactly what she was thinking when she finally fell asleep on the couch that night.

TWENTY-TWO

At seven o'clock the next morning, battling a monster hangover headache, Maggie called Tiger and asked to change the format for Saturday's show, to bring in patients of Dr LeBlanc's who were involved in the pay-to-participate research. Maggie avoided mention of the juvenile blood since that part of the investigation had not been shared with the public. Instead she focused on the legal young blood, with an emphasis on the idea that it could increase the longevity and quality of life of older patients. Tiger loved it.

Maggie enlisted the help of Nadine, the woman whom she and Mark had talked to over chicken salad, to connect with three patients who were all anxious to talk about their experiences with Dr LeBlanc on the air. All three were from the Santa Cruz and Naples area and had agreed to an in-station interview, Maggie's preferred method for talking with people. She had found that eye-to-eye contact elicited an intimacy that phone calls could never replicate.

Saturday morning, thirty minutes into the first interview, Tiger mouthed, 'Marconi Award', through the window. The phone lines hadn't let up since Maggie introduced the first guest. She wasn't interested in a broadcast award, but she did hope the information might at least illuminate other roads into the investigation. Through her phone calls to a dozen different patients the day before, she'd discovered that for a man devoted to helping others improve their quality and quantity of life, Dr LeBlanc had made a lot of enemies.

'My name is Wilbur Montesano. I am seventy-six years old. I am a retired high school English teacher. Millionaire. And master gardener.'

Maggie laughed. 'Millionaire and teacher don't often coincide.'

'You'd be surprised what a little knowledge and significant discipline will produce. Did you know, there are more millionaire teachers than there are millionaire doctors in the United States?'

'That's a stat I've not heard,' Maggie said. 'Tiger. Get that on the docket for next week. What does it take to be a millionaire?'

'Hard work and commitment are what it takes, and too many people today don't have either quality,' Wilbur said.

Maggie liked the guy. He had walked into the broadcast booth wearing golf pants and a crisp button-down shirt, the epitome of health and vitality at seventy-six.

'Let's talk about commitment,' Maggie said. 'I understand you committed significant amounts of your hard-earned retirement money to Doctor LeBlanc's research efforts. Tell me why you chose to do that.'

'Look. I invested well and made some good real estate decisions. I have zero debt. I worked hard for forty years so I could retire and enjoy life. But here's the thing. I don't want a long life riddled with disease. I want to be strong enough and healthy enough to get outside and enjoy the world.'

'Sounds like a reasonable plan.'

'That's why I don't get the judgmental attitudes. I've done my research. What LeBlanc was looking into isn't exactly new, but it's not been thoroughly explored. The fusion of young blood and old blood has great promise. But there hasn't been the support from the scientific community.'

'There's probably a reason there's no support,' Maggie said.

'Probably not the reason you think. Have you looked into federal grant projects? The politics of funding? The doctor was interested in the science, not the bureaucracy that drags everything down to a slow crawl.'

'So you're fine that he didn't have the scientific credentials to—'

Wilbur cut her off. 'That's why I joined! I'm seventy-six years old. Nobody else is taking this serious. And from what I've seen from Doctor LeBlanc's initial trials, there is real merit here. If I wanted to be a part of this, then I had to pay. Sure, I'd like to do it for free. But that's not an option.'

'You know, there are people who are accusing the doctor of getting rich off their blood money.'

'Don't be dramatic. Have you seen the machines that are required for this type of research? It's not cheap.'

A message scrolled across the computer screen in front of Maggie. Tiger was messaging: 'Take call on Line 3. Dr Meagan Rossi. Hot call.' A hot call was Tiger's term for a screened caller who is angry or has an opposing viewpoint from the current or previous caller.

'All right, Wilbur. Let's get an opinion from the medical community. Doctor Meagan Rossi is on the line. We appreciate the call, doctor. Before we get into specifics, can you start with your background?'

'I'm a specialist in plastic and regenerative surgery.' She had a thick accent, most likely South American, but she enunciated well. Listeners would have no problem understanding her. 'I'm actually here for a conference this week. And I'm amazed listening to your caller that he could be so cavalier with his life.'

Maggie muted his mic and put a hand up to keep Wilbur from responding. She wanted the doctor's input first. 'Why cavalier? He seems very tuned in to his health.'

'Just because someone knows how to run an experiment doesn't mean they have the patient's best interest at heart. I know through firsthand experience how dangerous trials can be for patients. The risk of infection from blood-borne pathogens is just one issue.'

Wilbur leaned into the microphone and Maggie took the mute off. 'If you've had some bad experiences, then perhaps you should study Doctor LeBlanc's methods. I'm not aware of any of his patients getting infections.'

The doctor huffed into the phone. 'Listen to me. There are clinics popping up all over the world claiming to offer stem cell treatments and pay-to-participate research. Some of these places operate without any scientific basis. People have died from poor patient care, from taking treatments that are unsafe and often useless.'

'Aren't you making a big leap, assuming Doctor LeBlanc fits into that category?'

'Google his credentials! This is pure exploitation!'

For the next ten minutes, Maggie basically sat back and allowed Wilbur and Dr Rossi to duke it out over the airwaves. When the conversation turned too clinical, Tiger twirled his finger in the air to wrap it up, then pointed to the waiting room where Maggie's next guest was waiting.

Before she hung up, the doctor got her last jab in. 'Your listeners need to get involved. Stem cell research is huge. Stem cells have the potential to grow into other types of cells, like blood and bone. They even have the potential to grow into other organs at a rapid rate. However, due to the possibility of great monetary gains, there are people involved who are doing more harm than good. The research on young blood is in its infancy. The same thing will happen here if protocols aren't put into place.'

By the time Maggie got the doctor off the air her eyes were rolling back in her head and Tiger was waving his arms. Callers were hanging up, bored with the conversation. Maggie had come to learn that people wanted to be informed, and they wanted to play an active role in their communities, as long as they didn't have to think too hard or spend any money.

Maggie's next guest, Arlene Harmyer, sat in the chair opposite Maggie and hunched her shoulders down around the mammoth white handbag sitting in her lap. The deep grooves in her forehead and around her eyes spoke of a woman in a constant state of sorrow. Maggie had asked her to tell her story.

'When Donald got diagnosed with Alzheimer's, I didn't know what to do. We're old-fashioned folks. I never drove. Donald took care of everything outside the house. And I took care of everything inside. So when he got sick I didn't hardly know where to turn. That's when our family doctor told us about Doctor LeBlanc.'

'So you were referred to LeBlanc by another doctor,' Maggie said, ready to nudge the story along. 'And did you end up participating in the study?'

'We did. It cost us seventy thousand dollars before we finally had to give up. I had to put Donald in a nursing home. He never got a minute better. And I lost all our retirement money. We lost our house. I live with my daughter and her kids now.'

Maggie could imagine Dr Rossi pumping her fist in the air.

'Did Doctor LeBlanc understand that you were using your retirement money for the study?'

'He did. After the fifth treatment I asked if we should keep going. I couldn't see any improvements, and the money was just flying out of our bank account. He told me to hang on, that his findings had shown that the tenth treatment was when things got better. We only made it to the ninth treatment before we ran out of money.'

'And the treatment ended at that time?'

'My son-in-law . . .' Maggie passed Arlene a tissue and asked if she was sure she wanted to continue. She nodded and said, 'He was so angry. He went to the doctor's office and tried to get our money back. Or at least some of it. He told him we were losing our house, but that doctor didn't care. He had what he wanted.'

Tiger patched through a caller at that point who was a neighbor to the Harmyers. As she described how she had watched the family lose all their money, and how she felt the doctor had taken advantage of these elderly people, Maggie noticed a woman standing in the production booth talking to Tiger. He stood as well, arms clasped in front of him, nodding his head and frowning.

As Maggie tried to interpret Tiger's body language, she watched in shock as the woman turned to face her. The woman leaned across the audio console and banged on the window. It was a soundproof broadcast room, but the soundproof only worked to a certain degree.

Arlene looked behind her at the woman banging on the window, and back to Maggie, her eyes wide.

'Arlene, we appreciate your time today. I know how hard this was for you to come into the station. We're going to take a break. Callers hang tight.' Maggie clicked off for an unscheduled station identification break and stood to put a hand on Arlene's shoulder. 'You stay here. Don't worry about this.'

The woman had seen Maggie walk out of the booth so she met her in the hallway.

'I will have you fired before this is over,' the woman said.

Tiger stepped between the two women. 'Maggie Wise, this is Jillian LeBlanc, Doctor LeBlanc's wife. She's upset about the show today.'

'Have I not been through enough? I was at the funeral home, planning for my husband's burial, when I received an urgent phone call from a friend. She tells me that my husband's name is being dragged through the gutter.'

'Mrs LeBlanc, I'd like to extend my condolences,' Maggie said.

'Spare me.'

Maggie exhaled slowly, trying to defuse the situation. 'My intention was never to defame your husband's name. The research he was performing is new to most of us. We're trying to understand it better. There's a great deal of confusion and misinformation, and that's what we're looking at.'

Jillian wore a white pantsuit with her black hair tied up in an elegant bun behind her head. Diamond earrings twinkled in her ears. The manicured exterior looked at odds against her uncontrolled anger. The whites of her eyes bulged and her pupils were dilated to the point that Maggie wondered if she'd taken something.

'You are a liar! You couldn't care less about the truth. Do you know what it's like having your own friends talking about this ridiculous young blood nonsense? It's humiliating.'

Maggie saw a ribbon of sunlight illuminate the hallway and turned to look at the entrance door where a man in his early eighties had entered and was listening to the woman's accusations. Maggie was certain the man was her next guest.

'Mrs LeBlanc, your own husband referred to it as young blood,' Maggie said. 'I have a printed copy of the interview if you'd like to read it.'

'I don't care what you printed. You're taking what he said and turning it into something horrible. You make it all sound like some cheap tabloid scandal.'

Mark had told Maggie that Santa Cruz PD had not made public the information that LeBlanc was responsible for the kidnapping of the two girls. And LeBlanc's death was still being reported as a suicide. Maggie wasn't sure what the cops were waiting on, but she was fairly certain Mrs LeBlanc didn't know any of the details. She wondered how Jillian's husband's kidnapping of little kids to steal their blood for his research would play into her cheap tabloid scandal scenario.

'I'm not altering his words at all, Mrs LeBlanc. The people we're interviewing came to the show today because they wanted a voice.'

'Oh bullshit. I know how this works. You pay these people off and they'll say whatever you want in order to boost your ratings.'

Maggie noticed the sunlight again and looked up to find her next guest leaving the station.

'Unfortunately, Mrs LeBlanc, public radio has no budget for payoff money. We are simply searching for the truth.'

TWENTY-THREE

The Tamiami Trail cut through the bottom half of Cypress City, bringing in coveted travelers on their way to or from the Everglades National Park. The Chamber of Commerce had tried to attract tourism to the town for decades, but it amounted to a few swamp tour boats and fishing guides. Cypress City was just far enough away from the water, both ocean and swamps, that it was hard to entice visitors to make the small town a vacation destination. Maggie figured the biggest economic gain from tourism went to the gas station owners who fueled travelers up on gas and junk food before the long haul through the Everglades.

Cypress City Elementary School was tucked away in a tree-lined neighborhood made up of small single-family homes and modulars, three blocks from Howard Street, where the O'Neals lived. Kelly had decided a Saturday afternoon meeting, at a place away from the house, would be best. Amaya had already experienced people in Cypress staring at her, talking about her, asking inappropriate questions – some by well-meaning but ignorant people, some by people whose intent was clearly to hurt.

Maggie parked her car in the empty parking lot behind the school and spotted Kelly and Amaya sitting side by side on a bench just outside a fenced-in playground area.

Kelly was smiling, watching her daughter tell an animated story. She was a scrappy girl, freckle-faced like her mom, with the same lopsided grin.

Maggie made it to within a few feet of the bench before Kelly saw her and stood.

'Hey, Maggie. Thanks for coming.' She tugged on Amaya's T-shirt sleeve and the girl stood. 'This is Amaya.'

The girl put her small hand out and Maggie shook it, noticing her solemn expression.

'I'm Maggie. It's good to meet you.'

She nodded. 'It's good to meet you too.'

'Amaya was telling me about a boy that got sent to the principal's office yesterday for scattering BBs across the floor.'

'Did he get a paddling for that one?' Maggie asked.

'No. They aren't allowed to paddle kids anymore. But he got sent home. The teacher was going over to his desk to get the rest of the BBs but she slipped on some and fell. She started crying.'

'I bet you never get sent home from school, do you?'

She glanced at her mom. 'Are you kidding? She'd kill me.'

Kelly had Amaya tell Maggie about the school and her teachers and her friends, obviously trying to move them past the awkward first few minutes. Maggie finally decided to cut her loose.

'Your mom tells me you might want to be a police officer someday.'

Amaya nodded again. 'Yeah. I had to write a paper on what I want to be someday. That's what I picked.'

'I thought maybe we could run up to the Dairy Twist. I could tell you a little about what it's like. That sound OK?'

'Sure.'

Kelly ruffled Amaya's hair and smiled at Maggie. 'I'll see you guys back at the house in a while.'

On the way to the ice cream shop, Maggie talked about her time as a street cop, including the paperwork and the interviews, the importance of asking questions. Like most kids, Amaya eventually got around to asking if Maggie carried a gun. And if she'd ever had to kill someone.

'I've had to fire my gun a few times. Those were bad days. The TV shows make it sound exciting, but it's pretty scary. That's the stuff that gives you bad dreams at night.'

'You have bad dreams from being a police officer?'

'Sometimes. I don't so much anymore, but I used to.'

'Because you're retired?'

'Yep. You have many bad dreams?'

Amaya shrugged and Maggie let it go.

'So what makes you think you want to be a cop?'

'I figure it'd be fun. You'd be driving around and be outside all day. It wouldn't be boring like sitting in school.'

Maggie had thought about taking Amaya to the Cypress City Police Department for a tour, but she was afraid one of the officers would recognize her from the kidnapping and say something.

'It depends. Sometimes riding around in your car can get pretty boring too.'

'Don't you have a partner?'

'Sometimes. It depends on where you're a cop. Sometimes you're by yourself each day.'

'I don't think I'd like that.'

By the time they reached the Dairy Twist, Amaya had loosened up and was full of animated tales about school and her mom and grandparents. She'd not mentioned her dad in any of her stories.

Maggie ordered a chocolate shake and Amaya said she'd have the same. They sat outside under an umbrella to sip them, glad for the shade from the brutal afternoon sun.

'Mom says you're on the radio. I told some of my friends at school that and they didn't believe me.'

'If you want, next time we could go by the radio station. I'll show you where we tape the show. I'll get a picture of you sitting behind the mic so your friends can see you.'

'That'd be cool.'

'Did your mom tell you that I did a radio show that played while you were missing? People listening to the show called in and one of them had a clue that helped the police track down the people who took you.'

'Nobody told me that.'

'Do you want to talk about it? About the kidnapping?'

She shrugged and her face grew red. 'I don't know. Sort of. But everybody acts like it's a secret. I feel weird talking about it. My best friend said her mom told her she's not allowed to talk about what happened.'

'Why's that?'

'I don't know.'

'Maybe if you talked about it now, it would make it less scary. Less weird.'

'I've been having these dreams where I'm lying in a room and I can't get up. I'm hooked up to machines and they're taking things from inside of me, but I can't get up or talk or scream. I'm just stuck there. My mom's been telling me how to wake myself up out of a bad dream. It sort of works, but then I'm afraid to go back to sleep.'

'You know the people who took you are all gone or in jail?'

'Yeah.'

'Do you understand what happened? And why they did it?'

'Mom said what they did was bad, but that it still might save somebody's life.'

'That's true. That research might help people someday. But what he did was still terrible.'

'Why'd he pick me?' Amaya asked.

Maggie hadn't anticipated that one. She'd decided, to the best of her ability, she'd be straight up with the girl, hoping the truth would make more sense than an overactive imagination.

'I think it was because the doctor needed blood or plasma from a young person. But he needed it to be a certain kind. That's why the technician at the plasma center figured out what type blood you had a few weeks ago. To see if you'd be a match. And you were.'

Amaya shrugged but remained quiet.

'Just because people seem nice, doesn't always mean they are. If something happens you aren't sure of, don't be afraid to tell an adult no. Then talk to somebody. Your mom or teacher or someone.'

'I don't know why the doctor didn't just ask. I bet I would have given him my blood if he'd said he needed it.'

'I think it's because the government says you're too young to donate.'

'Why does the government care?'

'Because they're trying to take care of you. Make sure you stay safe.'

Maggie could see the wheels turning in Amaya's head as she thought about that statement.

They finished their ice cream and Maggie said, 'If you want, I could drive you over to the park. You could show me where it happened. Maybe it wouldn't be so scary if you could talk about it. You can see that everything is still the same as before it happened.'

Amaya pulled her shoulders up, the same way Maggie had seen the girl's mother react, trying to muster up courage. She hoped Mark was right, that the kid would be a fighter, someone able to face chaos head on. Maggie liked the girl a great deal. She needed a chance at a good life. Amaya squinted at Maggie, considering the proposition, and finally nodded once. 'I'll go.'

Maggie parked in the elementary school parking lot and they took the route to the park that Amaya and her friends took. She said that she and some other kids played basketball or soccer most nights after school, but that she had to be home by 4:30 to wash up for supper. As they walked under the shady tree-lined block toward the park, Maggie quizzed Amaya about her favorite subjects in school, but when they reached the park entrance Amaya became quiet.

As they walked along the asphalt track toward the basketball court, Maggie filled the silence with stories about her and David coming to the park when he had visited Florida. Amaya didn't say a word, just walked and listened.

As they approached the empty basketball court, Amaya stopped.

'What's making you nervous?' Maggie asked.

Amaya pointed to an access road about a hundred yards to their right. 'That's where the van was.'

'What made you walk over to it?' Maggie asked, hoping she'd made the right decision to bring Amaya.

'That's my way home. We were done playing basketball. I was walking home. I cut through the grass there and that road takes me out of the park. Then I walk a block over to Howard Street where I live.'

'Did you notice the van when you were walking that way?'

'Not really.'

'When did you see it?'

'I don't really remember. I just remember the door opened and a guy got out. He was smiling and said my name. He said they were a transit van. It looked like the ones our school uses. He said mom asked if they would drop me off at my grandma's house. And he told me mom's name. I thought it was pretty cool I was going to grandma's house. And I got in the backseat and I don't remember anything else until I woke back up in the park.'

'You didn't recognize him?'

'He had on sunglasses and a baseball cap. He said my name so I thought I knew him. Mom said he was the guy from the plasma clinic.'

Maggie didn't think it was the time to give her a safety lecture. She figured she'd heard plenty of them in the past few days. 'Do you want to walk home together? I'll be with you, so you won't need to be scared.'

Amaya started to cry and turned from Maggie, angrily wiping tears off her face.

'Hey, it's OK. We don't have to do this. It's probably just too soon. You don't need to rush this.'

'I want to play with my friends. But I can't walk home anymore.' Amaya spoke through angry tears. 'I'm always afraid someone will pick me up.'

'You know it's normal to feel that way. When crimes happen to adults, they feel the same way. Sometimes it takes people a long time to feel back to normal again. But you'll get there.' Maggie put her hand on Amaya's shoulder and gently turned her back toward the way they had come in. 'I bet you could come play basketball and get a ride home with your mom or someone else. Maybe you can do that in a few weeks. That'll give you something to work toward.'

Amaya sniffed and nodded, but was silent on the walk back to the elementary school. Maggie worried she'd made things worse. Once they got into the car to drive back to Howard Street, Maggie apologized to Amaya for upsetting her.

'I was hoping this might make you feel a little less scared about things. I sure didn't mean to upset you,' Maggie said.

Amaya shook her head but was silent the rest of the ride home. Maggie looked over at the girl and saw her staring out the front window, focusing on nothing. Maggie felt sick that she had just asked the little girl to revisit a place that would forever be toxic in her thoughts.

'I'm sorry, Amaya. I shouldn't have asked you to go back there.'

Amaya looked at Maggie as if she was trying to discern whether Maggie actually understood the fear that she couldn't yet put words to.

When Maggie pulled the car up in front of the house, Amaya didn't make a move to get out. She stared out the passenger window, past the rows of push lawnmowers and toward her dad's workshop with its doors closed.

'You want me to walk you inside?' Maggie finally asked.

'I haven't seen my dad in two days.'

Careful, thought Maggie, wishing she had some idea how to navigate a conversation with a hurting ten-year-old. 'I'm sure you miss him. I bet your dad is pretty upset about what happened to you. He might even be angry at himself that he couldn't protect you. It's probably hard for him to talk about it.'

'I heard my dad tell mom that he wanted to kill that doctor for what he did to me. Mom started crying.'

Maggie wondered how much Amaya knew. There'd been a fair number of times when a juvenile had held the answers to a homicide investigation.

'You know, that's a saying people use. They talk about killing other people when they're really angry,' Maggie said. 'Especially when it's something they're angry about and they don't know how to fix. You've probably even heard your friends say it at school.'

'Yeah. But I think he really meant it.'

TWENTY-FOUR

Danny G and The Blue Orchids met in the side parking lot at six that evening to share a medical marijuana joint and a six pack before hitting the stage at eight. Their Friday shift had been moved to Saturday due to a wedding reception that had taken over the restaurant. Maggie had received a text from Danny after she left Amaya's house that he had information to share about the radio show. Maggie figured a head full of Danny G and a sip of tequila before her shift at

The Foxxy Den was just what she needed to drown out the worries of the day.

She'd sent Mark a text asking him to stop by as well, but she wasn't holding out much hope. He'd not answered her two previous phone calls. She assumed his silence had to do with Kelly O'Neal, which had started to piss her off.

Maggie refused the joint being passed between Danny and Whitney, and instead took a beer from Buffalo Bruce who was stretching his calf muscles by propping one foot at a time on the bumper of Danny's Malibu. For an eighty-something-year-old man, he still knew his way around a drum set, and he claimed the nightly stretches were key.

As the rest of the band went inside to warm up, Danny pulled Maggie aside.

'I heard your show today. Damn good. Pretty freaking weird stuff.'

'Thanks. Could you tell the interviews fell apart?'

Danny grinned, always keen on drama. 'Not at all. What happened?'

Maggie explained how the doctor's wife showed up, accusing the radio station of dragging her husband's good name through the muck.

'That's not what I hear. A buddy of mine called while I was listening to your show. He knows you're a friend of mine. He wanted me to let you know that the doctor swindled him out of hundreds of thousands of dollars.'

'Why didn't he call the show?'

'He's pretty private. I had no idea he had that kind of cash. And he doesn't want other people knowing either. He's a tight ass, so I couldn't believe he gave that kind of money to some whack job.'

'He was part of the blood study?'

'He said he and his wife went to a seminar the doctor had a couple of years ago. It was to get people to buy into a new business called The Vital Life Clinic. He said the clinics would have machines, some kind of plasma machines, but I can't think what he called them.'

'Plasmapheresis machines?'

'That's it. The patient goes in and the machine takes out

their blood and spins out the plasma. Then they put the blood back in with clean plasma from young, healthy patients. My buddy told me the doctor had all kinds of research showing the health benefits. How this would cure Alzheimer's, even extend life. The clinics were supposed to go up throughout Florida and California over a five-year period. He and his wife invested half a million dollars and they haven't seen proof that even a dime of it had been invested. They filed a class action lawsuit about six months ago with some other investors. He figures they're screwed now that the doctor's dead.'

'I appreciate the information. You care if I share his name with the police?'

Danny gave Maggie a piece of paper with a name and phone number on it. 'He told me to pass along his name. I figure this is like a get out of jail free card. This ought to buy me some insurance with the coppers, right?'

'I'll let Mark know that's your expectation.'

Maggie turned down a seat next to Agnus in front of the bandstand and opted for a stool at the bar. As the band played their first set, Maggie finished her first tequila, remembering her internal promise to cut back. She'd just waved a finger at Serena to get another when she felt two hands run up her back and rest on her shoulders, then a pair of familiar lips in her ear. 'Hey, pretty woman. Wanna buy me a beer?'

She slid off the stool and wrapped Mark in a hug. 'You bet I do. I was afraid you were avoiding me.'

'I was.'

'I appreciate your honesty.'

'I miss you, Maggie. But we need some ground rules. Unless you have news to share that will help solve the LeBlanc case, I don't want to discuss it. I'm worn out with the investigation and the media, and I don't want to argue about it with you. Are you good with that?'

'Absolutely,' said Maggie. 'Does that mean I shouldn't ask how your day went?'

'Yes. We can talk about water pollution. The plague. Hurricanes. Anything but blood.'

'Fair enough. I have to get the girls ready. Want to meet at my place after my shift?'

'I'll see you there.'

One of Maggie's favorite places to hang out and unwind was the dressing area in The Foxxy Den. It reminded her of the dressing room at Madame D's, a place filled with drama and excitement, where Maggie could sit back and absorb the theatre without having to go onstage herself.

When she had started working at the club, she'd convinced Mel to install proper lighting around the makeup mirrors that matched the lighting on stage in the bar. For a little dive in the back of a strip mall, Maggie thought the production was fairly well done, and the girls seemed to appreciate the effort. Some of the places they worked were horror stories, but most of the girls had to work a circuit in order to pay their rent, and options were limited. Dancing at one club typically wasn't enough because men didn't want to see the same girls every night. There were stories about girls making six figures stripping, but Maggie had never met any such girls.

Seven to eight o'clock was happy hour in The Foxxy Den. The girls had an hour to dress and prepare for the night while the men loaded up on cheap alcohol. Maggie was organizing the makeup tray when all four girls entered in shorts, T-shirts and flip-flops. Sassy and Cassondra both went to the sinks to wash their faces for makeup while the other two girls opened the dressing closet. With so few dancers they were able to store their personal costumes on site, another luxury compared to most of the clubs the girls worked at, where theft wasn't uncommon.

Maggie watched as Cassondra poured cheap vodka into a cup with orange juice. She said she couldn't dance without loosening up before she went onstage to face the men. Maggie hated to see someone so young go down that road and realized what a lousy role model she made.

'I saw your boyfriend on TV last week,' Sassy said, patting her face dry. 'Is that why you were asking about Andre O'Neal?'

Maggie nodded.

Cassondra laughed. 'That is some weird shit. Who in their

right mind would want to mix little kid blood with their own blood? That's just disgusting.'

'What are you talking about?' Felecia said. 'I quit watching the news. It makes me angry.'

Maggie provided a rundown on the parts of the investigation that had been made public, ending with the doctor's supposed suicide.

Ana Sofia presented her back to Felecia to zip her dress. She looked confused by the conversation. 'Why would he have to kidnap little kids for their plasma? Why didn't he just buy it?'

'Because these were little girls. One of them was only ten years old,' Sassy said.

'So?'

'So, in America there's laws to keep you from taking advantage of little kids.'

'If my kid is healthy, and they can donate blood and make a pile of cash, why is that a bad thing?'

'What the hell is wrong with you?' Cassondra said.

She looked hurt at the response. 'It's not like he'd be selling his soul. He'd be giving his plasma. Big deal.'

'All the doctor did was hook two patients up to the same machine they use in the plasma centers. Right?' Felecia asked.

Maggie nodded. 'The doctor had two machines in his office that some investor from China had paid for. A man from Australia had the beginnings of Alzheimer's. He had blood withdrawn from his body and his plasma removed. Then the doctor hooked up the two little girls and mixed their cleaned plasma back in with his.'

'So how does blood help Alzheimer's patients? If it works, it would be a miracle treatment,' Sassy said.

'There's research studies where pairs of surgically joined rats shared a blood supply for several weeks,' Maggie said. 'They claim the older rats made improvements on basic decision-making and thinking tasks.'

'If the kid doesn't suffer, and they find a cure for Alzheimer's, what's so bad?' Felecia said.

'This feels like one of those teenage movies, where a certain class of people give up their body parts so that others can live,'

Ana Sofia said. 'It's like some dystopian world with separate classes of people.'

'I don't care what it cures, you shouldn't be making money off your kid,' Sassy said.

'And what about the money your mom made off you when you did the tv commercials when you were a little kid?' Felecia asked.

'And look where that got me. A regular at The Foxxy Den.'

With Mark on her mind, Maggie finished her shift early and found him lying in bed watching TV when she got home. Before the David Letterman rerun had finished, they lay side by side on top of a tangled mess of sheets, thoroughly satisfied.

Mark reached for Maggie's hand and said, 'I'm ready to break the ground rules.'

'You have something good?'

'It's a doozy.'

'Am I allowed to express my opinion? Or am I just supposed to be quiet and listen?'

'That's an excellent question,' he said. 'Let's go with be quiet and listen, until I ask for an opinion.'

'Agreed, let's hear it,' she said.

'You know I told you the suicide bothered me. It didn't fit the doctor's personality or lifestyle?'

'Yes, you made that clear. I assume you were correct, otherwise you wouldn't be bringing it up.'

'What happened to be quiet and listen? Any cop could see that scene looked set up. Chief Osbourne got a crime scene expert from the state to examine the room. Osbourne had already determined the blood pattern from where he bled out didn't make sense.'

'How so?'

'First off, keep in mind the doctor's blood alcohol level tested at .26, and from everyone we talked to, including his wife, he was an infrequent drinker. His wife said he only drank when he was really stressed.'

'OK. So when he supposedly slashed his wrists, he was wasted.'

'Yes. Now the suicide. When Osbourne and I studied the

photos of the pants that the doctor was wearing, there were stains where the blood had spurted from the initial cut. But there weren't significant stains on his thighs where his arms would have lain as he bled out. They should have been saturated. As intoxicated as LeBlanc was, after he slit his writs, I felt confident his arms would have dropped to his lap. Instead, it looks as if his arms hung down behind him. The crime scene guys said there was also splatter out away from the chair, on either side of it.'

'It seems reasonable that his arms would have fallen down to his sides, especially if he was that drunk,' Maggie said.

'But when the receptionist found LeBlanc, his hands were lying in his lap. We have the initial photos. If he'd died that way, his lap would have been full of blood, and it wasn't.'

'That's a problem,' she said.

'Here's the best part. The coroner found cloth fibers embedded in the skin around his upper forearms. The bloodstains were consistent with having gauze covering his arms in this area. And we found strips of gauze in the trashcan in the office with matching fibers. The coroner also stated that it looks as if someone took a rag and carefully smeared blood on the doctor's arms after he bled out to disguise where the gauze had been tied.'

'Jesus. You think his arms were tied to the chair while he bled out?'

'I think he was tied to the chair so he wouldn't move around and make a mess. It was important to the killer to make it look like a suicide.'

'Have you narrowed the list of suspects?'

Mark let go of her hand and rolled over on his side to look at Maggie's profile. She remained on her back, grinning at his scrutiny.

'Honestly? We expanded the list. I could give you twenty people who won't admit to wanting him killed, but who say he got what he deserved.'

'You think the whole slashing of the wrists and bleeding out all over the floor of his office was symbolic for the killer?'

'That's my theory,' he said. 'It's not difficult to imagine the conversation as the blood doctor bled out all over his floor.'

'Have you ruled out the Baxters?'

'Yes. They had driven to Miami that day to visit the girl's grandparents. Their alibi is good.'

'How about Andre?'

'I don't know. The guy is a mess. But we have no evidence that directly links back to him. We have a security guard that says he saw a small dark-colored vehicle that matches the description of Kelly O'Neal's car. He says he saw it around ten o'clock the night of the murder, but it was dark, and he couldn't be positive on the color or make of the car. So it's basically worthless. She says she was home that night, with her daughter as an alibi. There's no reason to believe she's not telling the truth.'

Maggie stared at the ceiling, running the conversation she'd had with Kelly through her head. She was fairly certain the car they thought Andre was driving to the doctor's office was actually being driven by Kelly. But the police had taken her off the suspect list. And then there was Maggie's conversation with Amaya. Would telling Mark that Amaya heard her dad say that he wanted the doctor dead make a difference? Hatred didn't make a man a killer, it just provided the motivation.

Maggie pushed the thoughts out of her head. 'When do you make this public?' she asked.

'Tomorrow. Osbourne is doing a news brief at nine in the morning.'

'Can you imagine the media monster this will turn into when they find out this guy kidnapped little girls for their blood? It's like a science fiction movie.'

'Don't forget the rats,' Mark said. 'I've now seen diagrams of the rats sewn together. Imagine those visual aids all over the national news.'

After Mark left, Maggie spent a restless Sunday morning, struggling with the possible legalities of the case, and her own involvement. She had planned on contacting a friend of hers about the logistics of setting up an overseas bank account, and more importantly, the legality of accepting money gained from an interaction with a person involved in a criminal investigation. Obviously, the kidnapping was an illegal act, but that wasn't how the money had been gained. Kelly gained the money through the sale of her daughter's plasma to the doctor. But Maggie wasn't clear whether the act of paying someone for a child's plasma was illegal. Common sense said it should be, but common sense wasn't the rule of law.

Having retired from homicide, Maggie's knowledge of certain criminal acts was limited. And being out of the profession for several years didn't help. If Kelly had asked her opinion before the fact, she'd have told her absolutely not, you're dabbling in extortion. But the doctor had offered the money freely, as payment for a service. And Kelly had accepted. It was more complicated because Kelly had also served in the capacity of confidential informant, and had learned of the monetary offer during that time. If the police discovered that she took the money, it might boil down to whether a prosecutor wanted to indict a woman whose child had been kidnapped, and experience had taught Maggie that predicting a prosecutor's next move was a crap shoot.

Maggie found her friend's phone number, but after ten minutes of deliberation decided not to call. The guy was a year from retirement with the Major Crimes Unit in Cincinnati. Maggie was certain he could offer a sound opinion, but with the bizarre details of the case going public, she was afraid her questions would draw further scrutiny, something Kelly O'Neal did not need.

Instead, at four o'clock that afternoon, Maggie sat on the couch in her living room and stared out into a turbulent sky. She was certain the temperatures were still pushing ninety, paired with ninety percent humidity, but the fast-moving gray clouds and whipping palm trees looked cold and forbidding. Ocean storms had worried David while they gave Maggie a rush. The power of the wind and the waves crashing into the shoreline, lashing rain, with the tops of fifty-foot trees whipping around like rag dolls, all created a desire inside her to run out into it to absorb the energy.

The storm that blew up that afternoon had her thinking about David, how he would warn her away from the windows in their condo, not allow her to answer the landline telephone during a lightning storm in case of electric shock. As a child in Indiana, he'd lived through a tornado that had destroyed their home while his family sat out the storm in the basement. Maggie and David had been as opposite as two people could possibly be, but he had always claimed they fit together perfectly, like two puzzle pieces.

Maggie walked to her desk where she kept her favorite photograph of David. They were sitting on a porch swing at a friend's house. David's arm was around her shoulder and her head rested next to his, both of them smiling. She regretted it, but she'd come to remember their life together as either pre-cancer, or everything that followed. This was a pre-cancer photo, when life had been easier.

She set the photo down and considered the stack of medical records. She opened the accordion file and found David's doctor's business card. Without much forethought, she dialed the number and was shocked when the doctor answered.

'This is Doctor Remus.'

'Good afternoon. This is Maggie Wise, David Wise's wife. You treated him back in—'

'Of course! I remember David well. We aren't supposed to have favorite patients, but I can't help it. David was one of my favorites. He was a good man.'

Maggie smiled. It was how anyone who knew her husband reacted. How an irascible cop ended up married to a man with not a mean bone in his body was beyond her.

'I'm sorry to call you on a weekend. I really didn't expect you to answer. I finally got the courage to read through his medical records and had a few questions. Do you have a minute?'

'Absolutely. I use Sundays to catch up on paperwork, so good timing. Give me a minute to pull his file.'

'No, it's fine. I don't have anything specific. You had kept me updated on the research for a while, but I tuned it out for a long time. It was too hard. I just wondered if anything positive ever came out of the trials.'

'I'll be glad to send you the study in full.'

'Not necessary.'

'David was part of a phase three clinical trial. In a nutshell, we found that eighty percent of the patients who took the trial drug lived twice as long as those who didn't. Honestly, given the mortality rate, the results weren't what we'd hoped, but it's led to a better understanding of treatment options, and that's critical.'

'What you're saying is that David was in the twenty percent group.'

'That's correct. The worst part of my job as a researcher is making a connection with a patient and knowing things aren't working in their favor.'

Maggie felt her chest tighten and let go of the remaining questions she'd been prepared to ask. In the end, they didn't matter. The study had failed her husband.

'I have a secondary question that has nothing to do with the study. When you were working with David, I was a homicide cop in Cincinnati.'

'Yes, I remember that.'

'I'm living in Santa Cruz now, and I'm consulting on an investigation about a doctor who was involved in blood research for aging patients.'

'You're kidding. The Santa Cruz blood doctor?'

'That's the one.'

Dr Remus laughed. 'I was just eating lunch in the cafeteria this afternoon and heard the story break. It's crazy. It sounded like the doctor was kidnapping young children in order to satisfy his research.'

'That's the gist of it. I wondered what your opinion is of the pay-to-participate research. If you think it's valid.'

'Absolutely not. It sends most of us over the edge. It's bad science.'

'How does a person tell the difference between a proper clinical trial and a scam? From what I've read, some of the pay-to-play research has benefited people.'

'I agree with that. Reluctantly. The need for research is infinite, and the money to fund it is not. That's the crux of it. So privately funded research certainly has its place, but patients must be extremely careful about signing on. There is a distinction between legitimate research and entrepreneurs making money off of desperate people. Patients can do themselves more harm than good.'

Maggie's throat tightened, and she was back to her own

private regrets. 'A dying patient can experience harm from all different sides.' She cleared her throat to be able to continue. 'I found notes in David's file, anecdotal notes that you had written, where it was clear that David only did the trial because of me.'

'What do you mean? David signed up for the trial, and was accepted, because he fit the protocol.'

'But he stayed in it way past the point where he needed to.'

The doctor sighed. 'I see.'

'He was exhausted, and he still made the trips to Florida, knowing that he was dying, because he thought it gave me hope.'

'I've been working with dying patients for over twenty years, Maggie. I've watched families deal with death a hundred different ways. Some face it head on, and want every morsel of information. Some hide the truth, some lie, some look for distractions to get through the day. Some take sleeping pills and booze. And when I say some, I'm talking about both the patients and the family members. It's not just the patient that suffers. The only thing I've learned is that there aren't any rules or guidebooks that have all the answers. You can read all the blogs about dealing with cancer that you want, but it comes down to what works for you. And from what I saw, David was happy taking care of you. That made him happy. He stayed strong for you and I don't think that's a bad thing. There's nothing wrong with being a hero.'

TWENTY-FIVE

The national media coverage was more overwhelming than anyone had predicted. News vans descended on Santa Cruz first, camping outside of the Baxters' home, outside the girl's private school and the park and golf course where the girl had been abducted and then dropped off. And then Amber Hope, Santa Cruz's version of shock-commentator Nancy Grace, got involved. Young blood was the new laser focus of her syndicated news show and radio show, providing updates that were nothing more than guesswork, stirring up viewers with speculation because an hour is a long time to fill with actual facts.

Before Amber Hope became involved, the O'Neals had managed to avoid the spotlight. Maggie had watched the Baxters, with their sprawling Santa Cruz home and extravagant lifestyle, morph from media darlings to questionable parents, reminiscent of the JonBenét Ramsey case. And then Amber turned her focus on Andre and Kelly.

Danny sent Maggie a text, telling her to check out the show. Maggie grabbed the remote and sat down on the couch.

The backdrop was a dilapidated house and a side yard filled with rusted out push mowers with weeds growing up through the rows. Maggie noticed the trees rustling in the wind and assumed the news media had set up a live feed outside their home.

'Does this look disturbing to you?' The camera closed in on Amber's furrowed brow. 'I mean, I'm not one to judge, but this is not a normal way to raise your kids. Rumors have swirled around this family from the beginning, and one has to wonder. Would the sale of the child's blood help move that family out of the nightmare they are currently enduring?' Her wide-eyed shock morphed into a knowing smile. 'I mean, come on. What could it hurt, right? You set it up with a doctor who promises to take excellent care of your little girl. Someone who promises it won't hurt the tiniest bit. Someone who tells you, if you do this for me, then I'll do this for you. I'm just saying. The doctor wasn't above kidnapping little girls. Who says the rest of these characters weren't in on the act as well?'

Maggie watched in shock, realizing how accurate the description was, but how far from the truth her portrayal was. Kelly O'Neal had accepted money, a sizeable sum of money, from the doctor as payment for her daughter's plasma. But she'd only accepted the money after the doctor had kidnapped her daughter. This was her vengeance as a mother. But Maggie had seen media shaming. If the story broke that Kelly had received money in an overseas bank account in exchange for her child's blood, she would be overrun with social media rants, most likely facing the same death threats as other parents who had been tried and found guilty in the court of public opinion. Maggie felt increasingly uncomfortable with her part in the cover-up. She'd begun to worry she'd offered bad counsel to Kelly O'Neal, but by the time she had approached Maggie, the deed was done.

She pressed the pause button on her remote control to freeze the screen and leaned forward to stare at the image of the house behind the talking head. She noticed a figure behind the screen door, too short to be Andre or Kelly. Maggie pressed play again and the figure disappeared, probably pulled away from the door by Kelly.

She flipped from CNN to Fox News and found a segment on blood research. A panel of experts were debating the merits of private scientific research and the need for either more or less government oversight. She tried to imagine what it would be like sitting in your home while your life played out across every screen in the nation.

Maggie turned the TV off and called a friend of hers, a cop in Cypress City who she knew through Mark. She'd been to his house for a pitch-in and remembered seeing a basketball hoop in a barnyard beside the house. Maggie called and explained what she needed. The cop said he was working third shift and offered the barn lot to Maggie anytime she wanted it. Next, she called Kelly, who was thrilled to get Amaya out of the house and away from the circus in the front yard.

An hour later, Amaya left through the back door and cut through a neighbor's backyard to meet Maggie on Maple Drive.

Amaya got in the car grinning and out of breath, clearly excited by the intrigue.

'Did you give them the slip?' Maggie asked, smiling at the girl's expression.

'Yep. Mom wants you to call her to tell her I made it.'

Maggie gave Amaya the cell phone and had her place the call. After a half-dozen OKs from Amaya, she hung up. Maggie assumed she was receiving a litany of unwanted instructions from her mother.

'Before you drop me off, we have to call her again so she knows to look out for me.'

'No problem. We'll do it.' Maggie pulled her car away from the curb. 'I have a friend who lives out of town with a basketball hoop. I figured you might be tired of being cooped up in your house. Thought you might need to let off some steam.'

'Definitely. I can't even walk outside. Mom made me stay home from school today. It's like I'm in jail.'

'How do you feel about all this?'

Maggie glanced over at Amaya and she shrugged a shoulder. 'It's just weird. I don't know why anyone cares about us.'

'I think some people care because they know what happened to you was wrong. And they want to know someone is being punished for it.'

'But that doctor is dead. So why are they still here?'

'Now they want to know who killed the doctor. People are just nosy. They care about other people's business.'

Amaya was quiet for a minute but Maggie could sense she was holding back.

'What's bothering you?'

'I heard some kids at school yesterday saying it was my dad that killed the doctor. Is that why the news people are at our house?'

Maggie sighed. The girl was facing stress most adults couldn't comprehend.

'I know that what your dad said to your mom, about wanting to kill the doctor, is bothering you. But no one else knows that. Your dad was angry when he said it. These news people just want something to talk about. People don't have enough excitement in their own life so they harass other people. But you and your family don't need to worry about it. What happened to you was wrong. But you haven't done anything wrong yourself. And neither has your mom or dad. OK?'

Amaya nodded but didn't look convinced in the least. 'I just want all of it to go away. I want to go back to normal again.'

'Have you gotten to talk to your dad about any of this?'

'No.'

'Has he been at home at all?'

'I heard him come home last night. But I was in bed. He came into my room but I didn't say anything.' Amaya's voice had grown quiet. 'He sleeps on the couch now.'

'Do you know where your dad goes at night? Maybe I could talk to him for you.'

Amaya snapped her head around to Maggie. 'That'd be good. I heard him and mom fighting about it. He goes to Little Tom's. Mom is mad that he drives home all the way from Everglade City when he's been drinking.'

Maggie slowed the car and turned into the barn lot. A rusted basketball goal was nailed to the barn over a concrete pad. 'I'll see if I can talk to him tonight. I can't promise you anything. But maybe it'll help.'

Amaya got out of the car and Maggie tossed her the basketball. They started out passing back and forth to warm up, then shooting hoops and playing horse. By the time the sun fell behind the barn, they were well into a game of one on one, with Maggie working up a sweat like she'd not done in months. The exertion felt good, and Amaya laughed and hollered and yelled foul just like any other ten-year-old kid playing barn-lot basketball.

It was eight o'clock before Maggie parked a block away from Amaya's house and called Kelly.

'Are the news vans still out front?'

'Only one. The local van left. They parked in our front yard and I called the police to file trespassing charges. They pulled away about ten minutes later.'

'How about I walk Amaya back through the neighbor's yard?'

'That would be great.'

'The neighbor isn't going to come out after us, is he?'

'No. They're good people. I called them earlier and told them what was going on. I'll let them know you're coming through.'

Maggie hung the phone up and saw Amaya looking down, picking at a fingernail.

'You ready to head home?'

'Not really.'

Maggie wasn't sure where to go with that answer. She needed a therapist on call. 'How come?'

'It's just too weird. I want to be normal again.'

'I bet the news vans are all gone by tomorrow. They can't afford to keep people out here. And some other big story will come along.'

'I don't want to go back to school.'

'What's your mom say about that?'

She shrugged. 'She wants to go talk to someone about it.' Her voice was flat. She'd lost all of the joy from earlier in the evening. Ten-year-old Amaya looked as beat down by life as her parents.

'You know, I was a cop for a long time. And one thing I can promise you is that the things you see in the news this week are gone by the next week. People have short memories. It won't be long and your friends will have forgotten all about this. They'll have moved on to playing soccer at the park.'

Amaya looked over at Maggie as if she desperately wanted to believe that was true. Maggie felt her heart break for the little girl.

'Just get through tomorrow,' Maggie said. 'And each day after that will get better. I guarantee it. And I'll do whatever I can to make sure of it. Deal?' Maggie put a fist out, and Amaya bumped back.

'Deal.'

Amaya showed Maggie the safest way to sneak back home without detection. She followed Amaya down a fence line overgrown with weeds and scrub trees, and then directly through another neighbor's backyard.

'You sure it's OK we're walking through here?' Maggie asked.

Amaya said nothing, but kept her eyes on the sliding glass door on the back of the house. A woman in her late sixties slid the door open and ran outside, waving an arm in the air.

Amaya grinned back at Maggie and motioned for her to follow.

The woman ran out to meet them holding a paper plate covered in plastic wrap. 'I didn't want those rascals to hear me. Your mom said you were going to be coming through here. I've been waiting on you. Who's your friend?' she asked.

'This is Maggie. We were playing basketball. We didn't want the news people to see us so we came the back way.'

'Well, heavens, yes. You come the back way any time you want. Ms Maggie, it's good to meet you. You take good care of this girl. She's a sweetheart.'

They left, with Maggie trailing behind Amaya, running along the back side of Amaya's property and in through the kitchen door where Kelly was waiting, laughing at Maggie's expression.

She dropped onto a kitchen chair. 'I am too old for this. She wore me out.'

Amaya tore the plastic wrap off the plate and handed a cookie to Maggie. 'She makes the best chocolate chip cookies in the world.'

'Is that why we walked through her yard?'

Amaya nodded as if the answer was obvious.

'That's enough,' Kelly told her. 'You get upstairs into the shower.'

'Am I staying home tomorrow?' she asked.

'One more day. I think it's best. Then you'll have the weekend so things hopefully blow over. Then it's back to school on Monday. Summer break is almost here.'

Amaya pumped a fist in the air and ran for the back of the house.

'I hope she thanked you for taking her tonight,' Kelly said.

'She did. But it wasn't necessary.'

'Have you heard anything new?'

Maggie considered Kelly, knowing she had already shared too many details about the investigation.

'Please, keep me in the loop. I promise you I won't say anything.'

'It will come out tomorrow anyway. The police are officially ruling the doctor's death as a murder. There's a news conference scheduled for the morning.'

'What made the difference?' Kelly asked.

'I need you to keep this confidential until the police release the details. Gauze was used to tie the doctor's arms to the chair where they found his body. Someone sliced his wrists to make it look like suicide, and tied his arms down to make sure he couldn't get up.'

Kelly winced at the description. 'That's horrible. Are they any closer to knowing who did it?'

'Not that I've heard.' Maggie stood and moved toward the kitchen door to leave.

'I can't begin to thank you for what you've done for us, especially for Amaya. You're her new hero.'

'That's the one thing I'm not. Don't let her think that or she'll be disappointed,' Maggie said. Before leaving she turned to face Kelly. 'I think you ought to know. I asked and Amaya told me where Andre's been hanging out in the evenings. At a bar called Little Tom's. Does that sound right?'

Kelly crossed her arms over her chest and leaned against the kitchen counter. 'Amaya told you that?'

'I told her I'd like to talk to Andre, and Amaya offered up the name. I'd appreciate it if you didn't bring it up with her. It would be nice if she thought she had someone on her side who wasn't her mom.'

Kelly nodded, reluctantly. 'What do you want with Andre?'

'I just want to talk to him.'

She looked irritated but shrugged. 'Well, Amaya is right. That's where he hangs out. He doesn't want to get caught at a bar around here, so instead he drives out of town and somehow thinks that's safer.'

After leaving Amaya's house, it was nine o'clock before Maggie started the thirty-minute drive to Everglade City. The drive down the Tamiami Trail into the Everglades was beautiful in daylight, with occasional alligators sunning themselves along the canal and white and black swooping water birds making their way into the wetlands. But night driving was a straight twenty-mile shot to Highway 29, and then another five miles toward the coast. Everglade City was called the Gateway to the Ten Thousand Islands, a chain of islands and mangrove islets along the coast, with the most famous being Marco Island, just south of Santa Cruz.

Agnus often talked to Maggie about selling her oceanfront estate and move to Keewaydin Island, a seven-mile stretch of barrier island where the homes were off the grid, but often still extravagant. She'd made it clear that she thought Maggie could ferry her to and from civilization when necessary, meaning every Friday for Danny and The Blue Orchids, every Tuesday for Senior Bingo Night, every Thursday for euchre night at Betty's house – the list went on. As much as Maggie appreciated what Agnus had provided for her, she'd rather live in a cardboard box than serve as a ferry captain seven days a week.

Off the main drag in Everglade City, it was clear the town of five hundred people was still recovering from the last hurricane. Even in the dark, Maggie could see that a number of homes were still boarded up, with residents most likely waiting on insurance checks to rebuild. Maggie wove her way around quiet streets until she spotted a neon sign hanging in the window of a one-story redwood cottage on stilts. The sign read 'Little Tom's Bar and Grill'.

Inside, Maggie surveyed the room. A pool table and a scattering of tables and chairs were mostly empty, aside from two guys playing pool in the far corner. One man sipped a beer at the end of a fifteen-foot bar, where he stared up at a baseball game on the wall television. Maggie looked closer and recognized the man as Andre. Apparently sensing Maggie's stare, he looked down into his drink, obviously wanting to avoid company. Maggie sat on the stool next to him.

She turned slightly toward Andre. 'Hey, sorry to bother you. My name's Maggie Wise. We met a week or so ago at the park in Cypress.'

Andre nodded but kept his head down. 'I saw you come in. I figured you were here for me.'

'Can I buy you a beer?'

'Sure. Why not.'

When the bartender approached, Maggie ordered a Dos Equis and another Miller for Andre.

'Look, I apologize for tracking you down like this. I just wanted to talk for a minute.'

'Kelly stick you on my case?'

'Nope.'

'Amaya told you?' Andre looked at Maggie, his eyebrows raised.

'She did. But not to give you a hard time. I just asked where you were and she told me.'

Andre raised a hand up to stop Maggie. 'That girl don't give anybody a hard time. And I know you been seeing her. I want to be pissed off about it, but I can't say much, seeing how I'm not there myself.'

The bartender sat the beers down and Maggie drained half of hers for courage. She'd been dreading the conversation. She didn't anymore know how to talk to Andre than she did Amaya. Working homicide, she'd talked to plenty of family members in crisis, but the immediate crisis had often ended with a murder. Her discussions centered around one purpose: find the killer. But that wasn't her intent with Amaya or Andre, and Maggie acknowledged that part of her problem was that she wasn't even sure what her intent was.

'I guess Amaya is why I'm here,' Maggie said. 'You don't need me to tell you what a great kid you have.'

'Nope. That's pretty clear to me.'

'Here's the thing. I'm not here to judge. I lost my husband a few years ago after a fight with cancer that I didn't handle very well. I get your situation is different, but guilt's hell, no matter how you're living with it.'

Andre nodded slowly. 'You got that part right.'

'I can tell you that it wasn't until I saw a counselor from the VA that I finally started getting my shit together.'

Andre said nothing, but he sat motionless, obviously listening to what Maggie had to say.

'What I learned is there are a lot of things in life that are out of our control. Horrible diseases, greedy doctors looking to get rich off little kids. You can't protect your kid from every unseen danger. And beating yourself up over those things, day after day after day, is no good for you. And it's no good for your family. For a long time I felt like anything close to good in my life was something I didn't deserve.'

Andre nodded but kept his head down.

'I guess my point is, you still have a daughter to go home to. And she needs you something fierce right now. I can help. And I'm sure as hell glad to. In fact, I'd be honored if you'd let me keep coming around. But what Amaya really needs is you.'

'I don't even know what to say to her. How do you explain what happened so it makes sense to a girl her age? A kid who thought everyone in the world was good until now?'

'You don't need to have all the right answers. Hell, you don't need any answers. She just wants you to be there with her. To let her know it's all going to be OK.'

'And what if it's not OK?'

Maggie tipped her beer back. She'd anticipated the question but hadn't formulated much of a response.

Maggie and Andre both startled as a pool stick came down between them, smacking hard on the bar. They both turned and faced a tall man with broad shoulders and a thick beard, looking to be in his thirties.

'We been talking,' the man said. 'You look like the guy we saw in the news. The guy whose kid got kidnapped. Is that right?' His words were too loud for the quiet bar, and had the boastful tone of a drunk with a grudge.

Maggie spoke before Andre could respond. 'Hey, we're just trying to drink a beer and have a conversation. It's all good.'

The man listed sideways and then slammed the cue stick on the bar again so hard it broke in half and flew across the room. Maggie looked back for the bartender who had gone into the kitchen.

'I don't give a shit whether you have a conversation. We just want to know if this is the guy who was selling his kid's blood for money.' The man's words were slurred and he struggled to stand straight.

Maggie watched Andre grab hold of the neck of his beer bottle with his right hand, and she put her arm on his shoulder, hoping the bartender would come out and run interference.

'Hey. You got the wrong guy,' Maggie said. 'We're just having a beer. This is not the guy you want. We don't want any trouble.'

Maggie noticed the other guy walking toward them. His arms were bulked up and covered in tattoos. As Maggie tried to deflect his attention from Andre, the tall man took his pool stick with both hands and brought it down horizontally, over the top of Andre's head, before he knew what was happening. The man pulled the pool cue up and under Andre's neck, choking him as he fell back off the barstool and into the man's chest.

Maggie spun her stool around, pulled her legs up and planted both feet into the chest of the tattooed man, sending him flying back into a set of tables and chairs which clattered to the floor as he sprawled into them.

The bartender ran out from the kitchen holding a phone in the air, yelling that he was calling the cops.

Andre was kicking his legs out, trying to push off from the bar to send the man behind him off balance. He was attempting to pull the cue stick off his throat, but the guy was leaning backward and pulling up, cutting off Andre's airway.

As Maggie started toward them, Andre lifted one leg up off the ground and dug the heel of his boot down the man's shin, causing him to release the cue stick and drop to the floor. Andre turned and pounced, putting both knees on the man's chest before throwing a series of quick punches to the face.

'Andre!' Maggie shouted. 'Stop! You don't want to do this!'

The bartender tried to push Andre off as the guy with tattoos struggled up from the floor and headed for the door, leaving his friend to fend for himself. Both Maggie and the bartender grabbed for Andre's arms to pull him off. He landed one more blow to the guy's nose before they dragged him away.

They shoved Andre into a chair and the bartender went back to help the kid stand in the midst of the mess of tables and chairs.

'You and your friend get the hell out of here!' the bartender yelled at the two men.

Andre attempted to stand from the chair, wiping the blood flowing from his nose onto his T-shirt. His eyes were unfocused and full of rage.

'Hang on, Andre. It's over. Just sit down,' Maggie said.

The man who'd wielded the cue stick was bent over at the waist, wheezing and trying to catch his breath. He headed toward the door where his friend had just exited without another look toward Andre.

The bartender walked behind him. 'You come back again and the cops will escort you to jail. Your money is not welcome here.'

Andre sat in the chair, still breathing hard with anger, and touched his throat where the stick had rubbed the skin raw.

The bartender poured Andre and Maggie a free beer for their trouble. Maggie considered turning it down, but figured what the hell. She was due a couple of beers after the day she'd had.

While Andre calmed down, Maggie helped right the tables and chairs that had scattered across the floor. When she glanced back at Andre, she realized she'd seen the same uncontained fury in his eyes as when they were at the park searching for Amaya. Maggie assumed that Andre left home in the evenings because he didn't know how to contain his rage. And she realized, if Andre had wanted to kill the doctor, he wouldn't have coaxed him into getting drunk and tied him to the chair. He'd have beaten him to death.

TWENTY-SIX

Maggie woke early Saturday, frustrated she was still sore from barn-lot basketball, and the bumps and bruises from the bar fight. The healthy living she had intended to pursue once she moved to Florida had not materialized, and the daily half-mile walk on the beach didn't appear to be doing much good.

After finishing her radio show, Maggie spent some time organizing her desk and found the phone number that Danny had given her. She considered calling Mark, but decided to scout the guy out since he had specifically asked for Maggie to contact him.

Flip Linville picked up just as the phone was going to message.

'Damn phone. Sorry. This is Flip.'

'This is Maggie Wise. Danny Giardiello gave me your name and number in reference to a radio broadcast about Doctor LeBlanc.'

'Danny G! Hell, yes. I love that guy. And this is no BS, I listen to your radio show every week. Danny knows I'm a fan. So as soon as I heard your show I was like, oh, hell no. The media are portraying this guy as some kind of research god on the verge of a major discovery, but I'm telling you here and now, he was a con man. Plain and simple.'

'How do you know this?'

'Because the son of a bitch scammed me out of half a million dollars!'

'In return for what?'

'A stake in his business. I don't know what kind of scientist he was, but he was a hell of a salesman.'

'Danny said you attended an investor's meeting?'

He laughed. 'I wouldn't call it a meeting. It was more of a gala. The guy was selling youth. It was held in a tech center, all bright white and glossy. The audience was sprinkled with pretty young girls and guys wearing clothes that showed off youthful bodies and flawless skin. My wife and I got into an argument about it on the way home that night. She thought the whole thing was creepy, but I was like, babe, the fountain of youth has been around for centuries, and he's promising it. With a simple blood transfusion! And I did enough research to find out there was legitimacy to what he was saying. His problem was finding pharmaceuticals to buy in. They don't like plasma because it's a human byproduct. And the college researchers? Where's the altruistic draw? They aren't going to support some researcher interested in reversing the signs of aging. So he went private. And that's where we came in.'

'And when you went to the seminar, you were convinced it was a good idea? A money maker?'

He laughed again. 'Oh, yeah. I knew three of the other investors in the meeting. We ended up getting together the next week to talk about the offer, and all four of us said it was a no-brainer. The guy was poised to make millions. We've just not seen the milestones toward the millions that we were promised.'

'Would you mind meeting with me to talk through the details?'

'I'll do you one better. I'm part of a group of investors who are in the process of filing a class action lawsuit against LeBlanc. Who knows what happens now that he's dead. We'll go after his estate, but then we're fighting his wife instead of him. We're probably just screwed. But some of us get together for dinner every couple of weeks. More therapy bitch session than legal strategizing. But you're welcome to sit in tonight. We're meeting at Esposito's at seven for dinner and drinks.'

Maggie called Mel and asked if he could find a replacement for her shift at The Foxxy Den that night. He assured her that his sister had no social life and could use some excitement.

Free from her commitments, Maggie drove to Old Santa Cruz to eat lasagna and garlic bread coupled with most likely one too many Negronis. Esposito's was known for its boisterous wait staff, outstanding Italian food, and an atmosphere where customers felt welcome to stay and relax after a long meal. Eating at Esposito's was more of an event, so Maggie had high expectations for the conversation. She had called Mark and explained where she was headed, but he agreed that inviting a cop to the meal would undoubtedly change the conversation and the vibe – a hazard of the job.

Maggie arrived at 7:10 p.m., allowing Flip time to prepare his tablemates with the news that he'd invited a guest. The hostess seated her at a chair next to Flip, who introduced her to his wife Hellen, and the three other couples.

When Flip finished the introductions, his wife welcomed Maggie and explained that her husband's nickname came from his little brother, who couldn't pronounce Phillip as a toddler. 'But the cute mispronunciation is now considered a family curse because Flip grew into his name and never grew out of it. This is my burden to bear as his wife.' She smiled at her husband and then back at Maggie. 'Just giving you fair warning.'

And from there the conversation spun into a lively discussion about the renovation project at one of the couple's vacation homes, and then to stories about vacations, and eventually funny vacation disasters. Maggie enjoyed the chatter but remained quiet, listening to the group of people who had obviously become good friends.

After dinner, a round of drinks was ordered and the mood grew heavier. Bill and Lawrie Small, the couple who were renovating their vacation home, appeared to be in their mid-fifties and gave the impression of having old family wealth. The husband did something with technology stocks and his wife was a celebrated glass sculptor who had studied with Chihuly. Flip had told Maggie on the phone that Bill was the person who had actually filed the suit and was the main contact with the attorney.

'So what's the word?' Flip said. 'Do we still stand a chance?'

'Just for my own understanding, can you explain your interest in our meeting here tonight?' Bill asked. He looked directly at Maggie.

'Absolutely. I'm actually coming at this from a completely different angle. I've been helping one of the families whose daughter was kidnapped by the doctor.'

Lawrie broke in. 'That was one of the most disturbing things I have ever heard. To kidnap a child, drug them, and violate them? It's just almost too bizarre to contemplate. And you really believe that Doctor LeBlanc knew what was happening?'

Maggie nodded. 'He did. The plasma exchange took place in his office, under his supervision. Both girls were drugged the entire time they were away from their families.'

'As horrible as that is, I'm not sure what it has to do with our situation,' Bill said.

'The family wants justice. Someone needs to pay for what happened to their daughter. I'm trying to understand LeBlanc's business so that I can help the family pursue their own course of action.'

'Meaning the family is filing suit as well?' Flip asked. 'Jesus, I hadn't even thought of that. We need answers, and we need them fast.'

Bill frowned. 'I've called the attorney's office twice and left messages with the secretary. I also sent emails. I've heard nothing.'

'Is that typical?'

The question came from the wife of the third couple, Ed and Angela, who were introduced as hospital philanthropists. Middle-aged and attractive, the couple looked like spokespeople for the health and vitality movement.

'We've had good communication to date, but I'm not surprised they aren't rushing to respond,' Bill said. 'The main thing to remember is that the suit hasn't even been certified yet. I've asked for an update, but the secretary said she wasn't able to share that information. The attorney will need to respond.'

'The class action is a consumer fraud suit?' Maggie asked.

'That's correct. But federal law requires any class action suit to go through a series of four tests before being certified. And that's just the first hurdle. It could take years before anything significant happens. Meanwhile, I don't know how

LeBlanc's estate plays into this. I want to know from the attorney what our options are, and what kind of time restraints.'

'Meanwhile,' Lawrie gave the rest of the table a knowing look, 'we each have five hundred thousand dollars of our retirement sitting in someone else's bank account ready to disintegrate.'

Ed looked directly at Lawrie. 'We don't live in Santa Cruz and drive Bugattis because we're careful. We're successful because we take chances.' He tapped a forefinger on the table. 'But we also don't allow people to steal our money. And that's exactly what happened.'

Flip said, 'If these attorneys aren't responsive, I think we look elsewhere. We seize LeBlanc's assets. We go after his estate. We take every penny we can get.'

'Won't that be his wife's money at this point?' Lawrie asked.

'I don't care who's holding it,' Flip said. 'I put it there to begin with, and I intend to get it back.' He glanced around the table at the couples nodding their heads in agreement. 'We all intend to.'

The conversation turned to legal speculation for quite some time, and Maggie remained quiet, figuring they didn't want her opinion. She was clearly out of her monetary league. But when the legal wrangling died down, Maggie jumped in. 'You saw the news that LeBlanc was murdered. Can you speculate on who might have hated him enough to have committed murder?'

Angela, who had said little through the legal debate, pointed to each person around the table. They all laughed, including Angela. She said, 'Yeah, when I heard the news story about the kids getting kidnapped, I could have murdered him myself. Someone beat me to it, but I was angry enough. The sick bastard.'

Flip scooted his chair back and crossed his leg, looking as if he was getting ready for his next move. 'OK. So who's going to tackle the elephant at the table?'

They looked at each other uncomfortably. 'Come on. Maggie's not a cop. She's just asking a question. And each one of us here is thinking the same thing. David Anthony blew a damned gasket the last time we met. Like, literally came unhinged.'

Bill glared at Flip. 'I don't want to talk about someone who isn't even here to defend himself. He was angry.'

'He doesn't need to defend himself! We were all angry,' said the other man.

'What's said at Esposito's, stays at Esposito's. Capiche?' Flip looked at Maggie and she nodded.

Bill looked unhappy about the turn of the conversation but said, 'One of the other investors who typically attends the monthly dinners retrieved financial statements from LeBlanc's medical practice. He really burrowed into LeBlanc's assets, and it was a nightmare.'

'How so?' Maggie asked.

Bill laughed and lost his self-possessed businessman's composure. 'That's why it was a nightmare. I can't even explain it. There appeared to have been at least two accountants involved, and neither of them are still in business. One of them has been indicted on money-laundering charges over another client's money. The other one seems to have fallen off the globe. And the financials made it impossible to figure out where the investments are housed.' He swatted his hand. 'I can't rehash this again.' He glanced at Lawrie, whose eyebrows were furrowed with worry as she listened to her husband.

'None of this money is worth a heart attack. We'll sell everything we have and live in a trailer before I let this drama kill you.'

'Absolutely,' Angela said. 'These dinners are supposed to help us deal with this mess, not make it worse.' She stood and threw her napkin on the table and excused herself to the restroom.

Bill turned to Maggie. 'I'll be honest. I'm still uncomfortable with your interest. I don't see the connection between the family and our class action lawsuit, unless you're gathering information to share with their attorney.'

'That is not my intent at all. The family has never mentioned an attorney, although I have no doubt they'll be contacted. As I mentioned, I'm trying to find justice. If there were other associates working with LeBlanc who had something to do with the kidnappings, then I want to know that.'

The table remained silent and Maggie could sense that no one was buying her story.

'Hey, I feel like I may have turned the conversation in a direction you didn't want to go,' she said. 'I apologize for that. I'm going to head out. I appreciate you allowing me to join you. And I really do wish all of you the best.'

The men stood and shook Maggie's hand, apologizing for the heated conversation. Maggie paid her bill, glad to escape.

On the way home, she processed what she'd learned during the dinner. Flip inviting her to their meeting had obviously upset several of the group, but she wasn't clear on the reason. She assumed they felt as if she'd been invited into a private gathering that was none of her business, and Bill had clearly been concerned that Maggie was there seeking information for the O'Neal's attorney, something that hadn't crossed her mind until dinner. But she wondered if there were other reasons. When Flip brought up the name of the investor who'd blown a gasket, Bill had grown uncomfortable. He'd seemed concerned that Maggie was looking for information about the doctor's death, and Flip may have just outed one of their group.

TWENTY-SEVEN

Preoccupied with her own drama, Maggie almost drove past the car parked in front of Agnus's home. She glanced at the dashboard clock. Ten o'clock. Agnus's daily schedule did not vary, and Saturday was a non-party night. Her girlfriends did not call after eight thirty because she started the process of getting ready for bed at 'half past eight, on the nose'.

Maggie pulled in behind a silver Cadillac Seville and snapped a photo of the license plate with her phone before walking up to the front door.

She rang the bell and Agnus answered, looking flustered. She wore a pair of dress slacks and a brightly colored silk shirt and pearls. Her face was animated, her smile too wide.

'Hi there! Everything OK?' Agnus asked.

'Yeah, I was just driving by and saw a car out front. It's ten o'clock. Aren't you supposed to be in bed?'

'Agnus?' a male voice yelled from the direction of the kitchen.
'Oh, for goodness sake. I'm not a child, Maggie. I don't have a bedtime.'

'Yes, you do. Everyone who knows you knows you have a bedtime.' Maggie was irritated by Agnus's response but couldn't have explained why.

A man appeared behind Agnus, peering over her shoulder. 'What's this all about?' the man asked.

Maggie looked at Agnus with raised eyebrows, lost for words.

Maggie stretched out her arm. 'My name is Maggie Wise. I live just behind Agnus. I'm just stopping by to check on her.'

The man moved from behind Agnus and handed one of two martini glasses to Agnus to hold so he could shake Maggie's hand. Frowning deeply, he said, 'Agnus's safety is just fine.'

'Everything is just fine,' Agnus said, gushing. 'You're a sweetheart. Thank you for checking in on me. You go on and don't worry about me. I'll come see you tomorrow.'

Maggie left, shocked that the man hadn't even offered his name. At ten the next morning, when Maggie knew Agnus would be outside deadheading her daylilies, she walked over to check on her, hoping the silver car wasn't still parked out front.

'Beautiful day, isn't it?' Agnus said.

'If ninety-two and sunny at ten in the morning is your thing, then yes, it's a beautiful day.'

Agnus continued pulling the spent flowers off the long stalks and pitching them into the basket hooked over her arm. 'There's iced tea in a pitcher on the side porch. I figured you'd be over this morning to harass me. We may as well get this over with.' She placed her garden gloves and basket onto the ground and followed the concrete path to the side porch.

Maggie grinned, watching the woman march around the house, already anticipating the hell she was going to give her.

'Have a seat,' Maggie said. 'I'll pour.'

She prepared Agnus's tea with four teaspoons of sugar while she started in on the story Maggie was sure had been developing all morning.

'Before you go judging someone you don't even know, I'm here to tell you he's as good a man as you'll ever find. He worked as a copy repairman for forty years. That's how I met him. He was working on the copy machine at the senior center when I stopped by to pick up Carole Ann's lunch. He was working pro bono by the way.'

'A pro bono copy machine repairman. That's a new one.'

'I don't see you offering to fix their copy machine for free.'

'True enough,' Maggie said.

'Anyway, this was two weeks ago. And he's taken me to lunch three times since. So I invited him to dinner last night and we had a nice time. That's all there is to it.'

Maggie nodded. 'I'm glad for you. I'm sure he's a nice man. But there's a lot of men who'd be glad to take advantage of your situation. That's all I'm saying. Just be careful.'

'Be careful,' she said. 'And what exactly does that mean to you?'

'For one, you could shoot me a text if you know you'll be having late company. Or if you'll be out late yourself. Maybe let me know where you'll be going on your date if it's someone new.'

'Absolutely not. I am not losing my independence at this stage in my life. Try again.'

'I'm not asking because I want to check up on you. I don't care who you see. It's just about letting someone know where you are when you're with someone new. These kids who do the online dating do exactly the same thing.'

'I'm not a kid. And I'm not online dating.'

She tried to come up with a way to encourage Agnus to be careful without sounding like a father giving advice to his teenager. 'Just don't rush into anything, that's all. Make him earn your trust.'

Her eyes flared. 'Why are you being such a judgmental jackass about this?'

'How is me caring about you being judgmental?'

'What if I'd listened to all the people who told me not to let you move in?'

'I knew you'd bring that up.'

'Because, let me tell you, there were a number of my

girlfriends who thought I'd lost my mind letting some former cop turned alcoholic practically move in with me.'

'Alcoholic?'

She sighed. 'That's what you took away from what I just said? Yes, alcoholic. Your behavior at the time certainly indicated that you were one. My point is, I could see past that. And you haven't even spent five minutes with Roomy.'

'Roomy?'

She rolled her eyes. 'It's a nickname. For Romeo.'

'His name is Romeo?'

'You are a real shit. Why would you try and keep an old lady from an occasional thrill?'

'Because I'm a cop.'

'You're not a cop.'

'I was a cop for enough years to see too many nice women end up penniless, or worse, because of some guy offering a thrill.'

'Fair enough. I will not rush into anything. But I can tell you that not rushing when you're fifty-something looks a lot different when you're eighty-something.'

'OK, look. At this point, there's no way for me to be sly about this, so I'm just going to ask you straight up. What's Romeo's last name?'

Agnus's eyes narrowed. 'Why do you want to know?'

'Because I'm going to run a background check on him.'

All of the anger from moments before left Agnus's face. She looked crestfallen and Maggie felt horrible. 'Why would you think I'm seeing a criminal? You think that little of me?'

'Agnus, it's a background check. What you view as judgmental is nothing more than being careful. I was a cop for too many years. It's how my brain works. That's all.'

'You think I'm a stupid old woman not competent enough to take care of myself. This is why friends gripe about their kids. But I sure didn't think I'd have to deal with it with you.' Agnus scooted her chair back. Any other day and Maggie would have stood to help her get to her feet, but she knew better. After Agnus made it into the house, Maggie stood to leave. As she was walking away she heard the patio door slide open. Agnus hollered out, 'Jones,' then slid the door shut again.

*   *   *

Mark sent Maggie a text and offered to bring steaks and potatoes to grill for supper. By the time he arrived at six, Maggie had the fire in the firepit stoked up so it would burn down to coals when the steaks were prepped.

Mark walked into the kitchen, dropped two grocery sacks on the counter and pecked Maggie on the cheek before washing his hands. 'I'm sick of fast food. My arteries are seizing up.'

He pulled out thick ribeyes, baking potatoes and a bag of lettuce and assorted vegetables.

'Salad too?' Maggie said. 'We're having potatoes. Surely that meets the vegetable requirement.'

He ignored her complaints and gestured for her to wash the vegetables while he seasoned the steaks.

Maggie absently ran the peppers and cucumbers under the faucet as she told him about her dinner meeting with the investment group.

When she'd finished her summary, she asked if he knew the man who'd supposedly lost his temper at the last gathering.

'David Anthony,' he repeated. 'I don't think I've heard that name. But Santa Cruz PD did get a list of all the members of the class action suit. Over thirty people.'

Maggie whistled. 'Thirty? It sounded like the three couples at the table had each invested half a million. If that's an average investment, then the doctor was looking to bring in at least fifteen million dollars to start his clinics. And none of them have broken ground, according to the group last night.'

'So where's the money?'

'That's the big question. That's what has David Anthony coming unhinged.'

'I don't blame him.'

'I realize this isn't really your case,' Maggie said.

'No, there is no ambiguity here. This is absolutely not my case. What you are telling me is interesting, but the doctor was murdered in Santa Cruz. You need to contact Chief Osbourne.'

'I'm going to call Anthony. See if he'll do an advance interview for the radio show. Who knows, maybe I'll have a follow-up show for the investors and the class action suit.'

Maggie had been watching Mark slice a cucumber as she

shared her idea. His slicing slowed. She could tell he was stewing over something.

'You know, Maggie, we've only dated for about a year. So maybe this is just your personality. Maybe it's that you miss police work. Maybe you just need a hobby. But I don't get your obsession with this case.'

'I'm just telling you about my evening,' she said, surprised at the change in his attitude.

'But you can't let it go. It's not even my case, so you can't claim to be doing this for me.'

'I don't know if I can explain it so that it makes sense.'

Mark laid the paring knife on the cutting board and took a moment to respond. 'I wish you would try, because I'm coming up with my own conclusions, and they don't fare well for the two of us.'

Maggie backed away from him, shocked at the turn of the conversation. 'What does that mean?'

He turned to face her. 'I think you have a thing for this woman.' Mark's face turned red as he said the words.

'You can't be serious.'

'Don't placate me. I stopped by your house the other night and you weren't home. I called Danny to see if he knew where you were. I was going to track you down to see if you wanted to meet at Mel's for dinner. Danny told me you were over at Kelly's house. That you were taking her daughter out somewhere. It's not so much that I'm jealous, but I don't understand it. And I'm trying to.'

She wanted to pull him into her and assure him that he had nothing to be jealous of, but he hated coddling. She'd heard him say on several occasions, 'Tell it to me straight.' She just wasn't sure what straight was anymore.

'It's complicated,' she said. 'It has more to do with my past than anything happening right now.'

She had hoped when he heard that her reasoning involved her past that he would tell her he understood, and that she didn't need to go any further. But he remained quiet.

'I feel for this family,' she said. 'I want to do something to help them.'

'By getting involved in a murder investigation?'

She laughed at the absurdity of his question. 'Can you think of a better time to support someone?' His expression remained skeptical so she bit back her sarcasm to try again.

'Kelly wants what's best for her child, but do you have any idea how hard it is to give your kids what's best when you're living in poverty? She sells her plasma for extra money, Mark. Her husband was in the Marines and came back with his brain fried from sucking in fumes from the burn pits. And Amaya is stuck in the middle, this sweet-natured little girl that just wants a normal childhood.'

'You can't have it both ways. You can't play cop one day, and therapist the next.'

'Bullshit! Cops play therapist all the time. How many families have you talked through a crisis?'

'This is not the same thing. You're too attached to these people, and you've lost your objectivity.'

'I'm attached because I understand them! I grew up in a broken home, but I had an aunt that had my back. When things got too messed up with my mom, my aunt would step in and take me away to normal. She never judged my mom, but she showed me normal. She showed me there was another way out of the chaos. Someone needs to help this family find a way out.'

Mark frowned, but slowly nodded his head. 'I'm not trying to be a heartless bastard. I just don't want you to lose sight of how serious this is. You're getting drawn into something that could turn out very bad for everyone involved.'

Maggie sighed. 'It's more than just the investigation. This whole case has an eerie connection for me. I lay in bed at night and wonder if I'm making more of the coincidence than I should.'

'I don't understand what coincidence you're talking about,' he said.

'This whole medical drama has dragged me through David's research all over again. I know his was a legitimate medical study, but it's made me look at how I responded to his situation. And I'm not proud of it. Then there's Amaya and the awful circumstance that she's in. It's easy for people to sit back and judge the O'Neals for their decisions, for the terror that the girl experienced because her parents weren't careful enough. They didn't protect her. But I get it. My mom wasn't mother of the year material, but she did the best she could.' Maggie paused, and felt her face turn red. 'And I can't have kids of my own. David and I couldn't have kids because of me. I guess Amaya is a chance for me to maybe make a difference.'

Maggie choked up and Mark came toward her with his arms out, but it was her turn to back away.

He stopped, his expression full of regret. 'I'm sorry. I didn't realize.'

'I'm not good at this. I can't take sympathy for something I'm not proud of. That's why I don't talk about any of this. It's why I connect with Andre. I think the guy is so ate up with his failures that he can't do anything right. It's a never-ending loop.'

'Maggie. You aren't a failure!' He looked stunned at her self-assessment.

'You're missing my point,' she said, frustrated to have to put words to feelings she'd not even sorted out for herself. 'I'm not saying I'm a failure any more than Andre is, but telling that to the thought loop in your brain is just about pointless. I don't need someone telling me I didn't do anything wrong, or that it'll get better with time, or how I need to move on with my life. I've heard it all and then some.'

Maggie stopped talking. Mark was visibly pulling away from her, his arms crossed over his chest, and his expression hurt.

'Mark, I know this is messed up. It's why I don't bring this stuff up.' She took a breath and said what she'd not been able to verbalize until just that moment. 'I want to help that family because I don't have my own family to care for.' She paused. 'And I do miss being a cop. I miss getting up in the morning and having that purpose in my day, feeling like, even as screwed up as the job was, I was doing something important.'

Mark walked to the kitchen table and sat down. 'I don't know what to say. I feel like anything I say will be the wrong thing. Do you want me to go?'

Maggie sighed. 'Of course not.'

'I'm sorry for reacting the way I did. I was jealous and I've always hated that in other people.'

'You don't need to apologize.'

'So what do we do? I think I've managed to ruin dinner for both of us,' he said.

'You can't let a little emotion ruin a perfectly good steak dinner.'

He smiled. 'Compromise then. How about we skip the salad?'

'Absolutely. Straight to the steak.'

He stood and put his arms out and she went to him. 'You were being a good person, caring about this family, and I was being petty.'

She kissed his forehead. 'Don't give me more credit than I deserve. Just know that my crazy behavior doesn't have anything to do with us.'

TWENTY-EIGHT

After Mark left for work the next morning, Maggie set up her laptop on the couch to begin working on research for the radio show, but her thoughts kept returning to her conversation with the investors at the Italian restaurant. It was clear that Mark wasn't going to pursue the information. The doctor's murder was Santa Cruz's case and he wasn't willing to get involved. If she had information, she needed to funnel it through their office, although what she currently had wasn't anything more than a group of people gossiping.

She finally gave up on the radio show and started a search for David Anthony. Flip had mentioned that the man had a landscaping business, so tracking him down was fairly simple. There was only one David Anthony associated with landscaping in the state of Florida, and Maggie was surprised to discover that his business was located in Cypress City.

Fresh Cut was a company known all over south Florida, with the home office located about ten miles outside of downtown Cypress. Maggie pulled up what she could online. They offered maintenance and design services, and had two garden centers in the area, with another opening in Fort Myers in the next year. The owner had a strong social media presence that focused on politics and gender equality rights. Maggie found several photos of David marching in parades with his fists raised. In a photo that had run in the *Tampa Bay Times* several months earlier, he held a sign that read 'Men of Quality do not Fear Equality'. Maggie was surprised in a state that leaned right, that a business owner would be so openly left, but it hadn't appeared to hurt his business.

Maggie called and talked to a female who said David would be in the office all day. Thirty minutes later Maggie pulled down a gravel lane and passed a large sign that read 'Fresh Cut – South Florida's Largest Landscaper'.

She parked in front of a large garden center with a half-dozen greenhouses flanking each side. Pergolas shaded the front of the building with hanging plants and water misters which kept the air under the shade tolerable. Maggie entered and a young woman in her twenties said David was loading trucks out back, but Maggie could go hunt him down.

'He's the burly guy with the baseball cap on backwards shouting orders,' she said, laughing at her own description.

Maggie exited the back of the building and found two F350 pickups with fifteen-foot trailers being loaded with trees and five-gallon containers of plants. It didn't take Maggie long to find David Anthony shouting orders to a group of young laborers.

She stood to the side until there appeared to be a natural break in the action, then approached David and said, 'Mr Anthony, my name is Maggie Wise. I'm hoping I can take a few minutes of your time with a couple of questions.'

He looked annoyed. 'About what?'

'Doctor LeBlanc.'

He cursed and pulled his baseball cap off his head and put it back on. 'You an attorney?'

'No.'

'Cop?'

'No.'

David considered Maggie for another beat, then pointed to the garden center. 'I need air conditioning.'

Maggie followed him into a small office filled with gardening books and a drafting table with dozens of blueprints covering the top of it. David pulled two bottles of water out of the refrigerator and gave one to Maggie. 'Have a seat.'

Maggie moved a stack of file folders off one of the two chairs in front of David's desk and sat down.

'What do you need?' David said.

'I'm hoping to get some information about LeBlanc.'

David choked out a humorless laugh. 'Then you came to the wrong place. I got nothing.'

Maggie explained how she'd been working with the O'Neals, trying to figure out how to help the family understand what happened to their daughter, and who was responsible for her kidnapping.

David softened. 'Shit. That was bad news. Those poor girls.'

'I know you invested in the company, so I'm hoping you can help me understand how the doctor would go from using young blood from age-appropriate eighteen-year-olds, to young children off the street.'

Maggie listened as David explained the same rat research she'd heard repeatedly over the past week. Her goal for visiting David was to feel him out as a possible suspect. Get his guard down, get him talking candidly about the doctor. In Maggie's experience, it was an offhand remark that would often lead to a break.

'What made you decide to invest? It's hard to see the connection between landscaping and longevity research.'

'A buddy of mine convinced me to go to one of the investor meetings. LeBlanc had several. One in Santa Cruz. One in Miami. I think he even had a couple of meetings in California.'

'And you went to the one in Santa Cruz?'

'I did. It was something. Tan skinny girls with flawless skin and big boobs prancing around serving champagne off silver trays. Steroid boys with puffed-up muscles chatting you up about the latest health fads. It felt like a science fiction movie. It was all too perfect. You know how odd it is to walk into a room where half the people aren't bulging over their pants?' He patted his gut and laughed.

'Did you sign up that day?'

'No. There was a high-pressure pitch where individual salespeople met with each of us to talk about the *opportunity*.' He stressed the last word and rolled his eyes. 'I hung tight. I just wasn't convinced it was a sure thing. Then LeBlanc met with me personally two additional times. Once here, once at his office.' David shook his head. 'It's crazy looking back on it, but I felt like I was letting him down. Like his life-changing research depended on my commitment. I told him I could come up with $200,000, but to go beyond that would be putting my company, and all my employees, at risk.'

'How did he take that?'

David shook his head again, looking baffled as he remembered the encounter. 'He had this way of sympathizing that would validate your concerns, but somehow his purpose was always greater.'

'So you ended up signing on,' Maggie said, stating the obvious.

David appeared lost in his own thoughts. 'I got guys driving here from Immokalee. I pay a good living wage. These guys depend on me. And I leveraged the rest against my company because this doctor told me I would get a guaranteed return on my investment of twenty-five percent in five years. He brought financials with him with graphs and bound copies of research. Looking back on it, I don't know. Maybe it was all just smoke and mirrors. Because nobody seems able to tell us where our money is now. And I got a garden center that's supposed to break ground in six months and a half million dollars tied up in a bogus company with no idea how to get it back.'

'Can you get me a copy of your contract?'

'I've got it here in my office. I'll make you a copy. I'll make copies for anybody that wants one if you think you can help me out of this nightmare.'

Maggie drove to Santa Cruz and stopped at the police department downtown. She had no desire to talk with Kilbourne or Weston, but she had no other choice. She asked the desk sergeant for Kilbourne, hoping to at least avoid Weston. Five minutes later, Kilbourne appeared behind the counter and motioned Maggie back to his office, a cubicle with just enough room to hold two visitor chairs.

Maggie explained what David Anthony had told her.

Kilbourne made a copy and then examined the contract for several minutes and finally gave Maggie a skeptical look.

'I don't know what I can do with this. I mean, I think this

poor guy got screwed, but it's way beyond the Santa Cruz PD's ability to deal with it. Seems more like a civil matter.'

Maggie said, 'We're talking millions of dollars that this doctor scammed. And the investors don't have any idea where the money is, or how it will play out with the settlement of the estate.'

'I'll drop a copy by the county attorney, but he probably won't do anything with it. Again, it's a civil matter. This guy needs an attorney, not a cop.'

Maggie nodded. 'You don't think millions of dollars of missing money is motivation for murder?'

'There's a list of fifty people, and that's conservative, who despised the guy. But there's nothing linking any of those people to his office the night he was murdered. And there's nothing to indicate any of the investors are interested in anything beyond getting their money back. If you think about it, his death is doing nothing at all to help these people. They'll have a legal nightmare trying to get it all back. They needed him in jail, not six feet under.'

'I get it. But hatred doesn't always translate into common sense.'

Maggie could sense Kilbourne's scrutiny so she thanked him for his time and left. She walked to her car feeling the humiliating burn of someone publicly losing perspective.

It was well after lunch when Maggie finished at the police department. She'd intended on taking lunch to Agnus, but decided to do her one better and drove to Snappy's, Agnus's favorite donut shop, and bought a dozen. Next, she stopped at Starbucks and bought her favorite coffee.

Maggie pulled around the circular drive, glad to find no other cars in front of her.

Agnus met her at the front door wearing a pink tracksuit and bright white running shoes, smiling as always. 'Did you bring me a peace offering?'

'I did. Your favorite long john donuts and a caramel macchiato with a double shot of caramel.'

Agnus clapped her hands. 'Forgiven! Come on inside. I was hoping you'd stop by today. I can't stay mad at you for anything.'

Maggie followed her into the kitchen.

'I just got off the treadmill, so I can eat whatever I please.

You have impeccable timing.' Agnus sat two plates on the kitchen island and poured Maggie a cup of black coffee.

'Well, my timing the other night wasn't so good. I'm sorry, Agnus. I value your friendship more than anything else, and I clearly overstepped my bounds. I won't stop caring and I won't stop being protective, but I'll be more respectful.'

'Apology accepted. So what did you find out?'

'About what?'

'His background check. I know you ran it, whether you felt bad or not.'

'His record came back clean. Not so much as a speeding ticket.'

'Hmm. Old Agnus knew a little something after all.'

'I care about you. If I didn't care I would have driven right on by that silver Caddy in your driveway.'

'You gonna judge his car too?'

'I already did.'

'Give me another donut before I kick your ass. And next time, don't interrupt my date. I only have a limited number of them left in my life, and I plan to enjoy each minute.'

Maggie noticed a car drive by the kitchen window headed toward her house. She stood to get a better look, then sighed and kissed Agnus on the top of her head. 'Bad news. The police are after me. I better head that way.'

'Give me a call if you need bail money.'

'Will do.'

When she reached the front door, Agnus hollered after her, 'Come by tonight at six for dinner. I invited the crew over to meet Roomy. He's grilling out and I'm making cocktails. Danny G and the band will be here. Serena and Mark too.'

'You weren't going to invite me?'

'Not until you brought me treats and an apology.'

Maggie drove her car down the short drive and pulled in next to the Santa Cruz PD patrol car. Kilbourne and Weston were standing at her front door, arms crossed, watching her exit the car.

'What can I do for you?' Maggie asked. She leaned on the hood of her car so the two officers were forced to come to her.

'Mind if we go inside and talk? Get out of this sun?' Kilbourne said.

'I don't mind the sun. Feels pretty good today.' Maggie felt
the sweat drip down her temples and her rear end burn from the
hood of the car. She was counting on hundred-degree temperatures
at two o'clock in the afternoon speeding along the visit.

Weston walked up to her, obviously pissed at having to stand
outside. 'Then let's cut to it. What's your deal with the O'Neals?'

'What's my deal? What kind of a question is that?'

'Why don't you tell us about this relationship you've developed with the O'Neals?' Kilbourne said. 'Because from our
point of view, it looks pretty odd. What we see is a retired cop
out canvassing Collier County, tracking down rich investors,
trying to find someone with a motive to kill the doctor.'

Weston cut in, 'When we've already got the man with the
clear motive sitting in the next town over. Andre O'Neal's got
guilty written all over his face. And now we hear you've been
hanging out at the bars with him. Defending his honor. Kind of
odd for a female to be out taking on another man's problems.
Don't you think?'

Maggie gave Kilbourne an incredulous look. 'I just left you
two hours ago. You couldn't have talked to me then?'

Kilbourne pointed to the scab on Maggie's forehead. 'You're
fighting a young guy's game. You're too old for that shit.'

'Look, you're getting your uniforms sweaty. This is serving
no purpose. If you have a serious question, then ask it.'

'OK, how about this? Kelly O'Neal told us how you advised
her not to talk to the cops. You told her that she needs an
attorney. That the court has to appoint one for her if she can't
afford one. Why the hell would a former cop shut a suspect
down like that?' Kilbourne said.

'I don't care if you're screwing her on the side or not, you
still don't turn a suspect on a fellow cop,' Weston said.

Maggie slid off the hood of her car and took a step toward
him.

'You don't want to go there,' Kilbourne said, putting his arm
between Maggie and Weston. 'You throw a punch at a cop,
you're looking at a felony. I don't care who you are.'

Weston put his finger in Maggie's face. 'You need to get
your shit together.'

'Get off my property.' Maggie kept her voice level.

Weston walked back to his car but Kilbourne turned back to her. 'I'd suggest you tell us what you know before you end up on the wrong side of a jail cell. We've got no beef with you yet. But I think you're covering up for that couple. You're better off coming clean now, rather than getting dragged into their drama in front of a judge.'

Maggie walked inside her house and undressed. She threw her clothes on the floor and pulled on her swimsuit, heading straight for the water. She waded out, pushing against the surf, forcing her body forward until she finally calmed down enough to allow the waves to carry her up and down, in their rhythmic climb and release. Once she reached the ridge that fell off into deeper water, she swam another ten feet out and turned to follow the shoreline in the calmer water until her arms and lungs burned with the effort.

The vast aloneness of the ocean calmed her like nothing else could. No phones or people. Just smooth water gliding over her skin coupled with the thrill of what lay just beneath that deep ridge below.

She finally swam inland to the point where she could touch the bottom and stood to catch her breath, bobbing in the waves, feeling her heart rate return to normal. She walked slowly to the shore and down the beach to the house, ignoring the few sunbathers and dog walkers. With her body heavy from the exertion and her muscles aching, her thoughts had finally given way to the more primal physical needs for survival.

By the time she reached the house, her anger had lost its edge but settled in deep. She knew the cops were messing with her, trying to get her to say something she would regret later; she could let that one go. But she was disappointed in Kelly. Maggie had not imagined Kelly as someone who would drop a name. And had she realized Maggie's name carried so little weight, she could have saved them both some grief and said nothing. Maggie debated calling Kelly, but decided against it. It would serve no purpose. She also decided against telling Mark about the latest visit from the Santa Cruz PD. He'd already made his stand on the investigation quite clear to her.

TWENTY-NINE

Maggie and Mark entered the lanai behind Agnus's home and found Danny and Buffalo Bruce dangling their feet over the edge of the pool, watching Serena and Whitney play water volleyball. Agnus appeared to be offering Roomy direction on how to properly cook steaks on her grill. He appeared to be ignoring her.

'Hey, boss lady!' Danny yelled. 'Take a load off.'

Mark went to chat with Agnus, and Maggie sat next to Danny, glad to slip her feet into the cool water.

'What's up?' Maggie asked.

'Where you been hiding lately?' Serena asked.

'Working hard.'

'Hardly working's more like it,' she said. 'Want me to grab you a beer?'

'Nope. I'll serve you. What do you need?'

'Grab me a water and a bowl of chips and salsa,' she said.

Maggie served Serena her snacks poolside, and then greeted Agnus, who pecked her on the cheek, and Roomy, who grunted a hello.

Thirty minutes later, Agnus ushered her guests around the patio table for dinner, prodding each person to share stories, while she attempted to draw Roomy into the conversation. Maggie had never seen Agnus so manic. She laughed when a smile was sufficient, bustled around the table filling water glasses that weren't empty. Countless times she prodded Roomy, 'Isn't that funny?' 'Don't you just love that?' And his response was never more than a guttural noise or a head bob.

By the time dinner was through, Agnus appeared a nervous wreck. Maggie wasn't sure why she cared so much what everyone thought about this new man in her life, but Roomy clearly wasn't trying to make much of an impression.

Maggie and Mark stood to carry plates into the kitchen while Agnus passed around a plate of brownies she claimed she and

Roomy had made. As Maggie was loading the last of the plates into the dishwasher, Roomy walked into the kitchen empty-handed. He opened the refrigerator and rooted around but didn't remove anything. Maggie glanced over and found him leaning against the kitchen island, watching her wipe down the countertop with a dishtowel.

'What's up?'

'You got a good thing going here, huh?' Roomy asked.

'What do you mean?'

'I mean living here on the ocean with Agnus. I'd call that a good thing, wouldn't you?'

'I'd call it none of your business,' Maggie said.

'Well, I guess we disagree there. Agnus is my business. So whoever she has living in her gardener's shack is my business too.'

Maggie turned and leaned against the counter to give her full attention to the man. She didn't like the look of him. He had a soft face with a weak chin, a permanent frown and a jet-black combover. Maggie couldn't imagine what had attracted Agnus to him.

'Then I guess you need to take it up with Agnus. I have no intention of discussing my situation with you.'

'That'll change soon enough. You think you can sponge off Agnus and get away with it forever. But not on my watch.'

'I don't get your attitude. You don't even know me. If you care about Agnus, you'd want to make an effort to get to know the people she cares about. People she has cared about for *years.*'

Agnus rushed into the kitchen with her hands in the air like Edith Bunker. 'Cocktails are ready! Let's go you two! I have everyone's favorites all lined up.'

Maggie followed her out, glad to end the conversation. Mark caught her eye and motioned for her to sit by him at the patio table.

'Come on over here. I've already got your beer,' he said. She sat next to him and he grinned, scanning her expression. 'Agnus suddenly realized you and Roomy had both disappeared and she panicked. She's seen the cross looks between you two tonight.'

'He accused me of sponging off Agnus. He said I had it good living in her gardener's shack.'

'What an ass. He's playing alpha dog. Just let it go.'

'It's time to start looking elsewhere. I won't stay here with that guy in the picture. I don't need that kind of nonsense.'

'Come on, Maggie, he's pissing on the fence line. Don't pay him any attention. Besides, Agnus would be crushed if she heard you were talking about leaving.'

Maggie shrugged. 'This has always felt a little uncomfortable. I love Agnus and I love the ocean view, but it's awkward living somewhere like this for free.'

'You're going to let your pride kick you out of paradise?'

'I'm sure he isn't the only person thinking I'm sponging off an old lady.'

'Maggie, seriously. I get that you're mad, but don't go to Agnus and do something rash. You've seen her tonight. She knows there's an issue between you and Roomy and it's killing her. Just give it some time. I think it'll work itself out.'

THIRTY

The following afternoon, Maggie drove to the radio station to conduct research for her upcoming show on millionaires. She'd found nothing to support the claim from the schoolteacher who'd said there are more teacher millionaires than doctors, but she'd found several Santa Cruz real estate investors who had agreed to come on the show and discuss their path to wealth.

Maggie and David had begun saving ten percent of their salary for retirement the year they were married, and had increased it to twenty percent within a few years. A cop and a teacher's pension hadn't made them millionaires, but she had retired with enough money in the bank to live more comfortably than while she'd been working. She had a sizeable retirement account, and the money she had made from the sale of their home in Ohio was accruing interest.

She could buy her own damn home. She didn't need free rent from anyone. Romeo Jones had gotten under her skin more than Maggie would have thought possible. She hadn't realized how uncomfortable she was with her rent-free living arrangement, but she wasn't sure how to solve her own ego issues without leaving Agnus with an empty gardener's shack. And she sure as hell didn't want Roomy moving into it.

Maggie received a call from Mark as she was locking up the office.

'I think you ought to know. They just arrested Andre O'Neal for first degree murder.'

She leaned against the wall as if the wind had been knocked out of her lungs. 'Based on what?'

'I can't get into it right now. They're housing him in our jail temporarily. Santa Cruz's high-risk facility is at capacity. I need to get over there. It'll turn into a media mess when word gets out.'

'I appreciate the call.'

'You bet.'

'I'd like to go see Kelly. She's going to need support. The rumors about her husband have already been terrible. Are you good with that?'

'I figured you would. It's why I called,' he said.

'You might get blowback.'

'I'm not worried about that. However, I heard about the Santa Cruz officers stopping by your house again. Why wouldn't you tell me that?'

'Because I didn't want you to feel like you had to get in the middle. This is my issue, not yours.'

He hesitated. 'Just be careful. I know you need to go see her. But your name is showing up more and more in the investigation. People are quiet around me, but John said the Santa Cruz investigators have you listed as a person of interest. That doesn't mean too much at this point. Other than I want you to be careful.'

Kelly asked Maggie to park behind her house. She had her own car parked in a neighbor's garage and was keeping the house closed and locked. Andre had installed two air-conditioning units a few days back so that they could lock the house up at night. The talk on social media had turned against Andre, and Kelly had started to fear for their safety.

Maggie entered through the back door and found Kelly and Amaya sitting at the kitchen table looking exhausted, both of them with eyes red-rimmed from crying.

Maggie placed her hand on Amaya's back and the girl started crying again. Maggie knelt down on one knee beside her. 'How about a hug, Amaya?'

The girl laid her head on Maggie's shoulder and sobbed. Kelly turned away and left the kitchen. Maggie couldn't imagine the shame of seeing your child in that much pain.

After several minutes, Kelly returned with a cold washcloth for Amaya. She took it from her mom and sat back at the table, holding the cloth, sniffing and wiping her face on her T-shirt.

Kelly remained standing with her arms wrapped around her stomach. 'I called my mom. I want Amaya to go stay with her.'

'I'm not leaving.'

Maggie watched the girl, surprised at the anger in her words.

'Amaya, you can't stay here right now. This isn't a good place for you,' Kelly said. 'There's a counselor that grandma knows who can talk to you about what's happening.'

'So I can draw stupid pictures about my emotions? That doesn't change anything.'

'I know you don't understand this, but these are things you are too young to deal with. A kid your age shouldn't watch their dad get taken away in handcuffs. That's a terrible thing for anyone, but especially a girl your age.' Kelly sat in the chair next to her daughter. 'Just for a day or two.'

'I'm not leaving you.'

Kelly sighed, her shoulders slumped and frail. 'Let me think about it. But for right now, I need to talk to Maggie about your dad's case. This is adult conversation that doesn't concern you. Do you understand that?'

She nodded.

'I won't make you go to grandma's tonight, but only if you realize there are some things I need to talk about that you don't need to hear.'

Amaya stood without saying anything and walked out of the kitchen. They heard her close the door to her bedroom.

Maggie sat down at the table. As a cop, she'd been in a number of situations where kids were present during a parent's arrest. The first priority was arresting the suspect with no casualties. That typically meant that kids were swept to the side until the arrest was made and the scene deemed safe. There had been times when the cops in the room felt more anxiety over a kid's exposure to the ordeal than the parents did; the parents were so caught up in their own drama that the kids were afterthoughts. However, this one put Maggie on the backside of the arrest, dealing with the aftermath, and it was heartbreaking.

'I don't know what to do for her. She saw it all. Heard everything the cops said.'

'It seems like the truth is easier to handle than people whispering and lying, or even worse, not saying anything. Amaya will make up what she doesn't know. And that's almost always worse than the truth.'

'I would have agreed with that until this afternoon. The truth was pretty bad,' she said.

'Are you able to talk me through what happened?'

'Three cop cars pulled in front of the house with their sirens going. We had cops at the front and back doors, all yelling at the same time. One was yelling "everybody down". Another one in the back of the house was yelling for Andre to freeze with his hands on his head. I was so scared one of us was going to do the wrong thing, but I didn't know what they wanted. Amaya was sitting on the couch, terrified. Then one of the cops yelled for me to go sit by Amaya. Then they told Andre he was being arrested for first degree murder.' Kelly wiped the tears from her eyes using the cloth she'd given Amaya. 'I will never forget that moment. Amaya on the couch, pressed up against me. And when they said they were arresting her dad, Amaya's body went limp. I looked down because I thought she'd fainted. She looked up at me with this look, like she was trying to figure out if what they were saying about her dad was true or not. That question in her eyes, about her dad being a murderer, was the worst thing I've ever seen in my life.'

'Did the police give you any information?'

'I guess that depends on what you mean by information. They handcuffed Andre and took him out the front door and put him in one of the cop cars. Then they showed me the search warrant for Andre's workshop. Amaya and I sat on the couch while one cop stood at the front door, guarding us I guess, making sure we didn't interfere. The others went out into the shop. They were there for about a half hour. Then they came back in and said they were through. One of them said I should contact the Cypress City Jail Center for information about Andre. And they left. I looked out the front door and watched my neighbors standing outside with their cell phones videoing the whole thing so they can put it on Facebook.'

'Did you get a chance to talk to Andre?'

'No. I couldn't even say goodbye.'

Maggie lowered her voice. 'I have to ask you this. Do you think—'

Before she could finish Kelly started shaking her head. 'He didn't do it. I am telling you now, he did not kill that doctor. I would bet my life on that.'

Mark called Maggie at nine o'clock that night. 'This case gets more bizarre by the day. About the time I think Andre's the one, I hear something that has me shaking my head again.'

'The search warrant?' she asked.

'You got it.'

'For what?'

'The murder weapon. And they found it.'

'I thought they found the gauze in the trash in the doctor's office,' she said, 'along with the knife used to cut his wrists?'

'They did. The search warrant was for unidentified items used to carry out the crime. It sounded like complete BS to me. The warrant was only for the garage. And they found unopened packages of gauze tape located in a small brown paper bag under Andre's workbench. There were two rolls in the bag. That was it.'

'I don't even know what to say to that.'

'I had a similar response,' he said. 'Who would take home evidence linking you to the murder like that, unless it was a trophy kill, which obviously this was not.'

'And did they ask Andre about it?'

'No. He wasn't talking. They've assigned a public defender. They'll most likely get someone in there tomorrow.'

'I can't believe the prosecutor would go for an arrest over a couple of rolls of gauze tape.'

'Honestly, Maggie, I was in the observation room when they told Andre what they found in his workshop. He looked numb, like his thinking had just shut down.'

'What's the chief saying?' Maggie asked.

'I'm not done yet. A liquor store owner called and said Andre came into the store and bought beer the night the doctor died. This was around midnight, when Andre said he was home in bed sleeping. He lied about his whereabouts, and his wife lied for him.'

'Shit.' Kelly had told Maggie that she knew Andre didn't get home until four in the morning. The web around Kelly and Andre was expanding, and Maggie didn't like her own proximity.

'You said he bought beer. Did the store owner say if he bought whiskey too? Old Crow?' she asked.

'No. Only beer. But it doesn't mean he didn't already have the whiskey in his possession,' Mark said. 'Santa Cruz is trying to track down other surveillance tapes from the medical park where Doctor LeBlanc's office is located. We know Andre lied about being at home all night, but that doesn't put his car at the scene. And just because he had gauze tape in his workshop doesn't mean he committed the murder,' he said, 'at least in my mind. But the prosecutor agreed to the arrest.'

'I don't see a jury going for it. His attorney will say he's a mechanic. He's got gauze tape in his shop for accidents. Same as you and I have gauze tape in our bathroom cabinets.'

'I agree,' Mark said.

'No one is talking about Andre being set up? That someone planted the gauze in his shop?'

'John said Santa Cruz is convinced Andre O'Neal is their man, and this was the tipping point.'

'How did they know to look for it?'

'I've asked that question several times,' he said. 'All I heard was an anonymous tip. I assume it came in on a call line, but no one is saying.'

'I call bullshit,' she said. 'Everyone has seen the social media tirade against Andre. It wouldn't take a genius to plant something at the guy's house to feed the investigation.'

'But there's no one fitting that description,' he said. 'I think they have more than they're telling me. They've gotten pretty cagey around me over the past week. I'm sure it's my relationship with you.'

'All right then. Tell it to me straight,' Maggie said. 'What's your opinion?'

'Andre is being set up. The gauze under his workbench doesn't make any more sense than the doctor slashing his wrists drunk on Old Crow.'

'Agreed,' she said.

'But at this point, the only evidence points directly at Andre.'

THIRTY-ONE

Maggie woke to the low hum of the air conditioner and a blanket of cool air over her bed from the vent above her. The bedside clock read 4:45 a.m., but her body felt alert. The window was dark, still two hours from sunrise. She stared at the ceiling and considered the bottle of tequila on the desk in the living room, wondering if a shot or two would lull her back to sleep. She remembered David's plea to her just days before he died. He'd ordered Maggie to eat right and exercise. 'And stay away from the alcohol. That stuff will kill you,' he'd said, smiling at the irony. He had never touched alcohol, didn't like the way it made him feel, and yet there he was unable to lift his head from the pillow.

Aside from the need to escape her old life, Maggie had moved to Florida to have a healthier lifestyle. When she and David had visited, until he was no longer able to leave the condo, they had walked the trails around Collier County and Southwest Florida. Once he was wheelchair-bound, they took advantage of the boardwalk through the thick cypress swamp at the Big Cypress Bend. His favorite perch was a bench with binoculars looking up into a five-foot-wide bald eagles' nest, waiting for the thump of wings as one of the pair exited the nest to hunt. Walking with him along the beach or through the woods was one of her greatest pleasures in life. She cared for Mark a great deal, but hiking through the swamp wasn't his idea of a good time. And Maggie missed those days.

She dressed in walking shorts and a T-shirt, threw a bag of granola and a gallon of water in her backpack, and took off before the late morning heat could slow her down. One of her favorite hikes was the Bird Rookery Swamp Loop, and early morning, midweek in July, would most likely guarantee a solitary twelve-mile hike. It was one of the most remote areas of the state, and utilized old elevated logging trams to travel through the middle of a bald cypress swamp, through areas otherwise impassable on foot. On a leisurely day the hike would take Maggie five or six hours, but she planned a four-hour hustle to burn off energy.

By five thirty, Maggie had parked in the empty parking lot. Once her eyes adjusted to the pre-dawn light, she made her way down the half-mile boardwalk that ended at the start of a dirt and grass path. Four miles into the hike, light began drifting through the feathery cypress leaves and Maggie slowed her pace. She finally allowed her thoughts to wander beyond the rhythm of her steps. She'd used exercise as a way to de-stress her entire life, from track as a teenager, to hitting the gym after a homicide third shift before going home to David. She'd imagined the sweat and the hot shower afterwards pushing the toxins from her body so she could go home to him unpolluted.

Maggie stopped to watch a pod of baby alligators piled atop one another in the shallow canal that ran parallel to the logging trail. They lay motionless, drawing heat from one another in the cool morning, oblivious to the human ten feet from their nest. As she allowed her body to relax and her thoughts to wander, she realized it was her inability to escape the case that was eating at her. Mark was right. She'd become obsessed with it, but unlike her former job where she had learned to clock out and, for the most part, leave the cases at the office, she'd not found a way to shut her thoughts down here. But it was more complicated than the explanation she'd given Mark.

It was true that the parallels to her own life had drawn the chaos on her, but it was decisions she'd made over the past week that were keeping her up at night. Decisions she would not have made while she was a working officer.

Maggie acknowledged to herself that she believed in Kelly and Andre in large part because of Amaya. They needed to be innocent for their kid, for Amaya's future. But what if they weren't? Kelly had not mentioned the $75,000 sitting in an offshore bank account since she told Maggie what she'd done. But the information was never far from Maggie's mind. Kelly had already let the police know that Maggie was feeding her advice. What more might she add if they turned on her? Desperation was a strong motivator.

Ten miles into the hike, having made the loop through the swamp, it occurred to Maggie that as close to nature as she had been, she could never enter the deep heart of the swamp. The land was too thick and unforgiving, the alligators a slow and silent threat. The swamp was a humbling experience. The wetlands in the Everglades were one of the largest in the world, and Maggie used the vast solitary nature of the space to keep her place on earth in perspective.

And yet, before she pulled out of the parking lot, Maggie sent Mark a quick text. The hike had done little to separate the O'Neals from her thoughts.

Any word on Andre this morning?

Her phone buzzed in her hand. Not a good sign if the answer required a phone call.

'Chief Osbourne called this morning,' Mark said. 'Things aren't looking good for Andre. The gauze they found in his garage is medical grade. They don't sell it at WalMart or even in pharmacies. I called the medical supply company in Santa Cruz and they don't carry it for the general public. It's used by hospitals and clinics and sold in bulk. And the gauze found in Andre's garage matches the brand used at Doctor LeBlanc's clinic.'

'Think about what that means,' Maggie said. 'Assuming you agree that Andre was set up, that means whoever set him up had access to the gauze used at the clinic. This just narrowed the list of suspects by a huge margin.'

'Maybe. But the person could have gotten the gauze from any number of medical facilities. They didn't necessarily get it from LeBlanc's office.'

'How many medical facilities use that specific brand?'

'I can't answer that.'

'Is Santa Cruz looking into it?'

'Maggie. I'm not the Chief of Police in Santa Cruz. They have a boss telling them what to do. They don't need me interfering.'

'What do you know about LeBlanc's receptionist?' she asked.

'Maggie. Seriously. You have to stop.'

She laughed. 'You call and feed me information and then expect me to sit on it?'

'I'm keeping you informed as a courtesy, far more than I should. But you aren't a cop anymore. You have to let the investigation take its course.'

'I get it. Seriously. I appreciate you trusting me. I won't abuse it.'

The second Maggie got off the phone with Mark she called Kelly, asking if she could stop by. She agreed, saying Amaya would appreciate the distraction. She was going to spend the night at a friend's house that evening and she was beyond excited. The other girl's mother had called Kelly, asking if she thought it would be good for Amaya to have a normal night. Kelly was in tears recounting the conversation to Maggie. 'Someday, I will find a way to pay her back for her kindness. She probably has no idea how much this means to Amaya.'

The forecast that morning had said a chance of thunderstorms, and the drive to Cypress City made good on the prediction. Thunderheads rolled in from the Gulf of Mexico. Maggie wound the windows down as the temperature plummeted twenty degrees in a matter of minutes, smelling the fresh, pungent tang of ozone before the raindrops hit the earth. Thunder echoed for miles and lightning lit up the vast swaths of tomato fields stretching along the backroads.

When Maggie arrived on Howard Street, she parked in front of the house, glad to see the news vans were gone. She ran through the rain to the front porch and found Amaya bouncing around the kitchen.

'We're going to the movie theatre in Immokalee. We don't have school tomorrow because they have a teacher day.'

'Go get your bag packed, and when you're done, come back and you can tell Maggie all about it.'

The bathroom door slammed and Maggie grinned. 'It's nice to see a smile on her face.'

'You can't imagine. Amaya has a cousin who's a year older. She lives in Louisiana right on the bayou, and the girls get along great. They're both tomboys. They love sports and fishing. Anyway, my sister wants Amaya to go spend a week. I talked to her teacher today and she thinks it's a great idea. She'll just miss the last week before a six-week summer break. Amaya does good in school. So she'll be fine.'

'I can't imagine schoolwork is on her mind anyway.'

'No. Tonight is helping. It's probably helping ease my mind as much as Amaya's. I'm so afraid she'll be shunned at school, or made fun of. I had my share of that. I had hoped I would give my daughter better.'

'I don't know. Kids can be cruel, but they can also be decent human beings. And Amaya is a good kid. She doesn't strike me as the kind who would get picked on.'

'That's just what her teacher said.'

Kelly poured them both a cup of coffee and they sat at the kitchen table. 'I got a call today from Andre's lawyer.' She dipped her head. 'Public defender.'

'Same thing,' Maggie said. 'Your attorney passed the bar exam just like all the others.'

Kelly nodded. 'He seemed concerned. Asked a lot of questions. He wants me to meet with Andre tomorrow morning during visiting hours. I was hoping you could come with me too.'

'Why me?'

Kelly stood and looked down the hallway to make sure the bathroom door was still closed. She sat at the table again and took a long breath before speaking. 'The attorney said Andre confessed to murdering Doctor LeBlanc.'

Maggie stared for a moment in shock. 'Did you know this, before the attorney told you?'

'No! I don't know why Andre would have said anything, especially a confession. He knew from the last time the police were here, don't say a word until the attorney is there with you. I told him what you said about not saying anything to the police – that silence was the smart thing to do. Then the attorney told me that Andre would barely talk to him this morning. He said it was like Andre was afraid to talk. So he's hoping I can go in tomorrow morning and find out what's going on.'

'I'm not sure what I can offer. I think he'd be more inclined to tell you if I wasn't around,' Maggie said.

She shook her head. 'No. Andre respects you. He'll probably never be able to tell you that himself, but he appreciates what you're doing for Amaya. The night you drove to Everglade City to hunt him down made a big impression on him. He was actually trying with Amaya. He was talking to her again. It seemed like he was starting to deal with his demons. And then this.'

'Then I'll go with you.'

Kelly nodded once, but the tension around her eyes remained.

'There's something else I need to talk to you about before we go any further,' Maggie said.

'Sure. Anything.'

'You can't use me as a bargaining chip. It won't gain you anything. I'm not in good standing with the police department right now.'

'What are you talking about?' Kelly looked both confused and worried. Maggie figured she hadn't even realized she was sharing something best left unsaid, which was even more troubling.

'I had two cops visit my house. They were questioning me about my involvement with you and Andre.' Maggie put a hand up to halt the look of concern on Kelly's face. 'I'm not worried about that. What bothered me is that you told them that I said you needed to end the questioning with Andre. It's just not a good idea to name-drop with the police. It doesn't go over well with most cops.'

Kelly's expression had turned to surprise and confusion. 'That's not true! That's not how it happened at all.'

Maggie nodded slowly. 'It's OK if you did. I'm just explaining why you shouldn't in the future.'

'But I never mentioned your name. I told them to stop talking to Andre, like you told me to do. One of the cops asked me if I'd been talking to an attorney and I said no. Then he asked who I'd been talking to and I didn't say anything. He asked several times and I never answered. That's the absolute truth.'

'Then they're messing with me. They made an assumption and ran with it.'

'Why would they do that?'

Maggie took a mental step back. She knew exactly why they would do it. She'd done it herself too many times to count. It was part of the unwritten rules of the job. You said what needed to be said to get the case solved. There were countless times when Maggie had known the exact person who had committed a crime, but there were some investigations where knowing and proving weren't even in the same hemisphere. And when a cop *knows* who the killer is, he will put pressure where it's needed, in whatever way he can, within the law. It's not about a cop being a badass, it's about a cop needing the man who killed a little girl's mother with an overdose of fentanyl to go to jail. The fentanyl overdose had been one of Maggie's last homicide cases, and she'd made some enemies over the investigation, but the murderer was arrested. Yet in the world Maggie found increasingly hard to comprehend, the news media was more obsessed with pointing their fingers at cops than agreeing that the rapists, murderers and thieves needed locking away to pay for their crimes.

Maggie saw that Kelly was studying her closely. 'The cops said what they did because they are trying to catch a murderer. That's all it comes down to. It isn't personal, even though it feels that way at the time. I was angry when they showed up at my house, but I did the same thing a hundred times through my career. Sometimes it's the only way you get to the truth.'

Kelly frowned and seemed close to arguing the point when Amaya walked into the room dragging a bright pink suitcase and a unicorn sleeping bag.

Maggie stood to leave. 'I'm going to get out of here so you can get ready for the movies.' She pulled a twenty-dollar bill out of her pocket and handed it to Amaya. 'Buy you and your friend popcorn. Have a good time tonight. OK?'

Amaya grinned and thanked Maggie.

'And I'll see you in the morning,' she said, nodding at Kelly. Tears had welled in the corners of Kelly's eyes again, and her expression suddenly turned to dread. Maggie recognized the panic attack as Kelly turned toward the kitchen sink to hide her fear from Amaya.

The temperatures had remained in the low seventies after the afternoon rain, and the sky promised a beautiful sunset. Maggie took her laptop and a folding beach chair and walked down to the edge of the water to watch the sun drop into the ocean. She waved at the neighbor with the yappy dog who was doing the same thing fifty yards down the beach. Fortunately, he stayed put, apparently happy to enjoy the orange glow alone.

Maggie started with a Facebook search for Olivia Sable, the young receptionist working for Dr LeBlanc who had characterized Maggie as 'the arrogant talk radio lady'.

The public photos on Facebook and Instagram were of a blonde woman in her late-twenties who enjoyed showing off her tanned body. There were dozens of bikini photos and white-teeth selfies with suntanned boys photobombing in the background.

Then she found a post from Olivia on a site called Pop-Daddy. It was a fairly new site that linked friends by location and a list of self-identified attributes. The conversation that interested Maggie followed an innocuous photo of a half-dozen bathing-suit-clad twenty-somethings leaning into one another at the beach, arms draped loosely around shoulders with their Coronas lifted in a toast. The comments started with the typical, *Hey girl! Miss You!* And, *You look gorgeous! Call me tonight!* But the fourth comment down was from a girl identified as Sunshine Carrie, which Olivia had replied to.

> *Saw your boss man today!!!*
> *Seeing him tonight. $$$ ☺*
> *So lucky! Drink champagne for me!*
> *Diamonds are my best friend. You know that lol*
> *Miami?*
> *Probably ☹ Tired of that already*

Maggie saved the link, forwarded the post to her WKQE email account, and took a screen shot. She realized she was drawing some wide conclusions, but it looked as though Olivia was going to meet the doctor after hours for an expensive evening. Or perhaps the dollar signs represented his wealth. It also sounded as if the doctor was making them go to Miami, most likely to avoid his wife, and Olivia was tired of being forced out of town.

Maggie wrote down the date. The post was from 12 June. She searched social media for both Sunshine Carrie and Olivia's name, combined with the terms *boss* and *boss man*, but did not find any additional occurrences. She also found that Olivia had deactivated her account on the Florida HotSpot online dating site in May. It allowed her to keep the account online, but not post or receive new information. Maggie wondered if that's when an affair had started.

After an hour of stalking the young woman online, Maggie shut her laptop. It was impossible to imagine her buying Old Crow and convincing her boss to come back to the office to get drunk so she could slash his wrists. But there were plenty of instances where pretty girls convinced adoring boyfriends to commit horrendous crimes on their behalf.

The bigger issue was motive. Why would Olivia want her boss dead? If her goal was seducing him away from his wife, then why kill him before she got the wedding band? Unless, as Dr LeBlanc's receptionist, she had access to the money that the investors were missing. Embezzlement wasn't uncommon, and access to upwards of fifteen million dollars would certainly be enticing. Even a small portion of the money. Once she had it, finding a beach boy to stage a suicide at the doctor's office was doable. Even the police acknowledged the suicide setup was poorly executed.

Olivia would have seen the social media speculation around Andre, and Maggie could imagine her and an accomplice planning a murder scene made to look like a bad suicide attempt. She could imagine the logic: how would a guy like Andre O'Neal kill a fancy doctor? Get him drunk and slash his wrists.

Maggie watched the waves roll in to the beach, plotting through the details of the case: motive, means and opportunity were all tied up with Olivia. It was the first scenario that had made good sense to Maggie since the case broke.

It reminded her of a homicide she had worked in Cincinnati that involved a school district secretary who was in charge of payroll. She had paid herself an additional eighty-thousand dollars per year for three years, plus used several district credit cards, amassing a quarter of a million dollars in the three-year period. When her spending habits became more extravagant, her husband discovered the money in a bank account she had concealed from him. In response, he planned a long overdue vacation for them in Barbados, then shoved her over the edge of a bridge late one night, planning to take the money and flee the country after her funeral. There were no eyewitnesses to the crime, but a video camera – installed to catch a group of local kids who had been vandalizing the bridge – caught the fight between husband and wife, and the final blow to her head and shove over the edge. Back home, the community had been in disbelief that a church-going couple with two beautiful kids could go so wrong. What had surprised Maggie was that the media attention seemed less focused on the woman's murder, and more on the idea that a school secretary, a plain-Jane mom, would have the audacity to steal a quarter of a million dollars. Maggie had learned long ago that outward appearances often had little to do with morals or even common decency.

THIRTY-TWO

M aggie arrived at the Cypress City Jail Center ten minutes before their appointed time. Her identification was verified at a gate shack, and she was allowed through the ten-foot-tall chain-link fence with specific instructions for parking and proceeding to the processing door.

In the parking lot, she met up with Kelly who was wearing a pale-yellow dress and white heels, her hair hanging softly around her shoulders. She looked nervous and out of place in the austere setting.

'I thought the attorney would come too, but he texted and said he'd meet with Andre later. He wants an update after we're done.'

Maggie motioned for them to start walking but Kelly held back, as if having second thoughts. Maggie placed a hand on her back. 'We need to go. You can't be late for your allotted time or they won't allow you the visitation.'

Kelly took a long breath and bent to smooth her dress. Visiting a jail for the first time was scary enough on its own. Visiting a jail to find out why your husband had confessed to committing murder took scary to a new level.

Maggie started walking, talking to fill the space. 'Public defenders catch a lot of grief for not being more present, but most of them do a good job. Some of them have over a hundred cases at a time, so they don't have the time to spend with everyone like they do with paying clients,' Maggie said. 'But I'm confident Andre's attorney will be here when it matters.'

'Beggars can't be choosey.'

'There's no shame in using a public defender. I've heard them tell people who've offered to pay to go the free route instead, if it won't change their outcome. Sometimes a case is so obviously one-sided that it isn't worth paying lawyer fees just to get more face time with an attorney.'

Kelly glanced over at Maggie. 'I don't think that's the case here.'

'True enough. The goal here is to get it thrown out before it gets to that point.'

When they reached the front entrance, they presented their credentials again, walked through a metal detector and submitted to a hand wand. Next, they were shuffled to an attendant who had them fill out paperwork concerning their visit. The attorney had applied for visitation for two, something that wasn't always granted. Maggie explained it was a good sign, that Andre's attorney was already actively involved.

After storing their belongings and car keys in a locker, they sat in a waiting room with three long rows of metal chairs bolted to the floor. Maggie counted twenty people in the room, with two officers standing on the perimeter, watching and chatting.

She watched Kelly scan the room, picking up snatches of conversation loaded with anger and foul language and the frantic urgency of families trying desperately to deal with the bad decisions made by their loved ones.

'It's so loud in here,' Kelly said. 'I hadn't expected all these people.'

They listened as two names were called and two sets of families were escorted out of the room through a set of locked doors.

'Do you have a plan for what you want to say to Andre?'

'I just want to know what's in his head right now. I want to know why he would do this.'

'Why do you think he told the police he murdered the doctor?'

She turned to face Maggie, her eyes filled with pain. 'This sounds terrible to say about my own husband, but I think it was the easy way out.'

Maggie narrowed her eyes. 'How do you figure this is easy?'

'Because he's done now. It's out of his hands. I can see him thinking that now he's out of the picture, that Amaya and I can move on with our lives. We can leave him and all this drama behind us.'

'I don't think that's a thought process that would enter too many people's heads.'

She pressed her fingers into the corners of her eyes. 'People don't get Andre. He's not stupid. He's not crazy. He isn't dangerous. He just doesn't think like you and I do. He's a good man, but something awful happened to him in Afghanistan. Sometimes I get so angry over it I can't hardly stand it. But he won't admit it. I try to get him to go to the VA and get help but he sees it as a weakness. So I quit bringing it up.' Her hands gripped the handles on her chair. 'I read that shit on Topix about Andre, all the hate and the lies, and it makes me sick. Those people don't know him.'

'You need to block that website. Don't get sucked into that evil.'

They glanced over at the desk officer who stood to announce each new group. 'O'Neal and Wise. Meet the officer at door two in the back of the room.'

*   *   *

The visitation area was a long narrow room filled with five carrels divided by thick, floor-to-ceiling plexiglass. Within each carrel was a table that separated the visitor side from the jail side. The table stretched five feet deep, making physical contact difficult, but it allowed a more intimate connection than communicating through a phone or a plastic divider. The common belief was that frequent contact with family members during incarceration cut down on violence and was a strong motivator for good behavior.

Kelly and Maggie each sat in chairs facing the table with a locked metal door behind it. They didn't speak, both listening to the heavy sounds of the prison, clanking doors and buzzers and shouted orders. The carrel smelled of sweat and stress. They were sitting in the last of the five carrels, but they could see through the plastic dividers that the others were occupied. No one seemed to pay the rest of the visitors any attention. They had been told the visitation time was twenty minutes, which Maggie figured could feel like seconds or an eternity, depending on the situation.

Five minutes later, a light above the door lit up green and another buzzer sounded, followed by the loud clicks of a locking mechanism opening. Andre shuffled into the room in an orange jumpsuit. His feet were shackled but his hands remained free. Kelly cried as soon as she saw him, and his expression turned from overwhelmed to broken.

As Andre sat down, the guard behind him hooked his thumbs through his belt loop and ran through the rules. 'First and foremost, this is a privilege, not a right. If you do not follow the rules your visitation will be cut short with consequences. The only physical contact is hands across the table. You will have eyes on you during the entire visitation. Do not abuse this privilege. Keep your voices low so as not to bother other visitors beside you. You have exactly twenty minutes. If any of you in this room would like the visitation to end early, you press the button in the middle of the table and a guard will assist you. Any questions?'

By the time the guard had finished, Kelly had found tissues in her purse and stopped the flow of tears. As soon as the guard stepped out they reached across the table to hold hands.

'Are you OK?'

'I'm OK. It's sure good to see you though.'

'Are they treating you OK?'

'It's all right. It's not much different than you and Amaya sitting in that house lately. This just has bars.'

'Do you have a roommate?'

He grinned a little. 'I have a cellmate. He talks a lot. So I just listen. How's Amaya doing?'

Maggie scooted her chair back away from the table. She felt uncomfortable sitting next to them in what was probably the most intimate conversation of their lives. She saw Kelly squeeze Andre's hands, and Maggie looked away.

'She's doing pretty good,' Kelly said.

She went on to explain Amaya's trip to her friend's house, and the visit she was making to her sister's place in Louisiana for a week. Andre prodded her, asking details about mundane things. Maggie checked her watch. They'd already burned through ten minutes.

Maggie cleared her throat and scooted her chair closer to the table. 'Andre, I'm sorry to intrude. I know you just want to talk to Kelly, but I came at your attorney's request. And we've only got a few more minutes to figure out a plan.'

Kelly looked back at Maggie, her eyes worried. 'Andre, she's right. You have to help us figure out what's going on. When you left, you weren't talking to the police until your attorney was assigned. Then I hear the next day that you've admitted to killing that doctor. Why would you do that?'

'I don't need you to worry about it. I did what I needed to do.'

'You don't need me to worry? Why would you even say that? You're my husband and you're sitting in jail for a crime you didn't commit.'

Maggie watched tears well up in Andre's eyes but he said nothing.

'Damn it, Andre. You have to confide in me. You have to tell me what's going on so we can help.'

'There is nothing to talk about, Kelly. I did this for you, and for Amaya.'

Kelly's expression was panicked now, cognizant that the minutes were ticking by. 'You aren't even making sense.'

'Andre, if there's one thing I can't stress hard enough,' Maggie said, 'it's that you need to be completely honest right now, more than at any time in your life. You tell Kelly, and you tell your attorney, everything. Without the truth, they're shooting in the dark. And the wrong person is going to jail for murder.'

Andre hung his head for a long while, then finally looked directly at Kelly and squeezed her hands. 'They have you there. At the doctor's office that night. In your car. One of us is going to jail for it. Amaya needs her mom, Kelly.'

'Oh my god.' Kelly broke down sobbing.

Maggie tried to get Andre focused on the details. 'Who told you that they placed the car at the scene?'

Kelly interrupted. 'It's not like you think, Andre. I had nothing to do with that doctor's murder. You have to believe that.'

'Kelly, you can have that conversation later.' Maggie looked at Andre. 'We need to let the attorney know exactly what the police said to you. The police could have been leading you on, trying to force a confession.'

Maggie and Kelly both looked up at the light above the door that had turned from green to red, and listened as the locks clicked and the guard walked back into the small room.

'Can you just give us five more minutes?' Kelly said.

'No, ma'am. Everybody follows the same rules. Let's go, Mr O'Neal.'

Andre's eyes were cloudy and he looked confused as he stood from the table.

Maggie said, 'Andre. You tell your attorney everything. Be completely honest.'

Andre glanced back at Kelly as he walked out of the room.

They walked in silence through the parking lot back to their cars. When they reached them, Maggie said, 'Can we sit and talk a minute?'

They sat in Kelly's car where she cranked the air conditioner, pointing the vents directly at her face. Her hair was damp and hung limp, her forehead cut with worry lines. Before Maggie could speak, she broke down crying. She leaned her head on to the steering wheel and cried inconsolably. Maggie looked elsewhere, knowing there were no words that would help.

Once the tears stopped, Kelly wiped her face with tissues and leaned back in the driver's seat, spent of all emotion. Looking out the window at the gray jail complex in front of her, she said, 'What have I done? I was trying to make things right for Amaya, and I've put her own dad in prison for murder.'

'You didn't put Andre in prison. That's a decision he made.'

'But he made it for me! He knew he wasn't at the doctor's office that night, so he figured it had to be me. How is it that someone did something terrible to our family, and somehow my husband is now in prison and our family is destroyed? I can't even make sense of any of this anymore.' She looked over at Maggie, her eyes filled with light and determination. 'I have to make this right. Today.'

'Just hold up. You need to watch your step or you'll end up in the same place as Andre. Do you remember what I said to you before? How we were going to navigate the conversation carefully?'

Maggie waited for her to respond.

'Yes, I remember.'

'There are a series of events that have been set into motion, things the police aren't privy to. If you go to the police right now, offering up information you think will help Andre, you could make things worse for everyone. Do you understand that?'

Kelly took a moment but nodded her head.

'Andre is fine where he is right now. No one is hurting him. Right?'

'Yes.'

'We need to get a plan before you do anything. Understood?'

'But the police lied to Andre! You said the person that saw my car couldn't identify it other than saying it was a dark, older model car. They can't just openly lie to Andre. Isn't that entrapment, saying something that isn't true in order to get Andre to confess?'

'Entrapment is tricking someone into committing a crime in order to be able to prosecute. The police weren't doing that; they are allowed to say what needs to be said in order to get a confession.'

'Even lying?'

'If need be.'

Kelly looked shocked. 'You don't think that's wrong?'

'If it wasn't allowed, we'd have a lot of guilty people walking the streets. The police have to have some leeway.' She debated whether to push Kelly on the issue and decided her anger wasn't going to help Andre's case. 'You realize you're angry that the police told Andre something that is actually true? You were there that night. You *were* in that car.'

Kelly grew still but said nothing in response.

'I'm just trying to get you to keep things in perspective.'

'Then what do I do? Just let Andre sit there, having admitted to murdering someone to keep me out of jail? When I can tell the police it was me driving that car? That I drove there to get some kind of justice for my daughter?'

'Just slow down. You don't want to go to the police and open yourself to more scrutiny. Amaya doesn't need both her parents behind bars. Right?'

Again, it took her some time, but she finally agreed. 'I understand. But I have to go talk to the police. I need the details. I know you're being sucked into this more than you want, but would you consider going with me? Going there now?'

Maggie nodded. 'I'll go with you. But there's another piece to this that the police haven't shared. Can you keep this confidential?'

Kelly glared at Maggie. 'You need to ask me that at this point?'

'I do. This detail hasn't been made public. When you talk to the police today, you can ask about their search, but you can't let on that you know what they found.'

'I understand. I won't say a word.'

'The gauze that they found in Andre's workshop was medical grade. It's not sold in pharmacies or to the public. It's sold in bulk to medical professionals.'

'Meaning someone from the doctor's office planted it at our home?'

'The police were trying to find out how many other medical facilities in the area carry the same brand. With Andre's confession, I'm assuming the case is closed. But I'm still wondering, who would have access to the doctor's office?'

Kelly shrugged. 'Obviously the receptionist we met.'

'That's exactly what I thought.'

'But why would she kill her boss?'

'What if his death didn't have anything to do with the kidnappings? There's a large sum of investment money that hasn't been accounted for. I also have reason to believe she was having an affair with her boss. Maybe it was personal. Maybe Doctor LeBlanc wouldn't leave his wife.'

Kelly looked skeptical. 'You think the receptionist could have slashed his wrists?'

'I think she could have convinced someone else to.'

Officer James Offutt, one of Andre's arresting officers, entered the interrogation room and shut the door behind him. He introduced himself and sat across the table from them, laying a manila folder onto the table with a black and white mugshot of Andre paperclipped to the front of it.

'What can I help you with, ma'am?' he asked, looking at Kelly.

'I need to understand Andre's arrest. I'm sure it's what all wives say, but I promise you that my husband did not kill that doctor.'

Offutt nodded slowly, taking a moment to respond. 'I'm going to lay out for you exactly what we have in terms of evidence against your husband. We now have two eyewitnesses that saw a car registered in your name on the road leading to the doctor's office the night the doctor was murdered. Your husband stated that he was driving your car that night. He told officers Weston and Kilbourne that he came home at ten o'clock and went to bed. You substantiated that fact.' He paused and watched her for a moment. She didn't move. 'We know that is not true. Andre was out driving at midnight. We've got footage from a liquor store showing him buying a six pack.'

'Maybe he was home at ten o'clock and went back out later. I don't know about that. And maybe he drove by the doctor's office. He was upset that I went to the doctor's office with the police that morning. You can ask Chief Hamilton about that. He'll tell you.' Kelly glanced at Maggie but continued. 'Andre's torn up over all this. It doesn't mean he killed a man.'

'After your husband was arrested, we told him, either your

wife left the house the same time you did and went to that doctor's office, or you did. But we have a snatch of the license plate on your wife's car, placing that car on the access road to the doctor's office. We have the gauze tape that matches the tape used to tie the doctor's arms, found in the workshop at your house. So, I said to him – you killed the doctor or your wife did. And he said, I did it.' Offutt paused again, searching Kelly's face. 'We have his confession on tape.'

'How do you know that gauze is what was used on the doctor?'

Offutt went into a detailed explanation about the medical grade tape and the fact that it was only used by a handful of medical offices in the Santa Cruz area.

'You don't think someone could have planted that tape at our house to make Andre look guilty?'

'Who would that be?' Offutt asked.

Kelly ignored the question. 'So the investigation is closed? You aren't even looking for anyone else at this point?'

Offutt gave her a pitying look. 'Ma'am, your husband admitted to murdering the doctor. The case is closed. The best use of your time at this point is working with his attorney.'

THIRTY-THREE

Finding Olivia Sable proved harder than Maggie had imagined. Her social media posts stopped the day Dr LeBlanc was murdered. Plenty of friends had posted on multiple sites asking why she wasn't returning phone calls or responding to messages, but she had remained silent, at least on the public sites that Maggie had access to. Sunshine Carrie, however, posted hourly, leaving a trail of her whereabouts like breadcrumbs.

That day alone, Maggie had found two postings on Facebook. 'Sunshine Carrie was at TJ's Boston Lox, Santa Cruz, FL, with Olivia Sable and Chrissie Venetta', followed by a photo of a plate with a half-eaten bagel smothered in cream cheese, lox and capers. The next post said, 'Sunshine Carrie was at Gucci, Santa Cruz, FL with Olivia Sable'. The post was followed by a picture of the two young women taking a photo in front of a mirror in a brightly lit dressing room. They wore slinky dresses that looked like lingerie to Maggie.

Maggie spent the next half hour scrolling through Olivia's posts over the previous month, looking for people she spoke to regularly, as well as places she visited on a regular basis. Aside from a few comments from a person Maggie found surprising, she didn't find any stand-out information. She did, however, discover that Olivia attended a workout class twice a week from six until seven in the evening at a business called Cycling Nation, located just five minutes from the doctor's office. Maggie decided that if she'd not connected with Olivia by the next evening, she would wait outside the gym for a chat.

Maggie paid $4.99 to access the online Whitepages to find Olivia's address, as well as that of her parents', both located in south Santa Cruz.

After driving by Olivia's home and finding it empty, Maggie drove to her parents' home. At three o'clock in the afternoon, the upscale neighborhood was quiet; too hot for walkers and bike riders, and too early for rush-hour commuters rolling in from work.

Maggie pulled down the driveway of a Tuscan-style home with wrought-iron window boxes and ivy trailing up the walls. After waiting several minutes on the front porch, a woman in her late sixties answered the door, frowning at the intrusion.

'Yes?'

'Mrs Sable, my name is Maggie Wise. I'm a radio host with WKQE here in Santa Cruz.'

Her jaw dropped. 'You have to be kidding me. Now the media is going to hound her too? As if the police weren't enough? She is not here. And no, I will not tell you where she is. Leave her alone!'

Maggie was surprised when the door wasn't slammed in her face, but the woman remained standing there, her lips pursed in anger.

'I apologize for the intrusion. I'm not here to gather a story. My visit actually has little to do with the radio station, I simply

wanted to let you know who I was. I'm actually here representing one of the families of the two girls who were kidnapped.
I was hoping to ask Olivia just a few questions.' Maggie handed
her one of her business cards. 'If you could just share my
contact information with your daughter, I'd appreciate it. Again,
I apologize for the intrusion.'

The woman's expression softened at the mention of the girls,
but she said nothing else as she closed the door.

After leaving the Sables' home, Maggie drove to the doctor's
office, hoping to find posted instructions for patients. She found
a typed note on the front door that stated: 'Patients of Dr Oscar
LeBlanc may contact the following number to access patient
medical records'. Maggie wrote the number down and called
from her car.

'Hello, this is Lilly with Med Help Answering Service. How
can I help you?'

'My name is Maggie Wise. I'm a patient of Doctor Oscar
LeBlanc's. I was given this number and told you could help
me get my records.'

'Absolutely. I'll be glad to help.'

She put Maggie on hold for several minutes, then came back
with some unexpected news.

'One of Doctor LeBlanc's employees is taking care of records
distribution. She works two days per week. She'll be in the
office tomorrow from eight until eleven, and again the day after
tomorrow, same hours, if you'd like to stop by.'

'That's great. How do I make an appointment?'

'No appointment necessary.'

'And her name?'

'I'm sorry, I wasn't provided that information. But she'll be
glad to help you.'

'I also have questions about my investments in Doctor
LeBlanc's research project. Can you tell me who is taking care
of those details?'

'No, I'm sorry, Ms Wise. Med Help is only handling
medical records. I don't have any additional information about
investments.'

Rather than trying Olivia's house again, Maggie opted to
wait until morning to try the doctor's office. As far as she could

tell from an internet search, Olivia was the only full-time employee who had worked at the office

After receiving a group text from Agnus earlier in the day, Maggie showered and dressed and met the group at Mel's Class Act for dinner at six. The text had been vague, just a request from Agnus for everyone to *Please come.*

Maggie recognized all the numbers in the group text, which meant that Romeo hadn't been included. She wondered if dinner was going to be a surprise engagement announcement or a good riddance celebration, and decided that, regardless, she would make an appointment with a realtor the next day to begin searching for a home in Cypress City. Meanwhile, she would be gracious and thank Agnus for all she had done for her since her move to Santa Cruz. Agnus deserved happiness, and Maggie was determined to help her achieve that.

Mel Sharp was a former Alaskan fisherman who gave up the cold and the fish on New Year's Eve of 1999 in order to follow his daughter and son-in-law to Florida. His daughter's advice, after convincing him to move out of their basement and into his own apartment, was to do something he loved, something he thought he could be good at. Mel knew nothing about owning a restaurant, booking musicians or running a bar. But he wasn't afraid of fresh seafood, and he loved to eat and drink and listen to good music. Hanging above the cash register behind the bar was a framed piece of notebook paper with the brainstorming list that Mel had used when deciding that owning a 'classy' restaurant was going to be his new profession. His business brought him a great sense of pride, and Maggie respected the courage it had taken him to remake himself after realizing the Alaskan winters were not his idea of the good life.

But Mel also had a penchant for helping wayward souls. Between Mel and Agnus, most of the regulars at Mel's Class Act had received a handout or hand-up of some kind. Danny G credited Mel for starting his music career, which he was now able to do full time. He made decent money as a wedding singer, and he had enough contacts in south Florida that he stayed busy most weekends, while the new Vegas gig loomed large.

When Maggie arrived early at Mel's that evening, she found Danny signing a contract with a young couple who were sitting at a table in the back of the restaurant. Danny joined Maggie at the bar after the couple left.

'Fifty-thousand-dollar wedding. Can you believe that? For a one-night affair.'

Maggie shook her head. 'What a waste of money.'

'Agreed. But they're paying me two grand to bring the band. So I'm game. Nice kids. Her parents do something with offshore drilling in Louisiana, so money isn't much of a concern. Just making it a "perfect evening" for their guests is all that's required. I heard that fifty times tonight.'

'Sounds like a setup for disappointment,' Maggie said.

'When did you get to be such a cynic?'

'Birth.'

At six, Maggie and Danny moved into the restaurant where Mel had joined two tables together for the group of seven. Mel lit the candles at the table and placed silverware at eight places. Romeo was apparently on the list after all. Maggie noticed that Buffalo Bruce took a seat next to Agnus. He'd had a crush on her for years, but she'd never taken him up on his occasional requests for dinner, explaining that she didn't want to ruin a perfectly good friendship. Whitney and Serena sat on the other end of the table where they were quietly gossiping about something. Mark arrived and sat next to Maggie, with Danny directly across the table. Maggie had Mel bring out the first round of drinks on her. Mark kissed her on the cheek, and she felt a flush of happiness, realizing it had been days since she had relaxed.

With the appetizers served and people chatting amiably, Agnus tapped her wine glass with her spoon and motioned for Mel, who was serving a drink at the bar, to join them. He came to the table and took the empty chair next to Agnus.

'First, I want to thank you all for coming tonight. I don't need to tell you how important you all are to me. You reach a certain age and people start asking you what your secret is to long life and good health. Well, I can tell you my secret, and it's all of you. My good friends.'

Danny lifted his beer bottle and the table followed suit with a chorus of 'To Agnus.'

'It's been a tumultuous couple of weeks. I know I don't need to, but I want to explain myself. I'm no longer seeing Roomy.' Mark reached a hand down the table. 'I'm sorry to hear that, Agnus.'

'Don't be sorry. It was never meant to be. Maggie, please don't think this is about you, it's not. He didn't like you, and I didn't like that, but it's not why I broke it off. He just got too possessive.'

'A woman needs her freedom,' Bruce said.

'Indeed she does,' she said, smiling at Bruce. 'Here's the thing. I'm old. And I'm happy. But it doesn't mean I don't still have a hole in my heart that Jim used to fill. I thought when I met Roomy, and he started coming around, that he would fill it up. But he didn't. He was a worry. Love shouldn't be like that. So for now, I want to thank you for being my family. I value each of you.' Agnus raised her wine glass. 'To friendship!'

The group clinked glasses and several toasts followed until dinner was served.

Once the plates were cleared, Mel lowered the lights and pulled up a playlist of Frank Sinatra and Ella Fitzgerald, Agnus's favorite dance tunes. After Mark took Agnus several times around the dancefloor, she pointed to the table, claiming she needed a rest. The manic smile she had been carrying for several weeks had been replaced with a happiness that radiated from her on the dancefloor.

Maggie pulled her chair out and Agnus sat next to her. 'You look beautiful tonight.'

'I feel beautiful too!' Agnus said, laughing at her response.

'I want to bring something up, but it's not meant to dampen the spirit tonight. I think it's a good thing for both of us. Will you take it in that spirit?' Maggie asked.

'I'll try.'

'You'll assume this is all about Romeo, but it's only partially connected to him. You know how much I appreciate living next to you. The home you've given to me is an amazing gesture of friendship.'

Agnus nodded, her expression turning grim.

'I want to continue living there, but I need to pay you.' Agnus started to protest but Maggie laid a hand over hers to stop her.

'I know you don't need the money. But you can put it into an account for repairs. Or you can put it into an account where the money goes straight to charity. We can do an automatic deposit where you don't even have to look at the check.'

'This was never a problem before Romeo.'

'It was a problem for me. Blame it on my stupid ego, or my own psychosis. But I'd feel better about staying if you would allow me to do this.'

'All right then. I'll have my accountant set up an account and draw up papers for you to purchase the gardener's house on contract. We'll find a suitable charity for it. Does that make you feel better?'

'It does.'

Agnus patted her hand. 'Good. Then you better tell Danny to go rescue Serena on the dancefloor before Mel gets fresh with her.'

The evening ended with Mark following Maggie back to her place, a term she would gladly use now with no awkward hesitation. It was almost ten o'clock before they reached her house, and Mark had to leave for work by seven the next morning, but he requested a walk on the beach before bed. They stripped down to shorts and T-shirts and walked to the shore hand in hand.

'It was a perfect night,' Mark said. 'It was nice to see you and Agnus back to normal.'

'I agree. She's such a sweet lady.'

'I wish she'd get over it and hook up with Buffalo Bruce,' he said.

'No,' Maggie said, frowning. 'Can't you see there's no chemistry? There's no spark between them.'

'Bruce seems to think there is.'

'Bruce wants someone to share his life with. Agnus wants love. Two different things.'

They reached the shoreline and stopped where the water lapped against their toes. Under the moonlight, the water reflected like vast pools of spilled mercury.

'You think it's possible to have both? Friendship and love?' he asked.

'Absolutely! I wouldn't be standing here if I didn't think it was possible. I'm a pragmatist, but also a romantic.' She turned to face him. 'Can you deliver both?'

Mark placed his hands on her shoulders as she wrapped her arms around his back. He caught a shiny flicker of light and touched his finger to the tiny diamond earring dangling against her neck. He bent and kissed her ear, and followed along her neckline. She felt his body press against hers. He ran his hands down her back to rest on her hips, pulling her closer. She turned her head and said his name, searching for his mouth, her eyes bright in the moonlight. She dropped to her knees, pulling him down with her, and they lay in the wet sand, allowing the waves to splash onto them as the rhythmic surf drowned out everything but the moment.

THIRTY-FOUR

Maggie woke before her alarm and left Mark sleeping. In the kitchen, she whisked together eggs and a dash of cream, and sautéed mushrooms, peppers and tomatoes for scrambled eggs. By the time he wandered into the kitchen, she had the toast buttered and hot coffee on the table, with the eggs just coming off the stove.

Mark's eyes were puffy with sleep. He smiled at Maggie and she thought he was one of the most handsome men she'd ever laid eyes on. She realized the moment came with no comparison to David, an insight that she allowed to come and go without dwelling on the reason.

'This is a nice surprise,' he said.

'You need your energy. Get a good breakfast and I'll send you on your way.'

Midway through his scrambled eggs, Mark's eyes had regained their focus as he poured a second cup of coffee. 'I'm going to say something that's probably going to get me into trouble with you.'

'You have some cache built up after last night. Now's a good time to try me,' she said.

'I want to talk about the O'Neal investigation.'

She nodded once, maintaining a neutral expression. 'What's up?'

'I need to talk this through for my own benefit.'

'Sure.'

'I know that you don't believe Andre killed Doctor LeBlanc.'

'That's correct,' she said.

'Then I need you to have an open mind for a minute. Could he be covering up for his wife? Could he be confessing to murder in order to save his wife from prison? Because their car was at the scene. I'm sure you heard that one of the eyewitnesses got the first four digits from her license plate.'

'I did hear that. But I don't know when a couple of numbers has ever been good enough for a jury.'

'What you didn't hear is that the eyewitness remembered seeing a bumper sticker for Greenpeace on that car. Kelly's car has a Greenpeace sticker on it. I think we could most likely scan every car with a similar make and model in Santa Cruz, and none of them would have a Greenpeace sticker on the bumper.'

'That does complicate things,' she said.

'I agree with the Santa Cruz assessment of this case. One of the O'Neals was at the doctor's office the night of the murder. So it was Andre, or it was Kelly.'

'Just because they were in the vicinity doesn't mean they killed him. The guy was ate up with anger over what happened to his daughter. Maybe he was just driving by, trying to make sense of it all.'

'Come on, Maggie. There's no such thing as a naive cop.'

'For the record, I did not bring up the investigation. You did.'

He smiled and tipped his head to acknowledge the point. 'I honestly am trying to understand your point of view with this.'

'Then you want me to tell you what I've found?'

'I do.'

'You can't get mad at me for interfering,' she said, giving him a hard look.

'I won't promise that, but I still want to hear.'

Maggie grabbed her laptop and sat next to him at the table. She pulled up the screenshot of Olivia's post on her Pop-Daddy account. She watched as Mark read the exchange between Olivia and Sunshine Carrie.

'The way I read that post, Olivia was going on a date with her boss to Miami. She expected him to spend a significant amount of money on the date, but she wasn't happy that he was taking her all the way to Miami to avoid being seen by his wife.'

'I get where you're coming from, but I'm not sure why this is significant,' he said.

'Because someone from his office, or with intimate knowledge of his office, planted that gauze in Andre O'Neal's workshop. Someone murdered Doctor LeBlanc and staged it to look like the crazy dad that everyone's talking about on social media did it.'

'But what's her motive? If she's in love with the doctor, why kill him?'

'From my simple calculations, I believe he has upwards of fifteen million dollars in investments for his blood bank clinics. I think the doctor was so into his groundbreaking research that he didn't follow through with the details. He expected other people to be as passionate about his ideals as he was. We saw that with Ramone, the blood tech who was supposed to have taken care of the details with the young girls.'

'How so?'

'If you were in the doctor's place, wouldn't you have checked and double-checked the details on those girls being taken from their families? It's mindboggling to me that he trusted some blood tech to take care of the details. But I think that's his personality. He's the ideas man.'

Mark pursed his lips. 'OK. I'll give you that.'

'Then I talked to one of his investors and discovered there were at least two accountants involved with the investments. One of them was indicted on money laundering charges over another client's money. The other accountant has disappeared.'

'Did he take off with the money?' he asked.

'No one seems to know. The investor I talked to said the financials he had accessed made it impossible to figure out where the investments are housed.' Maggie paused. 'Again, this problem wasn't created overnight. This is a research doctor, someone who has taken on a monumental pay-to-play project, without the staff or means to carry out the details.'

Mark looked at his watch. 'This is all interesting. But I have to get to work. What does this have to do with the receptionist sleeping with her boss?'

'Because she's the one person who has access to everything we've discussed. Medical records, investments, patient accounts. She has the most to gain. She has the motive, the means and the opportunity.'

Mark narrowed his eyes. 'Motive sure, but means? You think she could have slashed his wrists?'

'Check out her social media feed. She's a beautiful girl with young, adoring guys everywhere. It's not too much of a stretch to believe she could have found someone to take care of the so-called suicide. Someone who could make it look like the deranged dad did it.'

'So what do you do about this? Do you want me to present your theory to Chief Osbourne? Because if you take it to him, I doubt you'll be well received.'

Maggie omitted the fact that she had plans to visit Olivia that morning. 'I'm not ready to say anything yet. Let me see what else I can come up with.'

Maggie arrived at Dr LeBlanc's office at nine and found three cars in the small parking area in front of the building. Presumably the BMW and Infinity were former patients, while the Mitsubishi belonged to Olivia.

Inside, Maggie found a woman in the waiting room stuffing papers and folders into a large leather bag while she talked on her cell phone. To the right of the waiting room was the hallway leading to patient rooms and the doctor's office. No lights were on. To the right of the hallway was the reception-ist's office where Olivia stood behind a partition. She nodded as a gaunt white-haired man who appeared to be in his eighties gestured with both hands, getting louder with each sentence. Maggie took a seat after the woman left and listened to the man grow more irate as Olivia explained repeatedly that she had no information about the investment part of Dr LeBlanc's office.

The man banged his hand on the counter and yelled, 'You tell me where my goddamned money is or I'll come back with someone who *can* get the money!'

Maggie stood and walked up to the man. He glanced at Maggie and continued. 'Don't give me this bullshit about not knowing where my money is either. That other lady may have bought it, but not me. I've been coming here ten years now, and you know more about this place than LeBlanc ever did.'

'Hey, buddy, this isn't her doing,' Maggie said. 'Get an attorney if you want to fight this. She's just the receptionist.'

The man turned to Maggie with bulging eyes, his expression one of disbelief. 'You're going to come in here and tell me how to conduct my business? Do you have any idea how much money these people sucked out of my retirement account?'

'Take it up with an attorney. All she can do is provide you with your medical records.'

The man looked back at Olivia, who nodded agreement. He uttered additional profanities but finally turned and left.

'You wouldn't believe some of the crazy people I've talked to over the past week.' Olivia closed her mouth and Maggie could see realization dawn. 'Oh wow. I recognize you. You're the radio lady.'

'That's me. I tried to connect with you over social media, but it looks like you've shut it all down.'

'You would not believe my life since all this happened. The police are at my house every other day. I had to hire an attorney. He's the one that made me get off all social media. I can't even log on. He wanted me to delete all my accounts.'

'Why would you need to do that?'

'I don't know. I was like, "no, I have friends on there all over the world!" I am not going to lose all my contacts. It's like I'm the one being punished. And I didn't do anything wrong!'

'Why are the police hounding you? You just work here.' Maggie tried for an indignant tone, full of sympathy.

'I don't know. I am so over all of this. I want out of this town so bad.'

'Maybe it's the rumors about you having an affair with the doctor that have the police interested. They assume you know something.' Maggie hoped she would get away with the offensive comment. She was guessing that the cops had taken note of Olivia's social media, same as she did. She guessed right.

'It's such bullshit! My personal life is none of their business.'

'Do you have another job? A way out of here?' Maggie asked.

'Oh, I'm getting out of here, for sure. I'm so over this place.'

'Where to?'

She shrugged a shoulder and studied Maggie, apparently realizing that the questions had nothing to do with the medical records she was supposed to be claiming.

'I ask because I might have a lead on a job opportunity for you.'

'No. I don't need it. I have plans. I'm just getting out.'

'What if I told you that I know your plans?' Maggie asked.

'What's that supposed to mean?'

'I know the game your doctor was playing. And I've got you figured out too.'

'You need to leave.'

'Or what? You'll call the police? I don't think you'll do that.'

'I don't know what you're talking about.'

'There are a large number of investors who are desperate to find out where their money is. A search for two previous accountants has come up empty. The legal quicksand around the investments is either a fiasco, or ingenious planning, depending on how you look at it.'

Olivia's face had grown rigid. She didn't flinch. She looked as if she had stopped breathing.

'I'm not sure you understand this yet, but you are playing with some dangerous people. I can make sure that you get your money and get out of town before all of this falls apart.'

'Why would you do that?' Olivia asked.

'To make a profit. Same as you.'

'Why would I trust you? I don't even know you.'

'You can view me as someone who takes care of things for people.'

'Like you took care of Kelly?'

Maggie lifted a shoulder in response.

Olivia didn't blink. 'I need to think about this.'

'That's fine.' She passed her the radio station business card with her cell phone on the back. 'You give me an answer by tomorrow morning at ten. Or I go to the police. Understand?' She nodded and Maggie left as another angry patient entered the building.

On her way home, Maggie listened to a voice message from Danny that said he was setting up the sound equipment for a first-time gig at a bar in Santa Cruz called Hex Appeal. The bar was located on the waterfront with twenty-dollar mixed drinks and a five-dollar cover charge, which Danny hoped would translate into full tip jars for the band by the end of the night.

Maggie arrived at the bar at around ten thirty in the morning and found Danny and Whitney plugging in the amps and guitars while Bruce arranged his drum set.

'Don't you guys have roadies taking care of this?' Maggie asked.

'We rely on the kindness of strangers and good friends,' Danny said.

Maggie spent the next half hour helping Bruce carry in the rest of his drum set, and then sat with Danny at the empty bar to drink a cold bottle of water.

'I didn't leave a message so you'd come over here and help, but thanks anyway.'

'You bet. I hope it's a money maker.'

'I figured out what I was making on the hour, between setup and teardown, practice and booking gigs.' He shook his head and grinned. 'It's not good. And if one more person tells me it's not about the money, I'll choke them.'

'Pretty high-class bar. Maybe you'll make some good connections.'

'The bar owner had heard about Whitney singing Motown and thought we'd be a good fit. We hung out here last week to get a feel for it.' He snapped his fingers. 'Which is why I called you. Remember telling me about the blood doctor's wife giving you crap about dragging her husband's name through the mud?'

'Yeah.'

'Well, I saw her here last weekend. She was with another lady tripping on the dancefloor.'

'Seriously?'

'She was dancing and drinking and having a hell of a good time. She didn't look like a woman who was distraught over her husband's good name. Or his death.'

'You sure it was her?'

'No doubt. Several people pointed her out so I took a photo. She was the talk of the bar that night.' Danny pulled his cell phone out. 'I figured you'd appreciate the irony. She's giving you hell about dragging her husband's good name through the dirt, and here she is a week after she buried him dancing it up with her girlfriend at a bar.'

Maggie took the cell phone and enlarged the photo. 'I'll be damned.' She handed it back to Danny, grinning. 'Do me a favor and forward me a copy of that.'

THIRTY-FIVE

The office of Thomas McBain, the defense attorney in Andre's case, was located in a residential neighborhood on the outskirts of Old Santa Cruz. The pale blue stucco office was tastefully landscaped with a small sitting area under a trio of twenty-foot-high palm trees. Due to its close proximity to the water, Maggie figured the small home was still in the two-million-dollar range.

She pulled behind Kelly's car in a small brick parking area.

'I'm sorry you've had to spend so much time on this mess,' Kelly said.

'I'm a retired cop with too many hours to fill. And I didn't have to spend any time on it. I've helped because I wanted to.'

'This all just makes me so nervous. I heard you tell Andre that we have to tell the attorney everything. We need to be completely honest so that he can help us. But I can't really do that, right?'

Maggie wiped a hand across her forehead, feeling the effects of the late afternoon heat. 'I told Andre that *he* had to tell the attorney everything. And I meant that. Just keep in mind the focus here is on Andre. It's not about you and what you did or didn't do.'

'Meaning I shouldn't talk about driving to the doctor's office?'

'Correct. Because he will want to know what you were doing there. At this point, unless you've told people I don't know about, you and I are the only people who know that fact. Is that true?'

'Yes.'

'Let's keep it that way.'

She sighed. 'I feel like I need an attorney to go with me to talk with my attorney.'

Inside the small home, a middle-aged Asian woman wearing a tasteful white pantsuit introduced herself as Simone. She thanked them for being prompt, then escorted Maggie and Kelly down a short hallway and into an office where an impeccably dressed African American man introduced himself as Tom. He gestured for them to sit at a small conference table where he joined them with a stack of papers.

He started the meeting giving Kelly his legal background and explaining to her how the public defender program worked. He described what she could expect out of his work with Andre, then jumped into the specifics of the case. Maggie was impressed with his professionalism, and his efficiency.

After summarizing the case against Andre, he said, 'I am quite concerned about your husband's situation because he is not being honest with me. It is abundantly clear that he is trying to protect you. I have explained that his motivation does not concern me. What I need is to understand the details so that I can provide the best defense possible.'

Kelly nodded but said nothing.

The attorney sighed, apparently hoping for more from her response. 'I counseled Andre to change his plea to not guilty. I will make the case that the police terrified him during the interrogation. That they blatantly lied, telling him that you were going to be arrested if Andre didn't admit to the crime.' He sat back in his chair and gave Kelly a long appraising stare. 'The problem is, Andre won't even discuss the matter. I cannot make him understand that you are not in danger.'

'I tried to explain the same thing, but he won't listen,' she said.

'Given his refusal to change his plea, I am recommending that we have Andre's mental state evaluated. We'll focus on his military record and his wartime injuries. But again, Andre won't discuss it. I need you to convince him this is his best option.'

Kelly shook her head. 'He'll never go for that. He'll go to jail before he allows someone to say he isn't mentally competent.'

The attorney threw the pencil he'd been twirling between his fingers onto the table. 'Do you understand the trouble your husband is in? We need to convince the jury that Andre was confused when he admitted to killing the doctor. That he was coerced into making a statement before his attorney was present. I need you to convince him that taking care of himself isn't going to send you to jail. Can you help him understand that? Because if you can't, your husband will most certainly be going to jail for the rest of his life.'

Back outside, Kelly turned to Maggie before getting into her car. 'I don't know how much longer I can keep this up. Nobody understands me anymore. The attorney thinks I'm screwing my husband over. My mom thinks I should file for a divorce. My neighbors think I should file a lawsuit against the doctor's estate. My sister wants me to leave Andre immediately and move to Louisiana. And nobody realizes half of Andre's problems were brought on by me.' She dug her keys out of her purse and clicked the unlock button, her brows furrowed in anger. 'On top of all that, I'm afraid to talk on my phone because I think it might be bugged. I know that sounds completely paranoid, but I swear my phone is acting weird, and I'm pretty sure someone is watching my house.'

Maggie noticed the attorney standing in the window at the front of the house, watching them talking. 'I wish I didn't have to say this, but you're probably right to be paranoid. It's most likely the media outside your house, the paparazzi looking for a story. It could be the police, but I doubt that at this point. I also heard rumors that the Baxters are talking about filing a civil suit against LeBlanc's estate. I heard they've hired their own investigators.'

'The worst part of this is the guilt. I've made a mess of everything. Amaya's trauma has gotten lost in all of this other drama. My own husband thinks I had something to do with that doctor's murder. And I know I should turn myself in and come clean about all of this. Andre doesn't belong in jail. But if Andre has to take care of Amaya full time, on his own, what then? I know this sounds terrible, but I'm not sure he's capable.'

Maggie could hear the anguish in her words, but she had no idea how to console her.

'So what happens if I do turn myself in?' Kelly said. 'What happens if I admit to pulling one over on the doctor, and then I get charged with murder? I swear to you, Maggie, I did not murder that man. It's not in me. It's not why I went to see him. I knew I had one night to get that money before the cops would get to him the next day. That's all there was to it.'

Maggie stared at her for a moment as a string of thoughts came together.

'What is it?'

'You hang in there. Keep your head down low. Give me a day to work something through and I'll get back to you.'

Maggie pulled from the driveway, thinking about Kelly's comment. She'd had one night to get the money before the cops got to him the next day. But what if someone else had the same idea? Who else knew they had one night to get to LeBlanc before the cops arrested him?

Driving back to her home, Maggie called Mark. 'I need you to think back on the order of events in the early part of the LeBlanc investigation.'

'Hang on. Let me get back to my desk.'

She heard his office door close and the creak of his desk chair. 'Go ahead.'

'Think back to the day before LeBlanc was murdered, back when you had just discovered that he had kidnapped the two girls.'

'OK.'

'Do you know if the Santa Cruz cops questioned his receptionist, Olivia, about the doctor's involvement?'

Mark didn't hesitate. 'No, I'm sure of that. They didn't want her tipping off the doctor before an arrest could be made.'

'What about the doctor's wife, Jillian LeBlanc?'

'She was a different story. One of the Santa Cruz PD officers had heard that she had a reputation for screwing around on her husband. He claimed they were in the process of filing for divorce. One of the officers questioned her that day. There was quite a bit of debate over whether that was a good move or not.' She listened as Mark flipped through his notes. 'I have written down here 3:30, but I'd want to confirm that. It was after Kelly O'Neal talked to the doctor that morning.'

'How'd the interview go?' she asked.

'It didn't produce much. I don't think they gave her too much information. It was more to feel her out, to see if she'd turn tail on him. Pissed off wife turned informant kind of thing.'

'So she knew the police were looking into her husband as a possible suspect, before he was murdered?'

'Yes, I'm confident of that.'

'And he was murdered that night.'

'I know where you're going with this,' Mark said. 'But she had an alibi. A friend was at her house that night. She'd gone to the bars and she came over and slept on Mrs LeBlanc's couch.'

'That's convenient. How reliable was the alibi?'

'I don't know. I wasn't involved in that part of the investigation. I just know the wife has never been a serious contender.'

'Didn't you tell me she was upset after she found out about her husband's death?'

'Well, yeah, but even if your marriage was in the tank you'd still be upset. She made the comment that she hadn't talked to him that night. That they sometimes went several days without speaking. Different schedules, that kind of thing.'

Maggie thought back to her conversation with Kelly: who else knew that the police were closing in on Dr LeBlanc? Jillian LeBlanc. Kelly O'Neal had figured out that she had one day to get what she needed from the doctor before the police closed in. Maybe Jillian had the same thought.

Maggie started to ask Mark if Santa Cruz had access to the computers from LeBlanc's office, thinking that Jillian may have gone to the office the night after the police talked with her to access the investment money before the police shut the accounts down. But Maggie also knew that LeBlanc had used his computer in his office that night to set up an offshore bank account for Kelly O'Neal.

Mark made a humming noise as if he was putting together the pieces. 'So Jillian could either endure the humiliation of watching her husband be arrested for kidnapping little girls, or she could fake his suicide and scam his investment money before someone else got access to it.'

'You have to admit, the idea has some merit.'

'I'm still listening.'

'At the beginning of the investigation, one of the officers mentioned that the doctor left his office the night he was murdered and used a security code to enter his house through the front door. Then he entered the code when he left as well. He said they subpoenaed the records from the alarm company to get exact times.'

'That's right. Santa Cruz shared the records. I have them on my computer.'

'What about the login/logout times? You're clear on those? The timing works?' Maggie asked.

'It was the alarm code records that helped narrow down his time of death.' She listened as he sorted through papers on his desk. 'We know that the doctor arrived home that night at 11:24 p.m., and left home again at 2:10 a.m. His wife remembered him leaving at around two in the morning. She said it wasn't all that unusual. They slept in different bedrooms because of his odd sleeping patterns. She stated that if he couldn't sleep in the middle of the night, he would get up and go in to work.'

'And the coroner agreed that LeBlanc bled out sometime after two thirty in the morning?'

'That's correct. I think he listed time of death as three a.m.'

'Would you be willing to share the alarm company records with me?'

'They looked at the time frame and everything checked out,' he said.

'I just want to take a look.'

He hesitated. 'I can get them to you, but obviously this is confidential.'

'Mark. Who else am I going to tell? I just want to take a look. I'll let you know if I find anything new.'

THIRTY-SIX

M aggie bought a drive-through hamburger and fries for dinner and drove home to examine the timings. She printed off five pages of documents from Beta Alarm Systems, with four of the pages consisting of legalese, and just one page with the security codes used on the day of the murder.

As she imagined, a code number was given, with the login and logout times. Maggie could see immediately that there was a problem. She went to the spiral pad of paper she'd been using for notes concerning the investigation and flipped back to a conversation she'd had with Kelly. She said she'd left the doctor's office, after setting up the overseas account, at 11:15 p.m. The documents showed that the doctor logged in at his home at 11:24 p.m. Maggie knew where the doctor lived, and figured it was at least a ten-minute drive, even on deserted streets at night.

Maggie called Kelly. 'Could I stop by tonight with a quick question?'

'Sure.'

'You'll be around all night?'

She laughed. 'Where else would I be?'

'Would ten thirty be too late?'

'No, that's fine.'

Maggie finished her paperback novel and watched reruns on TV until she found it late enough to drive to Kelly's. She wanted the traffic to be as close to what it would have been when Kelly made the drive on the night of the murder. As she'd done with Amaya, she parked a street over, under a tree with no streetlamp, and locked her car. Walking down the alley and around the house, she searched for anything or anyone that looked out of place. She walked around the side of the house and stood at the corner in silence. She heard a raccoon rustling around a garbage can next door and a barking dog a few houses away, but the rest of the street was silent. Seeing no one, she hoped it was simple paranoia on Kelly's part.

Maggie entered through the kitchen where Kelly had a pitcher of cranberry juice and vodka cocktail mixed and sitting on the table.

'I hope you don't mind. It feels awful drinking alone, so I thought I'd take advantage of your visit.'

'I'll take one. Thanks.'

She poured them each a juice glass full and led Maggie into the living room. The blinds were down with curtains pulled over them.

'New curtains?' Maggie asked.

Kelly smiled but looked embarrassed. 'I couldn't stand the gap between the edge of the blind and the window. I felt like someone was peering in at me through the cracks at night. With Amaya here, I had to be brave and convince her everything was normal. But with Andre gone and Amaya at my sister's, I've gotten paranoid.'

'I came in from the back of your property and walked around to the front. I didn't see anything out of place. No suspicious cars or people out on foot.'

Kelly nodded and sat down on one end of the couch, so Maggie took the other.

'How's Amaya handling being away from home?'

'My sister says she's doing great. She says the girls are having fun. When I call Amaya we tell each other stories about our day. I try to make her laugh. But it feels like we're just making it up.' She shrugged. 'I don't know. Maybe she is doing well. I sure hope so.'

'Nothing wrong with faking it. I think people call that having a good attitude.'

Kelly offered a fake smile and held her glass up. 'Cheers to that.'

'I came by tonight because I didn't want to call, in case your phone really has been compromised. I'm trying to put together a timeline from the night the doctor was murdered, and what the police are working from isn't jiving with the timeline you gave me.'

She frowned, as if not understanding. 'I told you exactly what I did that night.'

'Go back over the timeline again. From when you left his office.'

'It was eleven fifteen. I remember telling you that the next day. When I got in my car I looked at the time on the dashboard because I was hoping I would beat Andre home so I wouldn't have to explain where I was. I hadn't expected to be gone that long so I was worried about the time.'

'There's no doubt in your mind about when you left?'

'None.'

'So here's how it played out that night. You showed up at his office at eight o'clock, correct?'

'Yes.'

'You left his office at eleven fifteen. During those three hours he was helping you set up the offshore account.'

'That's right.'

'After you left, he supposedly left and went home. He was home from roughly eleven thirty until about two in the morning when he came back to the office. Sometime after he came back is when he was murdered. I'm wondering if he said anything to you about going home. You were sitting there with him for three hours, surely you talked about things.'

Kelly lifted a shoulder and made a disgusted face. 'It wasn't like we were making small talk. I hated the man. It was awkward and horrible if you want the truth. He was in and out of his office while we waited for things to set up. I would sit for long periods of time while he disappeared to somewhere else in his office. I'm sure it was so that he didn't have to sit there and stare at me.'

'So, when you left, you didn't see him acting like he was in a rush to leave?'

'No. He actually stopped me before I left to make sure he had the correct number to text me about when I would be bringing in Amaya again.' Kelly shuddered at the memory.

'Here's the problem. The coroner gave the time of death as three a.m. The police state that LeBlanc left his office and used his security code to enter his home at eleven twenty-four, and he left the house again at two ten.'

'No way. When I left his office, he had all the lights on, his computer was on. It would have taken him some time to shut everything up before leaving. No way could he do all that in nine minutes unless he lives just down the street.'

'I'm going to drive it tonight. Just to see. Maybe your clock was off by a few minutes. Maybe he did leave the lights and computer on and ran home for some reason, knowing he was going to come back. Maybe he was planning on meeting the person who murdered him at his office around three, and he went home to get something.'

'The three o'clock time of death doesn't really work either,' she said.

'How so?'

'If he left home at two ten and arrived back at his office around two thirty, that would be a really quick turnaround for the murderer. Someone had to have come in and gotten the doctor drunk enough to tie him down and slash his wrists in a half hour.'

Maggie cocked her head. 'The time of death isn't an exact science. I think give or take an hour would be reasonable. So it's plausible that his time of death was more like four in the morning.'

'Let's drive the route,' Kelly said. 'I'll go with you.'

'I appreciate the offer, but if I get pulled over outside the doctor's office, I'd prefer you weren't with me.'

Maggie had already examined several alternate routes, but given the time of day, with little to no traffic, only one route made sense. Maggie pulled down the tree-lined lane to the doctor's office, hoping that new surveillance cameras hadn't been installed since the murder. She turned her car around and started the timer on her phone, driving five miles per hour over the speed limit on the fastest route to the doctor's home. She encountered no traffic through the deserted business district to slow her progress. The trip took sixteen minutes and forty seconds, and that didn't include the time it would have taken the doctor to exit his car, walk to the front door, and enter the security code. Maggie took a screenshot and sent it to Kelly.

She texted back: *Great but how do you explain the time doesn't work without telling the police I was there?*

I'm working on it. Keep that positive attitude.

On her way home, Maggie pulled on to the Tamiami Trail and had to swerve to miss a group of drunken college boys in swim trunks and flip-flops stumbling along the highway median, probably trying to find their way back to their hotel. Maggie came to a stop at a red light and they walked in front of her car, flipping her off for no apparent reason. She noticed that two of the boys wore no shoes and tiptoed across the roadway, dodging shards of glass, until fat raindrops fell from the sky without warning, and they all took off running as the cold rain slid down their bare backs. Within minutes, the rain was coming down so hard all Maggie could see was the vague shapeless brake lights of the cars in front of her. She figured the rain would either sober the boys up in a hurry, or they'd end up sleeping it off in a parking garage until morning. Karma is a bitch, she thought.

She arrived home close to midnight, but instead of going to bed, she perked a pot of coffee and sat down at the kitchen table with the security code entries for Dr LeBlanc's house. She confirmed she was looking at the correct time period: the forty-eight hours from six a.m. Tuesday to six a.m. Thursday. Maggie noticed that what originally appeared to be one six-digit code was actually two codes, separated by one digit: 459200 and 459300. She noted that there was no way to tell whether a security code entry was for an entrance or an exit, to or from the home. She was fairly certain it was an older system based on the simplistic information. The couple had probably been using it for the past decade, and with no issues they'd not bothered to upgrade.

The cover page from Beta Alarm Systems contained contact information, and a direct line that was manned twenty-four hours a day for law enforcement. Maggie called the number and introduced herself as an officer working on the investigation.

She provided the case number that had been noted at the top of the paperwork.

'Yes, ma'am. How may I help you?'

'Can you confirm that there is no way to see login and logout access codes as separate entries?'

'That is correct. That information is accompanied with an upgraded system.'

'Then I'm hoping you can send me the same information as what was in the original file, but I need it for all of June and July.'

'Absolutely, no problem. We're always happy to help in an investigation. I'll have that ready for you within the hour.'

'I've got an alternative email to give you to send the report to.'

'Go right ahead.'

Maggie provided her Gmail account, surprised that the woman would send information to an email unrelated to law enforcement. She assumed the proper case number was all she needed for verification.

Ten minutes later, Maggie was looking at the codes used for the previous two months. She remembered the receptionist stating that the doctor arrived at work shortly before eight in the morning. Maggie looked through the months of June and July and found that the code 459200 was used every weekday morning between 7:30 a.m. and 7:45 a.m. During the thirty weekdays that Maggie examined, there were no instances of the code being used again before 5:30 p.m. However, the other code had been used sporadically throughout the day. It was clear that code 459200 was used by Oscar LeBlanc, and code 459300 was used by Jillian LeBlanc.

Maggie sorted through the papers on her desk and found the codes used for the night of the murder. Jillian LeBlanc's code had been used at 11:24 p.m. and 2:10 a.m. The entries hadn't been used by the doctor to go home and return to work that night. They had been used by his wife to leave the house, murder her husband, and return home.

THIRTY-SEVEN

After putting the pieces together, Maggie called Mark and asked to meet him in his office at seven the next morning to talk about problems she'd found with the security system login chronology. She worked until almost dawn, printing papers and getting documents in order to lay out her theory. When she arrived, she found that Mark had also invited John Desmond to sit in on the meeting.

Mark sat across the table from Maggie, saying little. She hadn't filled him in on the specifics, just asked him to meet with her. She was certain he was at least mildly concerned that his reputation in his own office was at stake over this. It was an odd feeling, presenting a case to officers who weren't colleagues. Working homicide, Maggie had needed to sell her theories many times throughout the years, but she'd been talking to a group of cops who knew her integrity as a police officer. John knew Maggie as a retired officer dating the chief of police. He was probably viewing this early morning meeting as a courtesy call.

After a brief summary, Maggie said, 'I believe that Jillian LeBlanc killed her husband.' She handed them copies of the phone records with the doctor's code highlighted in yellow, and Jillian's code highlighted in green. She started with the month of June, showing the doctor's pattern of leaving in the morning and coming home in the evening. She then showed Jillian's code, explaining that her lack of employment allowed her to enter and exit her home at various times during the day.

Mark interrupted. 'Could the codes be entered by another person?'

'The code isn't actually a numeric entrance. It's a key fob that registers when the person enters or exits. So, yes, a person could exchange fobs. You'll want to check the fob that's with LeBlanc's personal effects to make sure he was in possession of the one he'd been using the past two months. If they're like most couples, they each have their key fob on their keychain and don't think much about it. It's just the key they swipe to enter their home.' Maggie saw John making a note.

She had them turn to the last page of her packet which showed Jillian's code being used to exit and enter the house the night her husband was murdered. 'We were working on the assumption that the doctor had left his office to go home, and then returned to the office where he was murdered. That was based on his wife stating that he had come home and left again. And the security codes seemed to substantiate that. Except that it was Jillian that left, not the doctor.'

'Can we get data that shows whether the swipes were entrance or exits from the residence?' Mark asked. 'Just to confirm that she was exiting and entering?'

'The woman I talked to said it wasn't possible because this is an older security system. It would certainly be worth contacting their data department. They may have a data junkie that can access information that others can't,' Maggie said.

'Do you realize Mrs LeBlanc has an alibi? A friend spent the night on her couch,' John said. 'Her story checks out.'

'The way I understand it, the alibi is a drunk friend who passed out on Jillian's couch for the night. She may not even have noticed if Jillian left the house.' Neither officer spoke so Maggie continued. 'As you know, I've had problems with the idea that Andre would use the gauze to tie the doctor's arms, then bring it back and store it in his garage. Jillian LeBlanc is one of the few people who would know where the gauze was located, and would know that it was something that could be traced back to her husband's office. I believe she, or someone she had working for her, planted the gauze in Andre's workshop.'

'Then why would Andre admit to killing the doctor?' Mark said.

'Because Santa Cruz PD told him if he didn't admit to it, that his wife would be arrested,' Maggie said.

Mark glanced at John, and then back to Maggie. 'I appreciate you bringing this to our attention. John and I will go through this one more time and take it to Santa Cruz this morning.'

'I have one more bombshell.' Maggie opened a manila folder

and pulled out copies of a photo which she gave to Mark and John. 'Do you recognize the two women dancing in the photo?' John said, 'That's Jillian LeBlanc, and that's Olivia Sable.' He narrowed his eyes at Maggie. 'I thought Olivia was having an affair with Doctor LeBlanc. When was this taken?'

'The photo was taken at a bar in Old Santa Cruz the weekend after LeBlanc was murdered,' Maggie said.

John laughed. 'You gotta be kidding. Does Jillian know she's dancing with the woman who was screwing around with her husband?'

'That I can't answer. From the records I found online, it looks as if she's been LeBlanc's receptionist for ten years. I'm certain that Jillian and Olivia have known each other for a number of years. I found several interactions on social media between the two women.'

'Well enough to socialize, even while one is having an affair with the other's husband?' Mark said.

'What was the social media interaction like? Positive?' John asked.

'Olivia is active on several sites: Facebook, Instagram and a few others. I couldn't find much of a presence for Jillian, although she occasionally commented on Olivia's posts and photos. All the comments I saw were positive in nature.'

'Did you see them together at the bar?' Mark asked.

'No. A friend of mine snapped the photo. He said the two of them were the talk of the bar that night. They were both drinking heavily, both laughing and dancing. One lost her boss of over ten years, the other lost her husband. Seems like neither of the women were too upset over his death.'

John studied Maggie for a moment. 'Are you suggesting that Olivia Sable may be involved with Jillian in the murder of the doctor?'

Maggie glanced at Mark, who was watching her closely. It had been a positive conversation to this point, but she was about to step over the line.

'I had a talk with Olivia. Given my interaction with Doctor LeBlanc, it made sense to follow up with her, to feel her out.'

'What interaction are you referring to?' John said.

Maggie looked again at Mark, who nodded slightly. She

wasn't sure if Mark had shared with John that she had gone to LeBlanc's office before he was murdered.

'I met with Doctor LeBlanc about joining his research study. I was thinking about featuring his research on the radio show. I met Olivia that afternoon. After the doctor died, I got to thinking about his illegal affairs. For a doctor who is dealing with millions of dollars, he has a very limited office staff. I had a hunch that Olivia could play oblivious when she wanted, but that she probably knew a great deal about both his personal and professional affairs.'

Mark frowned. 'Santa Cruz interviewed Olivia extensively, on several occasions. I'm sure they were aware of that.'

Maggie could see the irritation in Mark's expression as she continued. 'After the doctor's death, Olivia was placed in charge of distributing patient records. I stopped by the office and waited until she had a moment to talk with me.'

Mark tipped his head back and groaned. 'Maggie. You shouldn't have done that. This is a police investigation.'

She ignored his comment and continued. 'I asked how she was holding up, if she had plans for moving on. She basically said she's tired of this town, tired of the police harassing her, and she can't wait to move. She said she had plans, although she wouldn't elaborate. I told her that I knew what the doctor's game was, and I also knew what her game was. The conversation turned tense in a hurry. She said she was calling the police.'

'Jesus, Maggie,' Mark said.

Maggie put her hand up to cut him off. 'I said I didn't think she would, and she dropped it. I said that she was up against some angry investors, but that I would help her take her money and get out of town before it all fell apart. She said she needed to think about my offer. I told her I wanted an answer today. If you want motive, there it is.'

'That should have been orchestrated by Santa Cruz. You had no right to go behind their back like that.'

Maggie interrupted. 'They wouldn't have taken me seriously. I tried repeatedly to get someone to look into other information and was treated like a nuisance. I believe there's an innocent man sitting in jail, so I won't apologize for skirting protocol.'

Mark frowned and took a moment to respond. 'Obviously

this is important information. But you've put me in a bad place with Santa Cruz. Do not contact Olivia. If she contacts you first, don't answer your phone. Forward any voice messages she may leave directly to Chief Osbourne. I'll call him as soon as we're through here.'

Maggie sat in her car, feeling the sting from Mark's words. She understood the territorial nature of police work, but she'd forgotten the extent of it. Mark was right. There were other ways they could have achieved the same result, but protocol could also grind an investigation to a complete halt.

She had one more task to complete before going home to spend the day on the beach with a bottle of tequila and a handful of ibuprofen for the morning after.

THIRTY-EIGHT

Maggie pulled up outside Kelly O'Neal's house and found her sitting on the porch in front of a fan reading a paperback novel. She stood and smiled as Maggie walked up the steps, and motioned for her to sit down.

Maggie responded curtly to Kelly's attempts at small talk and declined a drink. Slivers of conversation and details that had once seemed inconsequential had led to increased concerns about her involvement in Dr LeBlanc's death.

'There are details that the police have, new information, that could change everything in the investigation,' Maggie said.

She watched the smile leave Kelly's face and her brow furrow into worry lines. Maggie had figured Kelly would have one of two responses to that news. Hope, that her husband might be cut loose from jail. Or worry, that she herself might be facing legal issues. Maggie had her answer.

'What do you mean?' Kelly asked.

'Olivia Sable.'

Kelly grew very still. She pressed her lips together as if not wanting to discuss the issue.

'I talked with Olivia. She filled me in, Kelly. Why don't you quit playing me for a fool and tell me the truth?'

When Maggie had approached Olivia at the doctor's office, she had made a comment that Maggie had not been able to shake. When Maggie had told Olivia that she helped people get out of trouble, Olivia had responded, 'Like Kelly?' The offhand remark had made Maggie believe that the women weren't strangers. She felt confident that Olivia and Kelly knew each other. There was more of a history between them than Kelly had let on.

Kelly pulled her legs into her chair, curling up as if it wasn't ninety degrees in the shade.

'I know you must think I'm horrible,' she said.

'Just help me understand,' Maggie said, hoping Kelly would assume she was going on more than instinct.

'I did it for Amaya, for both of us, to help us start over. Andre isn't getting better. And he won't get help. His disability check is what gets us through. He barely breaks even with his mower business. Then Ramone approached me one day about this research that some famous doctor was doing in Florida.'

'Ramone, from the plasma center?'

She nodded. 'Ramone Anderson. It's true that he took Amaya's blood type, but it was several months ago. After he got it, he approached me one day after I donated. Amaya wasn't with me. He was telling me about this research, and how this doctor needed blood donations from kids aged ten to thirteen. He said the doctor paid well, and he asked if I would want to talk to him. At first I was like, no way. My kid isn't going to get involved with this. But then Ramone told me the doctor was paying two thousand five hundred dollars for each donation. My mouth dropped. I get paid thirty-five bucks!' She searched Maggie's face, but she offered nothing in return. 'Have you ever been poor, lived in the bad part of town? Did your kid ever qualify for free lunch at school? It's a humiliating way to live, Maggie. And twenty-five hundred bucks solves a lot of problems.'

'Did you meet with the doctor?'

'I only talked to him by phone. We never met in person.'

'So when you went to LeBlanc's office with the undercover officer, that whole thing was for show?'

'He didn't know we were coming. I knew when he heard my name he'd be shocked. And I did want to confront him about what happened to Amaya while she was with him.' Kelly was looking intently at Maggie, obviously trying to gauge her reaction. 'I'm so sorry I didn't tell you. But I needed your help. None of this really changes anything.'

'But why would the doctor go along with that meeting? Weren't you worried he'd blow your cover?'

'No. He knew how upset I was over what they did to Amaya. He didn't know what I was after. And he definitely didn't want anyone else knowing anything more than they had to.'

Maggie wiped her hands over her face, trying to keep the anger out of her demeanor.

'I had the one thing he needed. He needed Amaya's plasma for his rich patient's next treatment. There was no way the doctor was going to turn on me in that meeting. He obviously knew something was up, but he played dumb. He just thought I was there to get more money.'

'Which was the truth.' Maggie looked at her, shocked at how calculating she had been.

Kelly seemed to read Maggie's thoughts. 'The man took my daughter and didn't return her to me! He kidnapped another little girl and cut off all communication! I had no idea where they'd taken her. He put me through hell and he deserved everything I could throw at him.'

'So you sold Amaya's blood. Did she know what was happening?'

'She did. She knew it was a secret. She understood that it was important research, but that no one could know about it yet. Andre didn't know anything. He still doesn't. Amaya understood that she and I were doing this to help our family. My goal was to let her donate four times, and we'd have ten thousand dollars saved up for a down payment on a new home. I thought if I could get Andre out of there, move somewhere new, maybe it would be better for him.'

'What happened to your plan?'

'Amaya donated twice with no issues. I got paid in cash both times. I finally felt like I was getting some security for us. And then everything fell apart.'

'How so?'

'I wouldn't allow Amaya to donate more than once a month, and the doctor needed more. Ramone called me one morning and said they wanted to bump up Amaya's donation date by one week, just this once. I told him I couldn't get Amaya to the doctor's office that afternoon because I had a cleaning job. He said no problem. They would pick Amaya up after school. We agreed that Amaya would ride a transit van with him to the doctor's office. Olivia called me and walked me through exactly what would happen.'

'Olivia knew about all of this?' Maggie asked.

'She organized everything for LeBlanc. Of course she knew.'

'So Amaya knew the van was picking her up?'

Kelly shook her head. 'No, but Ramone said he would be there to explain things to her so I wasn't worried. But that's not the way it happened. He wore a disguise because he didn't want Amaya to recognize him in case things went wrong. When Amaya got in the van, he gave her something to knock her out. That was never supposed to be part of the plan. I swear that. I would never have allowed them to do that to Amaya.'

'So she got into the van without knowing him?'

'He called her name and said he was the school transit van driver. She's so trusting, she believed him.'

'Does Amaya remember being drugged in the van?'

'She doesn't remember anything. Just climbing into the van, and then it's blank.'

'Why would they do that to Amaya when she'd already given blood? This wasn't new to her.'

'Because Ramone decided they needed to pick up Amaya and the Baxter girl at the same time. He didn't want Amaya to know about the other girl.'

'Why the Baxter girl?'

'Just what you already knew. Ramone found a girl with the right blood type. He knew it from some community blood draw the parents did. But I didn't know any of this when they said they were picking up Amaya! I didn't know about the Baxter girl. And Olivia didn't either. It was the idiot Ramone letting

LeBlanc pressure him. He decided to get both girls at the same time and that's when everything snowballed. I was supposed to pick Amaya up at the office that afternoon, but instead I got a phone call from the doctor. He was adamant. He told me to stay away until they had things under control.'

'Jesus, Kelly. You knew where Amaya was the entire time we were searching for her?'

'It's not like I wasn't terrified the whole time Amaya was gone! And that bastard doctor did kidnap and drug her. I didn't know if she was safe. No one would answer my calls or talk to me.'

'Why didn't you just go to the office to see if she was there?'

'Because LeBlanc threatened me! All the doctor would say was that he'd taken her out of the city. He said he'd have Amaya taken away from me before he'd allow me to destroy his lifetime of research.' Her eyes shone with tears. 'The day I got in front of all those people who came out to look for Amaya was one of the worst days of my life. I felt like such a hypocrite. But I didn't know where Amaya was. I was terrified something awful had happened to her. The whole situation was just horrible. It's why I told you about Ramone, the blood tech at the plasma center. I figured if the police started looking into Ramone then the doctor would have to get Amaya back to me. I never could have imagined it would spin out the way that it did.'

Maggie felt nauseous, as if the room had flipped upside down. She wanted to shake Kelly. 'You knew where the Baxter girl was? You could have told those parents their daughter was safe?'

'But I didn't know where they were! I was terrified. That's why I came to you. I didn't know where else to go.'

Maggie watched her cry. She could see how one decision that had been made to better her family's life had led to a series of catastrophic events. But she couldn't understand how Kelly had let it go on so long given the devastation the lies had brought upon her daughter and another young girl.

'How could you do this to Amaya? You made her lie to countless people. As if all of the media attention wasn't bad enough, she had to lie about what had happened to her. To the doctors. The police. To me.'

'That's why I needed your help.'

'To keep the police off your back?'

Kelly took a long shaky breath. 'Remember, you came to me. Your cop boyfriend asked you to come talk to me about Amaya. I could tell you were a decent person. I just thought maybe you could help me out of the mess I'd made for Amaya.'

Maggie stood and walked away from her, unable to speak. She'd played into her hand from the beginning. And after all the time she'd spent with her, Maggie still didn't know whether she was a cold manipulator or a desperate mother trying to do better for her daughter.

Kelly followed Maggie to the corner of the porch where she stood looking out over the road, down into the river, muddy and full of debris from the rain the night before. Kelly stood next to her without speaking while she let her anger settle.

Maggie finally asked, 'What happened the night of the murder?'

'You know how you told me I should navigate our conversations carefully?'

Maggie felt her skin crawl. She had been such a fool. 'It's too late for being careful. If you had been honest with me from the beginning, I would have never given you that advice. We'd have gone straight to the police.' She turned to face Kelly. 'You have to make this right. You can't set Amaya up to live a life of lies.'

Kelly nodded but said nothing. She was quiet so long that Maggie assumed she was done talking, that she was giving in to the idea that the police would now be involved and taking over. But she finally spoke, her voice so quiet that Maggie had to take a step closer to hear her.

'After the undercover officer and I met with the doctor that morning, Olivia called me that evening. She said the doctor was a mess. He was talking about suicide. He said his research was ruined. That if any of this was made public, he would lose his license to practice medicine. He said he would kill himself before he went to prison. Olivia told me the cops were onto him.'

'How did she know that? The cops hadn't talked to her at that point.'

'Jillian told her.'

'Son of a bitch.' She turned to face Kelly. 'You know her too?'

'Not really. Just from Olivia. When she called, she said that the police questioned Jillian about her husband's possible involvement in the girls being kidnapped. So she knew the chances were good that he was going to get caught. And probably sooner rather than later.'

'I don't understand why the doctor's receptionist would have called to tell you this?'

Kelly tilted her head and gave Maggie a look that made it obvious she thought Maggie would have figured it out. 'Olivia is the one who gave me the idea to take the extra money. We were friends in high school, just a year apart. Neither one of us grew up with money. We lived down the street from each other. Her parents didn't get rich until her dad got in a car wreck and got a big insurance settlement.'

Maggie shook her head slowly, putting it all together. 'So you'd already received five thousand from the doctor for Amaya. But Olivia figured you could gouge him for quite a bit more, given the mess he was in.'

Kelly didn't say anything.

'And, let me guess, Olivia was doing her own gouging at that point. Probably his wife as well.'

Kelly said nothing.

'So how do we go from three women scamming a doctor, to murder?'

'It's not like that. After I finished talking to the doctor that night, I left. I wasn't there when it happened.'

'If you weren't there, how do you know what it was like?'

'Because he was suicidal.'

'You're telling me that you believe the doctor committed suicide?'

She nodded.

'Then how did his arms get tied to the chair?'

'I don't know. I swear. I haven't talked to Olivia since all of this happened. I'm sure she's as terrified as I am.'

'You have to tell the police what happened.'

'Maggie. Nothing has changed. You wanted me to stay quiet. To keep the money in a safe place for Amaya. That's not changed! It's the same amount of money as before. I don't know why you're so angry with me.'

'Kelly. You sold Amaya's blood for a profit.'

She interrupted, 'You knew that! You said yourself, you don't know that it's not legal to do that.'

'You lied to the police in an investigation. You covered up critical information in the kidnapping of two girls, and you kept relevant information from the police about the murder of a man.'

'Except for the kidnapping, you knew all this before and told me to keep quiet!'

'You allowed your daughter to be kidnapped and an entire community to search for her for two days!'

'But she *was* kidnapped! Once the van took her, they wouldn't communicate with me. I didn't know where she was.' Her eyes pleaded for understanding. 'You said yourself, Amaya needs me. I'm not a bad person. All I was trying to do was make things better for us. I swear to you.'

Maggie took a long breath. 'I believe that you want the best for your daughter. That's why you have to make this right. You can explain to her one day why you made the decisions you made. But you can't put these lies on her. You can't send her through life knowing that this twisted past she was a part of ended with a murdered man and her own father in jail. This is wrong, Kelly, and people have to pay for it. You have to pay the consequences so Amaya gets right from wrong.'

Kelly went back inside the house and Maggie listened as she cried. Maggie was done. Let the Santa Cruz cops have it. She finally walked toward her car, but turned when Kelly yelled her name.

Kelly ran out to the car, her hair a mess, face red and puffy, eyes filled with regret and worry. Maggie leaned against the car door and waited.

'I need you to let me explain this to Amaya before you go to the cops.'

Maggie said nothing.

'Let me go to Louisiana, to my sister's, and talk to Amaya first. Then I swear I'll come back and face whatever they want to throw at me. She can't watch me get hauled away in handcuffs like she did her dad.'

'I told you my opinion.' Maggie watched her taking in this information. 'This is on you now. But you're in a bad spot. After the police take Olivia and Jillian in, you'll be next. Your situation would be much better if you'd go to the Santa Cruz PD now and explain it all. This whole thing is so bizarre, you may not even have charges drawn against you. That'll be up to the prosecutor.'

Kelly nodded and her tears started again, but her crying had lost its impact. At that point, Maggie felt little more than exhaustion.

Maggie drove away from Kelly's and considered calling Mark and telling him everything. But the thought of the drama that the conversation would cause made her pitch her phone onto the passenger seat. He would be furious that she had known about the money from the beginning and not told him. He had shared vital information with her on the premise that it would remain confidential. She had not shared her own information back with him, in an effort to help Kelly, but at what cost? And when it came down to it, she'd been duped. After a lifetime spent in law enforcement, how could she have so easily been pulled into Kelly's schemes?

Maggie turned right onto the Tamiami Trail without much forethought, but when she continued on to Bonita Beach Road her intention was clear. Thirty minutes later she parked along a residential street in Fort Myers, a few blocks from the ocean, but the water wasn't her destination.

The Last Straw was located two blocks from the beach on a street called Lover's Lane. The street sign had an additional notice underneath it that read 'Dead End'. The irony had made her smile, and had been the reason she'd stopped at the bar the first time she was in town over a year ago.

The atmosphere was like a tonic: dimly lit, smelling of stale beer and peanut shells, with wood-paneled walls and old nautical paraphernalia hanging haphazardly from them. There were TVs at either end of the bar for those who wanted to avoid eye contact and conversation, and the bartender could either chat you up or sling beers all night long with no more than a head nod. Maggie was relieved to find the far seat at the bar empty, wedged against the wall behind a video machine, with no one within three seats of it.

She slid onto the stool and smiled when Kenny recognized her. 'What's up, stranger? I was afraid you'd dumped me for a new hangout,' he said.

'Nope. Just busy.'

He turned and several minutes later placed a tumbler of top-shelf tequila in front of her. She tipped her glass to him.

'Cheers, Maggie May. Here's to a better tomorrow.'

Maggie smiled. He and Sassy were the only two people who ever referred to her as Maggie May. 'I'll drink to that, Kenny.'

And she did. Pounding them back, each one an angry attempt to numb her thinking. She shuffled between regret over decisions she'd made over the investigation, to righteous indignation that she'd saved a man from wrongful incarceration and received nothing but reproach from Mark.

Six tumblers in, Maggie's body slumped against the wall. Her vision had blurred and she wasn't sure she could find the bathroom at the back of the room. She'd intended to stop at five, but a man had sat down beside her and ordered her another round. She'd ignored him, telling him she didn't want company. When the drink arrived and she'd still ignored him, he'd said she needed to grow a personality.

Henry had finally intervened and the man had disappeared, probably in search of another woman to harass.

She finally made her way to the bathroom, staying close to the wall, moving her hand from one chair to the next to steady herself. She felt the fog blacking out her peripheral vision and prayed all the way to the stall that she wouldn't fall because she wasn't sure she'd be able to stand once she hit the floor. In the stall, she tried to remember which way her car was from the bar. She couldn't remember for certain if the car was to the right of the bar when she faced the building, or when she faced the beach.

Weaving her way back through the chairs and tables, her attention focused intently on the barstool, she decided one more drink would do it for the night. She had known when she headed toward Bonita Beach Road that her night would end in this condition, and now here she was, ready to swear off the booze one more time. She glanced at her phone, wiping the spilled tequila from the screen, and stared at another missed call from Mark. He'd called and texted repeatedly but she just couldn't deal with a conversation. She figured it was her right to have a night where she didn't give a damn. Her head had to be clear before she drove, so she decided to finish her drink and sleep it off in the backseat.

The banging on her front door woke her. She opened her eyes wide enough to see the clock said quarter after nine. It took her a moment to realize it was daylight, so it had to be morning. Lying on her side, her head hurt so bad that she wasn't sure she could lift it off the couch. The banging started again and she heard Mark's voice. 'Maggie! Answer the goddamned door!'

She shut her eyes and slowly pushed herself up and into a sitting position. She prayed her car was in the driveway. The last thing she remembered was climbing into the backseat to sleep. With a wave of nausea she stood and limped to the front door, opening it, wincing at the bright morning sun behind him.

'I'm sorry. Come in.' She forced the words out, hands pressed to her temples. There was no point in trying to pretend she was anything other than hungover.

He slammed her door. 'Where have you been?'

'I went to Fort Myers. I drank too much and stayed the night.'

'Would it have hurt you to take ten seconds to send me a text last night to tell me that?'

'I'm sorry.'

'Do you know how many times I drove by your house last night? Drove by Mel's? Drove by Kelly O'Neal's? I was terrified something had happened to you. And you were sitting in a bar getting wasted.'

'I don't know what else to say.'

'You smell like alcohol, and you drove home like this? You're lucky you didn't get a DUI. Or kill someone in the process.' He stared at her but she couldn't keep eye contact. 'What the hell has happened to you? How could you be so selfish, so reckless?'

'I don't know what I can say other than I'm sorry.'

'What is it with you and the dark side? Most cops I know

retire and want nothing to do with it. They're burnt out on the drama. But you can't get enough of it. You drink too much. You disappear with no explanation to the man you've been dating for a year. You hang out with strippers at a low-rate bar for chump change. You decide to champion a family who's as dysfunctional as it gets. And for what? Why's it always have to be so dark with you? Put some light in your life, for God's sake.'

She felt the bile in her stomach rising.

He looked at her as if he were trying to comprehend something that made absolutely no sense. 'Why are you doing this to me, to us? Did you do this when you were married to David? Just take off when things got rough? Go get hammered in a bar and pass out, coming home when you damn well felt like it?'

Maggie wasn't sure she could speak without vomiting. These were her secrets. She had no desire to drag out her sad past.

'I asked you a question. The least you could do at this point is answer me.'

'A few times.' She finally made eye contact and saw the shock in Mark's face. 'I left twice while we were married. He forgave me.' Even as she said the words she realized how pathetic she sounded.

'I'm not so forgiving, Maggie. I can't understand how someone who supposedly loves me can take off and put me through the hell I went through last night. What you did was selfish. It's not who I thought you were.' Mark walked to the front door, but turned before leaving. His face had softened. He looked at her with pity, a reaction that hurt worse than his anger. 'You need to get the drinking under control. This is no way to live.'

THIRTY-NINE

After spending the day feeling as low as she had felt in many years, Maggie swallowed a second handful of ibuprofen and called Agnus. 'I need some normal in my life. Can you help me?'

'Honey, I'm as normal as they come. What do you have in mind?'

'Fire and water. No alcohol.'

'You got it. Seven on the beach.'

An hour later, with another bottle of water down and the ibuprofen finally penetrating the vise grip on her head, Maggie stripped down and stepped into her swimsuit. She set her watch to vibrate after half a mile. She swam along the ridge until she felt the buzz. She turned and began the strokes back, concentrating on the rhythm and her breathing. Once the swim was complete, she dried off and lugged firewood to the beach for a late steak on the griddle. At seven o'clock she threw two thick ribeyes over the coals and texted Agnus: *Ten minutes.*

Agnus made her way down the dune, smiling as always, with a woven basket hanging off one arm and a beach bag on the other.

Maggie sprinkled one last dash of salt and pepper over the steaks, then pulled them off to the platter to rest. She had a table and chairs set up with plates and silverware.

'I could smell those steaks all the way up at the house. We'll have Kevin down here with that damn yappy dog if we're not careful.'

'We're safe. Wind's blowing the wrong direction.'

'I made you a pile of homemade potato salad to die for.'

'You are a wonderful friend,' Maggie said.

She pulled Agnus's chair out for her, then pulled the table closer to avoid scooting her chair in the wet sand.

Agnus put two water bottles on the table and Maggie dished up the salad and tore a chunk of French bread off for each of them. She sat beside Agnus and raised her bottle.

Agnus touched her bottle to Maggie's and said, 'Here's to normal, honey.'

Maggie felt her throat close up and couldn't respond, afraid that she'd break down in tears.

After dinner they moved their beach chairs to the surf where they allowed the water to rush up against their feet.

'I assume whatever has you so tied up has something to do with us drinking water for supper? On top of Mark calling twice last night and stalking your house every hour,' Agnus asked.

'I screwed up big time. He won't be back after what I did.'

'You want to talk about it?'

'Nothing much to say. I left home, got drunk, and ignored the man I claim to love. On top of all that, I got played, Agnus. By a girl with a cute kid.'

'I guess there's worse people to get played by.'

Maggie dug her toes into the sand and decided that as much as Agnus would enjoy hearing the sordid details of the investigation, she was too tired to sort it all out.

'Sounds like the drinking had something to do with getting played. Maybe Mark can forgive that. You two were a good match.'

Maggie shook her head. 'I don't think so. There wasn't much excuse for what I did.'

'At least you're big enough to admit that.'

'You know what kills me? I always thought I was such a good judge of character.'

'I know that,' Agnus said. She reached over and patted her thigh.

'My own life is in the toilet, so why would I think I can figure someone else out?'

'I don't know why it's such a big deal. So you got played. It happens every day.'

'There's a lot of money involved. And a dead man. And she used me, a former cop, to bring legitimacy to what she did.'

'Are you in trouble?'

Maggie heard someone yelling her name from back at the house. 'What the hell . . .' she said.

'Ms Wise!'

Maggie stood and faced her home. Olivia Sable was standing just beyond the dune, waving her hand.

'This is not good,' Maggie said. She grabbed her cell phone and slipped it in the pocket of her shorts.

'Is she the player?'

'She's *a* player, but she's not the one.'

'Invite her on down. Sounds like an interesting evening.'

'I don't think that's a good idea.'

'Ms Wise!' Olivia waved her hand high in the air, as if Maggie couldn't see her.

'I'll be back.'

'If you need help, call my name and I'll come running.'

Olivia wore a short dress and high heels that were sinking into the sand. She stood awkwardly on one foot as Maggie approached.

'I called you today, several times. Why didn't you call me back?' she said.

'I don't think it's a good idea that we talk.'

'What's that mean?'

Maggie pointed toward the stepping stone path that led back to her house and watched Olivia hobble back through the sand to solid ground.

'There's no hidden meaning. I just can't help you.'

"I know you said I needed to tell you by ten o'clock yesterday, but I just wasn't ready. But I need your help now.' Olivia had taken on a big-eyed, pouty look that Maggie found disingenuous.

'Look. You are in trouble. You need to contact an attorney and tell them your situation. Be honest. If you can't afford an attorney, get Jillian to pay for one for you. But something tells me you can afford one.'

She opened her mouth as if Maggie had just told her something outrageous.

'You're a cop! Are you reading me my rights? Jillian told me you used to be a cop, and I told her you were just a scammer.'

'I'm a retired homicide cop from Ohio. I'm not reading you any rights. I'm not your problem right now, but I'm also not your solution.'

She moaned and shook her head. 'Oh my god. The cops are coming after us, aren't they?'

'Just tell them what happened.'

'This is such a nightmare. All because that doctor was a freak. You have no idea what Jillian and I put up with.'

'Tell it to the cops.'

She moaned again. 'People have no idea. He made us take the injections to make sure there weren't adverse reactions. We were guinea pigs for that monster for years.'

'Why didn't you leave him? Get a new job?'

'Because he was blackmailing us! He told me that he got into my computer at work and set up a bank account, at my personal bank, and was putting deposits there from the investment accounts.'

'How would he have access to your personal account?'

'Because I did my bills at work. He got on my computer and my logins and passwords were set to automatically log me in. He had access to all my bank accounts and credit cards. He had access to my private accounts for years and I didn't know it.'

'He used your own accounts to set up new accounts to deposit money?'

'Yes. He said if he ever went to jail that Jillian and I would go down with him. He set up overseas accounts for both of us. He'd dangle it over our heads, telling us when the clinics were up and running that the money would be ours. He said it would all be legal. That we would be receiving payments as partners in his business venture. But if we left before the business took off, he would tell the police we'd embezzled money from the company. And he had the paperwork to prove it.'

'Did you embezzle money?' Maggie asked.

'No! I swear to you, the most I ever took from him was a couple of pads of Post It notes, and he screwed me royally.'

'The night he died, how did you end up at the office?'

'He called me and asked me to come. I didn't just show up there in the middle of the night. He was crazy.'

'You went to the office thinking the doctor was suicidal?' Maggie said.

'Yes. He's always been temperamental. Like, he'd get furious with someone and rage around the office, even with patients in the other room. I'd told him multiple times to get a grip. But this was totally different. He was crying on the phone. Telling me how his life was over. He's never done that. It was horrible. So I called Jillian. I was like, "you have to come to the office, *now*. Oscar is going off the deep end."'

'I thought you were having an affair with the doctor? And you were still friends with his wife?'

She rolled her eyes. 'People are so stupid. The cops asked me about the Facebook post too. We were talking about the money. The doctor was putting money into our accounts. Paying us. Right? So it's not like we were doing anything illegal.'

'You mentioned going to Miami with him.'

She groaned. 'Not everything is about sex. Oscar wanted me to go to Miami to set up another investor meeting. I hated those trips. And honestly? He was so into his freaking blood research that he couldn't have cared less about sex with me or anyone else. Including Jillian.'

'What was he like when you got to the office?'

'He was so drunk. He was slamming whiskey. And he's not a drinker.'

'What time did you get to the office?'

'I don't know. He was drunk. Crying. Telling us his life was over. We started out trying to console him. Telling him it'd be OK. It was stupid. He just kept drinking. And then Jillian looked at me with this numb stare. She didn't say anything, but I swear I just knew what she was thinking. She went to the surgical drawer and picked up a scalpel and she handed it to him. She told him, "Here, do it." That's exactly what she said.'

'And that's all it took?'

'He took the knife,' Olivia said.

'So why would she tie his arms after she handed him the knife?'

Olivia's expression faltered. 'She tied his arms to keep him from getting up and making a mess.'

'You know how absurd that sounds? How did it happen? You tied him down? And then she cut? Or was it the other way around?'

'No!' Olivia shook her head, her eyes worried now, sensing the trouble she was in.

'I don't think Jillian LeBlanc would get her hands dirty. That's what you were for.'

'No! You are so wrong.'

'The police questioned Jillian about her husband's involvement in the kidnappings earlier that day. I think she called you and said things were going bad. She said that you had to do something before the cops got involved and found the money stashed in your accounts. You both knew you were out of time. Jillian decided to get her husband drunk enough that the two of you could kill him and make it look like suicide.'

'You are such a bitch.'

'Jillian forced the alcohol on him, shot after shot, to get him weak enough that she could tie his hands to the chair. Then it was your turn. Take the scalpel, slice each wrist, and you're a millionaire.'

'That's not true!'

'Your fingerprints are on that scalpel. The cops are on their way.' Maggie pulled her phone out and held it up.

Olivia saw that Maggie had someone connected to her cell phone, and Olivia's face turned red with fury, as if Maggie had been tricking her into her previous statements.

'I met Oscar,' Maggie said. 'He'd made some terrible decisions, but they were in the name of his research. He thought he was making a difference in the world. You were just after the money.'

'You have no idea what you're talking about.'

Maggie replayed in her mind Olivia's comment about LeBlanc putting money in her account and claiming he was going to set her up for embezzlement if she talked. Maggie thought it sounded absurd and decided to call her bluff. 'Olivia, the police know all about your accounts. Those accounts weren't set up by the doctor. You and Jillian have been syphoning off his research money. He was so consumed with the research that he paid no attention to the money. That was your job. He trusted that you were taking care of him, and all along you were fleecing him.'

'Jillian is the one who set up the accounts! Jillian was behind all of this! The money, everything was her idea. Everything was going bad. She convinced me to come to the office with her. When I got there, she already had him doing shots. She had a gun! I swear to you, she had a gun in her hand when I walked in the office. He was trying to talk sense into her, but she just kept pouring more shots.'

Olivia stopped talking suddenly, appearing to pull back in an effort to control what she was saying. She was so intent on proving her innocence that she didn't seem to notice the phone was back in Maggie's pocket. She took a long, slow breath and lowered her voice. 'I swear to you, I had no idea what she had in mind. She was still feeding him shots when she told me to tie his arms. I did it. I thought she was just messing with him.

Like, trying to scare him. And then she opened the drawer and took the scalpel and just cut him. She didn't even think about it. She just did it! It was horrible! He leaned back in that chair crying and bleeding and then he passed out.'

'So you did nothing while the doctor lay there bleeding out?' Maggie asked.

'I was like, "Jillian, we have to do something! This is so wrong." But she told me to shut up. After he passed out, she cut the gauze and put it in a plastic bag. I just left. I swear to you. I couldn't take it. She came over to my house afterwards to check on me.'

'That's odd you were so upset over his death. A buddy of mine saw you dancing at the bar with Jillian the next weekend. He said you two were the talk of the bar.'

'Because he was psychotic! You don't know what it was like, working for a psycho for almost ten years. I can't begin to tell you the weird shit he was into. Jillian couldn't take it anymore.'

'And then you took the gauze and planted it in Andre O'Neal's workshop to deflect the attention from you both.'

She shook her head. 'I don't know who did that. Jillian and I had no idea how that happened.'

'Who else would have had the need to plant evidence other than the murderer?'

Olivia finally broke. Her knees gave way and she crumpled to the ground where she cried until Mark pulled into the driveway in his Cypress City PD vehicle, followed by two marked SUVs from Santa Cruz.

Once the Santa Cruz PD officers had taken Olivia to the station, Mark left without saying goodbye.

Maggie went to check on Agnus. She'd long since left the beach. In the midst of the Santa Cruz officers questioning Olivia, Maggie had seen Agnus walking back to her house with her two bags hung over her shoulders.

It was after nine but Maggie figured the excitement might have kept her from going to bed. Through the light in the window at the back of her house, Maggie could see Agnus sitting at the kitchen table. She tapped on the French door and Agnus looked up, startled.

She called to her, 'It's Maggie! I'm just checking in.'

Agnus opened the door looking concerned.

'Excitement's over. I just wanted to apologize for the police in your driveway. I know that looks terrible in this kind of neighborhood. I'm sure you didn't bargain for this when you agreed to sell me the house.'

'Are you kidding? There ain't nobody that'll mess with me after the cops I've had around here lately. I'll be the talk of Santa Cruz. That crazy bad ass old lady that has the cops at her door every other night.' Agnus motioned for Maggie to step inside. 'Come on in and fill me in on the story.'

'Nah. You need to get some sleep. I just wanted to be sure this mess didn't have you shook up.'

'This old gal? It'd take more than a few cop cars to shake me up.' She studied Maggie for a moment. 'I know you don't want to talk about it, but I have to ask. I saw Mark's car. Did he come to check on you?'

'Not hardly. I wanted to get the police here and get the girl's conversation recorded without alerting her that I was calling the cops. So I called Mark's number on my cell phone and just hoped he would answer and listen to the conversation after I put the phone in my pocket. He said he thought I was harassing him at first and almost hung up. Then he heard me yell Olivia's name to tell her I'd be right there. He kept me on the line, recording everything, and got Santa Cruz headed our way.'

'That's good news then. You and he solved the case together. Maybe this will smooth things over between the two of you.'

Maggie smiled and shrugged, deciding not to tell her that Mark left without saying goodbye. They both turned to see headlights illuminating the palm trees along the driveway.

'You expecting visitors this late?' Agnus said.

'Not a chance. I sure hope whoever this is has the wrong address,' said Maggie. 'I need a break from humanity.'

'Maybe I better hang on. See if you need help,' Agnus said.

Maggie pecked her on the cheek. 'I'm fine. Go to bed and I'll fill you in tomorrow.'

Maggie felt her stomach turn as the driver turned into the parking area and she recognized Kelly O'Neal's car.

Kelly apologized for coming by unannounced and explained

that if she had called first she would have lost her nerve. Even in the dim starlight she looked pale and nervous.

'What's going on?' Maggie asked, opting to keep the conversation outside in the driveway rather than inviting her inside.

'I went to see Andre this afternoon. I told him everything. The money, donating Amaya's plasma, all of it.'

Maggie leaned back against her car, shocked at the news. 'How did he take it?'

'Some of it he suspected. Some if it cleared up worries he'd had about me. He thought I was having an affair, and that I was using Amaya to cover it up.' She shrugged. 'Not that what I told him was any better, but he seemed relieved.'

Maggie nodded. 'You let him know that he'll probably be released soon?'

'He couldn't believe it. He honestly thought he was going to spend the rest of his life in jail over this. I thought you'd want to know that it was Andre that planted the gauze in his shop.'

'What the hell? How would Andre get the gauze?'

She grinned. 'That's what I asked. He told me you can get anything on the internet.'

Maggie grinned back and nodded. 'True enough.'

'He said he called the medical answering service and said he had an allergic reaction to a wound and needed to know what kind of dressing the doctor used in his office. He said someone called him back within an hour. Then he got online and ordered a box to be delivered overnight to the house. Once he got it, he made an anonymous tip to the police that it was in his workshop.' She tilted her head. 'The police officer said it wasn't sold to the public, but Andre didn't have any problem getting it.'

'I don't think you give your husband enough credit,' Maggie said.

'I figured that out.'

'So Andre planted the evidence, knowing he'd seal his fate. He did it to keep you out of jail,' Maggie said.

Kelly turned away from her. 'It hit me yesterday after I talked to you, how many times I had told you that Andre wasn't a fit parent, that I was the parent that needed to raise Amaya. I'm more ashamed of that than anything else that's happened. Andre's the one truly good person in this whole sordid mess, and he took the fall.'

'I'm glad you told him,' Maggie said.

'I have one more favor to ask, and then I'll never bother you again, I promise.'

Maggie watched her closely, trying to figure her latest angle. 'What is it?'

'I'm hoping you'll go with me to the police station. I'd like you to be there while I explain everything that I did. I had packed my bags to drive to Louisiana to tell Amaya, but I was afraid if I left here that I might not return. I can't do that to Andre. He deserves better than that.'

'Of course I'll go with you.'

Kelly nodded once and pulled an envelope out of her purse. 'Actually, I lied. I have one more favor.' She offered a half-smile. 'I wrote a letter to Amaya. I hope you won't need to give it to her. But in case things go badly for me, I want her to understand the decisions that I made.'

Maggie studied her face, but more than fear, she saw hope in Kelly's eyes. Maggie opened her arms and wrapped her in a hug. 'I think you're going to be OK. I believe there are better days ahead for all three of you.'

The next day, Maggie wandered around her house, dusting and vacuuming, killing time, trying to stay busy. Her skin crawled with the realization that Mark was gone, the investigation was over, and her life was headed for a whole lot of empty that she didn't know how to fill. She poured the remaining tequila down the kitchen sink and regretted it immediately.

She took a run down the beach, imagining the sweat detoxifying her body, but the activity did little to still the self-reproach consuming her thoughts. She wanted to apologize, needed to apologize to Mark, but he'd not answered her call that morning, and what good would one more apology do at this point? After her shower she opened her cell phone and deleted his contact information.

At four o'clock, Maggie called Danny and asked him to meet her at Mel's. She arrived early and ordered a lime and tonic for herself and watched a baseball game on TV until he arrived. After he'd settled in with a beer and she'd given him an update on the young blood case, she took a deep breath and forced out the words she'd practiced throughout the afternoon.

'I spent the last several weeks trying to help a family I said was a mess, but I can't hide behind that anymore. At least the O'Neals have each other. I'm too screwed up to even keep a relationship.' Maggie looked down at her tonic water and flipped the lime slice into the glass. 'A couple of weeks ago, you told me people are either the fixer or the fixable.'

'I remember.'

Maggie nodded her head, trying to summon the courage to say what needed to be said.

'What's going on?' he asked.

'Mark's gone. And I need a fixer. I need a support, someone to hold me accountable. Can you do that?'

Danny looked stunned. 'You know I'll do anything for you, but I'm not sure you picked the right person for the job. Are you saying you want to quit drinking?'

She nodded.

'Don't you need somebody sober to help you stay that way yourself? Aren't those sponsors in AA recovered alcoholics?'

'I don't know. I've never done this.'

'I'm not making excuses. I'll do whatever you need. I just don't want to let you down.'

She drank the rest of the lime tonic. 'You're my best bet right now.'

'Then I'm your man. You call me any time, day or night. Maybe some of your willpower will rub off on me too.'

Maggie smiled. 'This is about me figuring out my life. I just need you to know that I'm making a commitment to stop.'

'I'm proud of you, Maggie.' He stood from the barstool and patted her on the back. 'Let's get out of here and go get a piece of pie. I need to tell you about a job opening I saw posted in the paper today.'

'Oh yeah?'

Danny left money for their drinks on the bar and grinned. 'Santa Cruz PD is looking for an experienced investigator.'

Lightning Source UK Ltd.
Milton Keynes UK
UKHW010354090121
376694UK00003B/138